THE SOUND OF THINGS FALLING

Juan Gabriel Vásquez

Translated from the Spanish by Anne McLean

BLOOMSBURY
LONDON • NEW DELHI • NEW YORK • SYDNEY

First published in Great Britain 2012
This paperback edition published in 2013

Originally published in Spain 2011 by Alfaguara
(Santillana Ediciones Generales) as
El ruido de las cosas al caer

Winner of the XIV Alfaguara Prize. Published by Alfaguara

This book has been selected to receive financial assistance from English
PEN's Writers in Translation programme supported by Bloomberg.
English PEN exists to promote literature and its understanding, uphold
writers' freedoms around the world, campaign against the persecution and
imprisonment of writers for stating their views, and promote the friendly
co-operation of writers and free exchange of ideas. www.englishpen.org

Bloomsbury Publishing Plc
50 Bedford Square
London WC1B 3DP

www.bloomsbury.com

Bloomsbury Publishing, London, New Delhi, New York and Sydney

A CIP catalogue record for this book is available from the British Library

ISBN 978 1 4088 3161 8

10 9 8 7 6 5 4 3 2 1

Typeset by Hewer Text UK Ltd, Edinburgh

Praise for *The Sound of Things F*

'The work reads beautifully. Vasquez's
exploring the darker corners of his count
probing his characters' intractable duality, and in questioning the frailties of memory, is compounded by his skill in evoking those instances when things change forever'
Independent

'A sobering book, *The Sound of Things Falling* makes a virtue of pained honesty about Colombia's recent past'
Literary Review

'Compelling . . . He holds his narrative together with admirable stylistic control as he shows a world falling apart and the powers of love and language to rebuild it' Anita Sethi, *Observer*

'The sense of loss and melancholy are superbly held in a novel that explores the pain and release to be found in revisiting the past' *Metro*

'One of the most original new voices of Latin American literature' Mario Vargas Llosa

'A thrilling new discovery' Colm Tóibín

'A masterful writer' Nicole Krauss

By the same author

The Informers
The Secret History of Costaguana

JUAN GABRIEL VÁSQUEZ was born in Bogotá in 1973. He studied Latin American Literature at the Sorbonne between 1996 and 1998, and has translated works by E. M. Forster and Victor Hugo, among others, into Spanish. He was nominated as one of the Bogotá 39, South America's most promising writers of the new generation. His previous books include *The Informers*, which was shortlisted for the *Independent* Foreign Fiction Prize, and *The Secret History of Costaguana*, which won the Qwerty Prize in Barcelona. His books have been published in fifteen languages worldwide. After sixteen years in France, Belgium and Spain, he now lives in Bogotá.

ANNE MCLEAN has translated Latin American and Spanish novels, short stories, memoirs and other writings by authors including Hector Abad, Carmen Martín Gaite, Julio Cortázar, Ignacio Martínez de Pisón, Enrique Vila-Matas and Tomás Eloy Martínez. She has twice won the *Independent* Foreign Fiction Prize: for *Soldiers of Salamis* by Javier Cercas in 2004 (which also won her the Premio Valle Inclán), and for *The Armies* by Evelio Rosero in 2009. In 2012 she was awarded the Spanish Cross of the Order of Civil Merit in recognition of her contribution to making Spanish literature known to a wider public. She lives in Toronto.

For Mariana, inventor of spaces and time

And the walls of my dream burning, toppling,
like a city collapsing in screams.

Aurelio Arturo, *Dream City*

So you fell out of the sky too!
What planet are you from?

Antoine de Saint-Exupéry, *The Little Prince*

CONTENTS

I

One Single Long Shadow

THE FIRST HIPPOPOTAMUS, A male the colour of black pearls weighing a ton and a half, was shot dead in the middle of 2009. He'd escaped two years before from Pablo Escobar's old zoo in the Magdalena Valley, and during that time of freedom had destroyed crops, invaded drinking troughs, terrified fishermen and even attacked the breeding bulls at a cattle ranch. The marksmen who caught up with him shot him once in the head and again in the heart (with .375-calibre bullets, since hippopotamus skin is thick); they posed with the dead body, the great dark wrinkled mass, a recently fallen meteorite; and there, in front of the first cameras and onlookers, beneath a ceiba tree that protected them from the harsh sun, they explained that the weight of the animal would prevent them from transporting him whole, and immediately began carving him up. I was in my apartment in Bogotá, 250 or so kilometres south, when I saw the image for the first time, printed across half a page of a national news-magazine. That's how I learned that the entrails had been buried where the animal had fallen, and the head and legs had ended up in a biology laboratory in my city. I also learned that the hippopotamus had not escaped alone: at the time of his flight he'd been accompanied by his mate and their baby – or what, in the sentimental version of the less scrupulous newspapers, were his mate and their baby – whose whereabouts were now unknown and the search for whom immediately took on a flavour of media tragedy, the persecution of innocent creatures by a heartless system. And on one of those days, while following the hunt in the papers, I found myself remembering a man who'd been out of my thoughts for a long while, in spite of the fact that there had been a time when nothing interested me as much as the mystery of his life.

During the weeks that followed, the memory of Ricardo Laverde went from being a minor coincidence, one of those dirty tricks our minds play on us, to becoming a faithful and devoted, ever-present ghost, standing by my bed while I slept, watching from afar in the daylight hours. On the morning radio programmes and the evening news, in the opinion columns that everybody read and on the blogs that nobody read, everyone was asking if it was necessary to kill the lost hippos, if they couldn't round them up, anaesthetize them and send them back to Africa; in my apartment, far from the debate but following it with a mixture of fascination and repugnance, I was thinking more and more intensely about Ricardo Laverde, about the days when we'd known each other, about the brevity of our acquaintance and the longevity of its consequences. While in the press and on the TV screens the authorities listed the diseases that could be spread by an artiodactyl – and they used that word: *artiodactyl*, new to me – and in the rich neighbourhoods of Bogotá people wore T-shirts saying *Save the Hippos*, in my apartment, on long drizzly nights, or walking down the street towards the city centre, I began to think stubbornly about the day Ricardo Laverde died, and even to force myself to remember the precise details. I was surprised by how little effort it took me to summon up the words I had spoken or heard, things I'd seen, pain I'd suffered and now overcome; I was also surprised by the alacrity and dedication we devote to the damaging exercise of remembering, which after all brings nothing good and serves only to hinder our normal functioning, like those bags of sand athletes tie around their calves for training. Bit by bit I began to notice, not without some astonishment, that the death of that hippopotamus put an end to an episode of my life that had begun quite a while ago, more or less like someone coming home to close a door carelessly left open.

And that's how this story got under way. I don't know what good it does us to remember, what benefits or possible penalties it brings, or how what we've lived through can change when we remember it, but remembering Ricardo Laverde well has become an urgent matter for me. I read somewhere that a man should tell the story of his life at the age of forty, and this deadline is fast approaching: as I write these lines, only a few short weeks remain before this ominous birthday arrives. *The story of his life.* No, I won't tell my life story, just a few days of it that happened a long time ago, and I'll do so fully aware that this story, as they warn in fairy tales, has happened before and will happen again.

That I'm the one who's ended up telling it is almost beside the point.

* * *

The day of his death, at the beginning of 1996, Ricardo Laverde had spent the morning walking the narrow streets of La Candelaria, in the centre of Bogotá, between old houses with clay roof tiles and unread marble plaques with summaries of historic events, and around one in the afternoon he showed up at the billiard club on 14th Street, ready to play a couple of games with some of the regulars. He didn't seem nervous or disturbed when he started to play: he played with the same cue and at the same table he always did, the one closest to the back wall, under the television with the sound turned down. He played three games, though I don't remember how many he won and how many he lost, because that afternoon I didn't play with him, but at the next table. I do remember, however, the moment Laverde settled his bets, said goodbye to the other players and headed for the corner door. He was passing between the first tables, which are usually empty because the strip-lighting cast strange shadows on the ivory balls in that part of the hall, when he stumbled as if he'd tripped over something. He turned around and came back over to where we were; waited patiently while I finished a series of six or seven cannons that I'd started, and even applauded a three-cushioned one briefly; and then, as he watched me mark my score on the board, he came over and asked me if I might not know where he could borrow a tape machine to listen to a cassette he'd just received. I've often wondered since what would have happened if Ricardo Laverde had asked one of the other billiard players rather than me. But it's a meaningless question, like so much of what we wonder about the past. Laverde had good reasons to choose to ask me. Nothing can change that fact, just as nothing can change what happened afterwards.

I had met him at the end of the previous year, a couple of weeks before Christmas. I was about to turn twenty-six, I'd graduated from law school two years earlier and, although I knew very little about the real world, the theoretical world of legal studies held no secrets for me. After graduating with honours – a thesis on madness as grounds for exemption from legal responsibility in *Hamlet*: I still wonder today how I got them to accept it, let alone award it a distinction – I had turned into the youngest lecturer ever to teach in the faculty, or that's what my elders had told me when proposing the idea, and I was convinced that being professor of Introduction to Law, teaching the basics of the career to generations of frightened children just out of high school, was the only possible horizon in my life. There, standing in front of a wooden lectern, facing rows and rows of baby-faced and disoriented boys and impressionable, wide-eyed girls, I received my first lessons on the nature of power. I was barely eight years older than these inexperienced students, but between us opened the double abyss of authority and knowledge, things that I had and they, recently arrived in the world, entirely lacked. They admired me, feared me a little, and I realized that one could get used to this fear and admiration, that they were like a drug. I told my students about the potholers who were trapped in a cave and after several days began to eat each other to survive: can the Law defend them or not? I told them about old Shylock, about the pound of flesh he wanted, about the astute Portia, who managed to prevent him from taking it with a pettifogging technicality: I enjoyed watching them gesticulate and shout and lose themselves in ridiculous arguments in their attempts to find, in the thicket of the anecdote, the ideas of Law and Justice. After these academic discussions I'd go to the billiard clubs on 14th Street, low-ceilinged places filled with smoke where my other life went on, a life without doctrines or jurisprudence. There, between small bets and coffee with brandy, my day would draw to a close, sometimes in the company of a colleague or two, sometimes with female students who after a few drinks might end up in my bed. I lived near by, in a tenth-floor apartment where the air was always chilly, where the view of the spiky city of bricks and cement was always good, where my bed was always open to discussions of Cesare Beccaria's concept of crimes and punishments, or a difficult chapter of Bodenheimer, or even a simple upgrade of a mark by the quickest route. Life, in those days that now seem to have belonged to somebody else, was full of possibilities. The possibilities, as I would later discover, also belonged to somebody else: they were gradually, imperceptibly extinguished, like a tide going out, until they left me with what I am today.

At the time my city was beginning to emerge from the most violent years of its recent history. I'm not talking about the violence of cheap stabbings and stray bullets, the settling of accounts between low-grade dealers, but the kind that transcends the small resentments and small revenges of little people, the violence whose actors are collectives and written with capital letters: the State, the

Cartel, the Army, the Front. We *bogotanos* had become accustomed to it, partially because its images arrived with extraordinary regularity in our news reports and papers; that day, the images of the most recent attack had begun to appear, in the form of a breaking-news bulletin, on the television screen. First we saw the reporter presenting the news from outside the door of the Country Clinic, then we saw the image of the bullet-riddled Mercedes – through the shot-out window we saw the back seat, broken glass, smears of dried blood – and finally, when all movement had ceased at all the tables and everyone had quietened down and someone had shouted to turn up the sound, we saw, above the dates of birth and the still fresh one of his death, the face of the victim in black-and-white. It was the conservative politician Álvaro Gómez, son of one of the most controversial presidents of the century and himself candidate for the presidency more than once. Nobody asked why he'd been killed, or who by, because such questions no longer had any meaning in my city, or they were asked in a mechanical fashion, as the only way to react to the latest shock. I didn't think so at the time, but those crimes (*magnicides*, they called them in the press: I learned the meaning of that little word very early) had provided the backbone of my life or punctuated it like the unexpected visits of a distant relative. I was fourteen years old that afternoon in 1984 when Pablo Escobar killed or ordered the killing of his most illustrious pursuer, the Minister of Justice Rodrigo Lara Bonilla (two hit men on a motorcycle, a curve on 127th Street). I was sixteen when Escobar killed or ordered the killing of Guillermo Cano, publisher of *El Espectador* (a few steps away from the newspaper's offices, the assassin put eight bullets in his chest). I was nineteen and already an adult, although I hadn't voted yet, on the day of the death of Luis Carlos Galán, a presidential candidate, whose assassination was different or is different in our imaginations because it was seen on TV: the crowd cheering Galán, then the machine-gunfire, then the body collapsing on the wooden platform, falling soundlessly or its sound hidden by the uproar or by the first screams. And shortly afterwards there was the Avianca plane, a Boeing 727-21 that Escobar had blown up in mid-air – somewhere in the air between Bogotá and Cali – to kill a politician who wasn't even on board.

So all the billiard players lamented the crime with a resignation that was by then a sort of national idiosyncrasy, the legacy of our times, and then we went back to our respective games. All, I mean, except for one whose attention remained riveted to the screen, where the images had moved on to the next news item and were now showing a scene of neglect: a bullring full of weeds as high as the flagpoles (or as high as the place where flags once flew), a roof over several vintage cars that were rusting away, a gigantic tyrannosaurus whose body was falling apart revealing a complicated metal structure, sad and naked like an old mannequin. It was the Hacienda Nápoles, Pablo Escobar's mythical territory, which had once been the headquarters of his empire, now left to its fate since the capo's death in 1993. The news item was about this neglect: the properties confiscated from the drug traffickers, the millions of dollars wasted by the authorities who didn't know how to make use of these properties, all the many things that could have been done and hadn't been done with those fairy-tale assets. And that was when one of the players at the table nearest the television, who up to that moment had not drawn attention to himself in any way, spoke as if talking to himself, but he did so out loud and spontaneously, like someone who, long used to solitude, had forgotten the very possibility of being heard.

'Well, let's see what they do with the animals,' he said. 'Poor things are starving to death and nobody cares.'

Someone asked him what animals he was talking about. The man just said: 'It's not their fault, anyway.'

Those were the first words I heard Ricardo Laverde say. He didn't say anything else: he didn't clarify which animals he was talking about, or say how he knew they were starving to death. But no one asked again, because we were all old enough to remember the Hacienda Nápoles in its better days. The zoo was a legendary place, a millionaire drug baron's eccentricity, that promised visitors a spectacle that didn't belong to these latitudes. I'd gone when I was twelve, during the Christmas holidays; I had gone there, of course, behind my parents' back: the very idea of their son setting foot on the property of a recognized Mafioso would have been scandalous to them, let alone the thought of him enjoying himself there. But I couldn't resist going to see what everyone was talking about. I accepted the invitation from the parents of a friend; one weekend we got up very early to make the six-hour drive from Bogotá to Puerto Triunfo; and once inside the ranch, after passing under the big stone gate (with the name of the property in thick blue letters), we spent the afternoon among Bengal tigers and Amazonian macaws, pygmy horses and butterflies the size of a hand and even a pair of Indian rhinoceroses which, according to a boy with a Medellín accent and camouflage flak jacket, had just recently arrived. And then there were the hippos, of course, none of which had escaped yet in those glory days. So I knew very well what animals the man was talking about; I didn't know, however, that those few words would spring to mind almost fourteen years later. But all this I've thought since, obviously: that day, at the billiard club, Ricardo Laverde was just one more of so many in my country who'd followed the rise and fall of one of the most notorious Colombians of all time with astonishment, and I didn't pay him too much attention.

What I do remember about that day is that he didn't strike me as intimidating: he was so thin that he seemed taller than he actually was, and you had to see him standing beside a cue to see that he was barely five foot seven; his thin mousy hair and his dried-out skin and his long, dirty nails gave an impression of illness or laziness, like land gone to waste. He'd just turned forty-eight, but he looked much older. Speaking seemed to be an effort for him, as if he couldn't get enough air; his hand was so unsteady that the blue tip of his cue always trembled in front of the ball, and it was almost miraculous that he didn't scratch more often. Everything about him seemed tired. One afternoon, after

Laverde had gone, one of the guys he'd been playing with (a man around the same age but who moved better, who breathed better, who is undoubtedly still alive today and perhaps even reading this memoir) told me the reason without my having asked. 'It's prison,' he told me, revealing as he spoke the brief sparkle of a gold tooth. 'Jail tires a person out.'

'He was in prison?'

'Just got out. He was in there for something like twenty years, so they say.'

'And what'd he do?'

'Oh, that I don't know,' the man said. 'But he must have done something, no? Nobody gets that many years for nothing.'

I believed him, of course, because nothing allowed me to think there was an alternative truth, because there was no reason at that moment to question that first innocent and ingenuous version that someone gave me of Ricardo Laverde's life. I thought how I'd never known an ex-convict before – the expression *ex-convict*, anyone would notice, is the best proof of that – and my interest in getting to know Laverde grew, or my curiosity grew. A heavy sentence always impresses a young man like I was back then. I calculated that I was barely walking when Laverde went to prison, and no one can be invulnerable to the idea of having grown up and gone to school and discovered sex and maybe death (that of a pet and then a grandfather, for example), and having had lovers and suffered painful break-ups and come to know the power of deciding, the satisfaction or regret resulting from decisions, the power to hurt and the satisfaction or guilt in doing so, and all this while a man lives the life without discoveries or apprenticeships that invariably results from a sentence of such length. A life unlived, a life that runs through one's fingers, a life one suffers through while knowing that it belongs to someone else: to those who don't have to suffer.

And almost without my noticing we began to approach each other. At first it happened by chance: I applauded one of his cannons, for example – the man had a knack for shots off the cushion – and then I invited him to play at my table or asked for permission to play on his. He accepted reluctantly, as an initiate receives a novice, in spite of the fact that I was a better player than him and that by teaming up with me Laverde could, at last, stop losing. But then I discovered that losing didn't matter much to him: the money he put down on the emerald-coloured felt at the end of a game, those two or three dark and wrinkled notes, was part of his daily expenditure, a debit already accepted in his budget. Billiards was not a pastime for him, or even a competition, but rather the only way Laverde had at that moment of being in society: the sound of the balls hitting each other, of the wooden counters on the scoreboard, of the blue chalk rubbing against the old leather cue tips, all this made up his public life. Outside those corridors, without a billiard cue in his hand, Laverde was unable to have a normal conversation, let alone a relationship. 'Sometimes I think,' he told me the only time we talked somewhat seriously, 'I've never looked anyone in the eye.' It was an exaggeration, but I'm not sure the man was exaggerating on purpose. After all, he wasn't looking me in the eye when he said those words.

Now that so many years have passed, now that I remember with the benefit of an understanding I didn't have then, I think of that conversation and it seems implausible that its importance didn't hit me in the face. (And I tell myself at the same time that we're terrible judges of the present moment, maybe because the present doesn't actually exist: all is memory, this sentence that I just wrote is already a memory, this word is a memory that you, reader, just read.) The year was coming to an end; it was exam time and classes were finished; the routine of billiards had settled into my days, and somehow given them shape and purpose. 'Ah,' Ricardo Laverde said each time he saw me arrive, 'you almost missed me, Yammara. I was just about to leave.' Something in our encounters was changing: I knew it the afternoon Laverde didn't say goodbye the way he always did, from the other side of the table, bringing his hand up to his forehead like a soldier and leaving me with my cue in my hand, but waited for me, watched me pay for both our drinks – four coffees with brandy and a Coca-Cola at the end – and walked out of the place beside me. He walked with me as far as the Plazoleta del Rosario, through exhaust fumes and the smell of fried *arepas* and open sewers; then, where a ramp descends into the dark mouth of an underground car park, he gave me a pat on the back, a fragile little pat from his fragile hand, closer to a caress than a farewell, and said, 'OK, see you tomorrow. I've got an errand to run.'

I saw him dodge the huddles of emerald sellers and head down a pedestrian alley that leads into 7th Avenue, then turn the corner, and then I couldn't see him any more. The streets were starting to be adorned with Christmas lights: Nordic wreaths and candy canes, English words, silhouettes of snowflakes in this city where it's never snowed and where December, in particular, is the sunniest time of year. But in the daytime unlit lights do not adorn: they obstruct, sully and contaminate the view. The wires, suspended over our heads, crisscrossing the road from one side to the other, were like hanging bridges and in Bolívar Plaza they climbed the posts, the Ionic columns of the Capitol and the walls of the cathedral like ivy. The pigeons did have more wires to rest on, it's true, and the corn vendors couldn't keep up with the tourists who wanted to feed them, and the street photographers couldn't keep up with demand for their services either: old men in ponchos and felt hats who seized their clients as if they were driving cattle and then, at the moment of the photo, ducked under a black cloth, not because the machine demanded it, but because their clients expected it. These photographers were also throwbacks to other times, before everybody could take their own portraits and the idea of buying a photo in the street that someone else had taken (often without them noticing) wasn't completely absurd. Every Bogotá resident of a certain age has a street photo, most of them taken on 7th Avenue, formerly calle Real del Comercio, or Royal Commerce Street, queen of all Bogotá streets; my generation grew up looking at those photos in family albums, those men in three-piece suits, those women with gloves and umbrellas, people from another time when Bogotá was colder and rainier and tamer, but no easier. I have among my papers the photo my grandfather bought in the 1950s and the one my father bought fifteen or so years later. I don't have, however, the one Ricardo Laverde bought that afternoon, although the image remains so clearly in my memory that I could draw every line of it if I had any talent for drawing. But I don't. That's one of the talents I don't have.

So that was the errand Laverde had to run. After leaving me he walked to Bolívar Plaza and had one of those deliberately anachronistic portraits taken, and the next day he arrived at the billiard club with the result in his hand: a sepia-toned piece of paper, signed by the photographer, on which appeared a less sad or taciturn man than usual, a man of whom it might be said, if the evidence of the past few months didn't convert the appraisal into an impudence, that he was content. The black plastic cover was still on the table, and Laverde put the image on top of it, his own image, and stared at it in fascination: his hair was combed, not a wrinkle in his suit, his right hand extended and two doves pecking at his palm; behind him you could almost make out the gaze of a couple of passers-by, both in sandals with rucksacks, and in the background, beside a corn cart enlarged by the perspective, the Palace of Justice.

'It's really good,' I told him. 'Was it taken yesterday?'

'Yeah, just yesterday,' he said. And then, out of the blue, he told me: 'The thing is, my wife's coming.'

He didn't say *the photo is a gift*. He didn't explain why such a strange gift would interest his wife. He didn't refer to his years in prison, although it was obvious to me that this is what loomed over the whole situation, like a vulture over a dead dog. Anyway, Ricardo Laverde acted as if nobody in the billiard club knew anything about his past; I felt at that moment that this fiction preserved a delicate balance between us, and I preferred to keep it that way.

'What do you mean coming?' I asked. 'Coming from where?'

'She's from the United States, her family lives there. My wife is, well, we could say coming to visit.' And then, 'Is the picture OK? Do you think it's good?'

'I think it's really good,' I told him with a bit of involuntary condescension. 'You look very elegant, Ricardo.'

'Very elegant,' he said.

'So you're married to a *gringa*,' I said.

'Yeah. Imagine that.'

'And she's coming for Christmas?'

'Hope so,' said Laverde. 'I hope so.'

'Why do you hope so? It's not for sure?'

'Well, I have to convince her first. It's a long story. Don't ask me to explain.'

Laverde took the black cover off the table, not all at once, like other players do, but folding it in sections, meticulously, almost fondly, the way they fold a flag at a state funeral. We began to play. During one of his breaks he bent down over the table, stood up again, looked for the best angle, but then, after all the ceremony, shot at the wrong ball. 'Shit,' he said. 'Sorry.' He went over to the board, asked how many cannons he'd made, marked them using the tip of his cue (and accidentally touched the white wall, leaving an oblong blue smudge among other blue smudges accumulated over the years). 'Sorry,' he said again. His head was suddenly elsewhere: his movements, his gaze fixed on the ivory balls that slowly took up their new positions on the cloth, were those of someone who'd already left, a ghost of sorts. I began to consider the possibility that Laverde and his wife were divorced, and then, like an epiphany, another harsher and therefore more interesting possibility occurred to me: his wife didn't know that Laverde was out of prison. In a brief second, between cannon and cannon, I imagined a man coming out of a Bogotá prison – the scene in my imagination took place at Distrital, the last prison I'd seen as a student of Criminology – who keeps his release secret in order to surprise someone, like Hawthorne's Wakefield in reverse, interested in seeing on the face of his only relative that expression of surprised love we've all wanted to see, or have even provoked with elaborate ruses, at some time in our lives.

'And what's your wife's name?' I asked.

'Elena,' he said.

'Elena de Laverde,' I said, trying out the name and attributing that little possessive preposition that almost all people of his generation were still using in Colombia.

'No,' Ricardo Laverde corrected me. 'Elena Fritts. We never wanted her to take my surname. A modern woman, you know.'

'That's modern?'

'Well, at that time it was modern. Not changing your name. And since she was American people forgave her.' Then, with a rapid or recovered light-heartedness, 'So, are we having a drink?'

Our afternoon dwindled away in drink after drink of cheap white rum that left an aftertaste of surgical spirit in the back of the throat. By about five, billiards had stopped mattering to us, so we left the cues on the table, put the three balls in the cardboard rectangle of their box and sat down in the wooden chairs, like spectators or escorts or tired players, each of us with his tall glass of rum in hand, swirling it around every once in a while so the fresh ice would mix in, smearing them more and more, our fingers dirty with sweat and chalk dust. From there we overlooked the bar, the entrance to the washrooms and the corner where the television was mounted, and we could even comment on the play on a couple of tables. At one of them four players we'd never seen before, with silk gloves and their own cues, bet more on one game than the two of us spent in a month. It was there, sitting side by side, that Ricardo Laverde told me he never looked anyone in the eye. It was also there that something began to trouble me about Ricardo Laverde: a deep discrepancy between his diction and his manners, which were never less than elegant, and his dishevelled appearance, his precarious finances, his very presence in these places where people look for a bit of stability when their lives, for whatever reason, are unstable.

'How strange, Ricardo,' I said. 'I've never asked you what you do.'

'It's true, never,' said Laverde. 'And I've never asked you either. But that's because I imagine you're a professor, like everybody else around here. There're too many universities downtown. Are you a professor, Yammara?'

'Yes,' I said. 'I teach Law.'

'Oh great,' said Laverde with a sideways smile. 'More lawyers is just what this country needs.'

It seemed like he was going to say something else. He didn't say anything.

'But you haven't answered me,' I then insisted. 'What do you do?'

There was a silence. What must have passed through his head in those two seconds: now, with time, I can understand. What calculations, what denials, what reticence.

'I'm a pilot,' said Laverde in a voice I'd never heard. 'I was a pilot, I should say. What I am is a retired pilot.'

'What kind of pilot?'

'A pilot of things that need piloting.'

'Well, yeah, but what things? Passenger planes? Surveillance helicopters? The thing about this is I . . .'

'Look, Yammara,' he cut me off in a deliberate, firm tone of voice, 'I don't tell my life story to just anyone. Do me a favour and don't confuse billiards with friendship.'

He might have offended me, but he didn't: in his words, behind the sudden and rather gratuitous aggressiveness, there was a plea. After the rude reply came those gestures of repentance and reconciliation, a child seeking attention in desperate ways, and I forgave the rudeness the way one forgives a child. Every once in a while Don José, the manager of the place, came over: a heavy-set, bald man in a butcher's apron, who topped up our glasses with rum and with ice and then went back to his aluminium stool beside the bar, to tackle *El Espacio*'s crossword puzzle. I was thinking of his wife, Elena Fritts de Laverde. One day of some year, Ricardo left her life and went to jail. But what had he done to deserve it? And hadn't his wife visited him in all those years? And how did a pilot end up spending his days in a downtown billiard club and his money on bets? Maybe that was the first time the idea, though intuitive and rudimentary in form, passed through my head, the same idea that would later reiterate itself, embodied in different words or sometimes without any need for words: *This man has not always been this man. This man used to be another man.*

It was already dark when we left. I don't know exactly how much we drank at the billiard club, but I know that the rum had gone to our heads, and the pavements of La Candelaria had become even narrower. They were barely passable: people were flowing out of the thousands of downtown offices on their way home, or into the department stores to buy Christmas presents, or coagulating at the corners, while waiting for a bus. The first thing Ricardo Laverde did on the way out was to bump into a woman in an orange suit (or a suit that looked orange there, under the yellow lights). 'Watch where you're going, idiot,' the woman said, and then it seemed obvious to me that letting him find his own way home in that state would be irresponsible or even risky. I offered to walk with him and he accepted, or at least didn't refuse in any perceptible way. In a matter of minutes we were passing in front of the big closed front door of La Bordadita Church, and then we began to leave the crowds behind, as if we'd entered another city, a city under curfew. Deepest Candelaria is a place out of time: in all of Bogotá, only on certain streets in this part of town is it possible to imagine what life was like a century ago. And it was during this walk that Laverde talked to me for the first time the way one talks to a friend. At first I thought he was trying to ingratiate himself with me after the gratuitous discourtesy (alcohol tends to provoke this kind of repentance, this kind of private guilt); then it seemed to me there was something more, an urgent task the motivations of which I couldn't quite understand, a pressing duty. I humoured him, of course, the way one humours all the drunks in the world when they start to tell their drunken stories. 'That woman is all I have,' he said.

'Elena?' I said. 'Your wife?'

'She's everything, all I have. Don't ask me to give you details, Yammara, it's not easy for anyone to talk about his mistakes. I've made some, like everyone has. I've fucked up, yeah. I really fucked up. You're very young, Yammara, so young that maybe you're still a virgin of these kinds of mistakes. I don't mean fooling around on your girlfriend, not that, I don't mean having fucked your best friend's girlfriend, that's kids' stuff. I'm talking about real mistakes, Yammara, this is something you don't know about yet. And a good thing too. Enjoy it, Yammara, enjoy it while you can: a person's happy until they fuck it up somehow, then there's no way to get back to what you used to be.

Well, that's what I'm going to find out in the next couple of days. Elena's going to come and I'm going to try to get back what there used to be. Elena was the love of my life. And we separated, we didn't want to separate, but we separated. Life separated us, life does that kind of thing. I fucked up. I fucked up and we were separated. But the important thing isn't fucking it all up, Yammara, listen carefully, the important thing isn't fucking up, but knowing how to fix the fuck-up. Even though time has passed, however many years, it's never too late to fix what you've broken. And that's what I'm going to do. Elena's coming now and that's what I'm going to do, no mistake can last for ever. All this was a long time ago, a long, long time ago. You hadn't even been born yet, I don't think. Let's say 1970, more or less. When were you born?'

'In 1970,' I said. 'Exactly.'

'You sure?'

'Sure.'

'You weren't born in '71?'

'No,' I said. 'In '70.'

'Well, anyway. Lots of things happened that year. In the following years too, of course, but mostly that year. That year our life changed. I let us be separated, but that's not the important thing, Yammara, listen up, the important thing isn't that, but what's going to happen now. Elena's coming now and that's what I'm going to do, fix things. It can't be that hard, can it? How many people do you know who've made up for going the wrong way halfway down the road? Lots, no? Well, that's what I'm going to do. It can't be that hard.'

Ricardo Laverde told me all that. We were alone by the time we got to his street, so alone that we'd obliviously started to walk down the middle of the road. A cart overflowing with old newspapers and pulled by a famished-looking mule passed us, and the man holding the reins (the knotted rope that served as reins) had to whistle loudly at us to get out of his way. I remember the smell of the animal's shit, though I don't remember it shitting at that precise moment, and I also remember the staring eyes of a child who was in the back, sitting on the wooden planks with his feet hanging down over the edge. And then I remember stretching out a hand to say goodbye to Laverde and being left with my hand in mid-air, more or less like that other hand covered in pigeons in the photo from Bolívar Plaza, because Laverde turned his back on me and, opening a big door with a key from another era, said to me, 'Don't tell me you're going to go now. Come in and we'll have a nightcap, young man, since we're having such a good talk.'

'I really have got to go, Ricardo.'

'A person doesn't have to do anything but die,' he said, his tongue a little thick. 'One drink, no more, I swear. Since you've already come as far as this godforsaken place.'

We'd arrived in front of an old, colonial, one-storey house, not carefully preserved like a cultural or historical site, but sad and dilapidated, one of those properties that pass from generation to generation as the families get poorer, until the last one of the line sells it to pay off a debt or puts it to work as a boarding house or brothel. Laverde was standing on the threshold and holding the door open with his foot, in one of those precarious balances that only a good drunk can pull off. Behind him I could see a brick-floored corridor and then the smallest colonial patio I'd ever seen. In the centre of the patio, instead of the traditional fountain, there was a clothes line, and the whitewashed walls of the corridor had been decorated with calendars of naked women. I had been in similar houses before, so I could imagine what was beyond the dark corridor: I imagined rooms with green wooden doors that close with a padlock like a shed, and I imagined that in one of those 3- by 2-metre sheds, rented by the week, lived Ricardo Laverde. But it was late, I had to hand in my marks the next day (to meet the unbearable, bureaucratic demands of the university, which gave no respite), and walking through that neighbourhood, after a certain time of night, was too much like tempting fate. Laverde was drunk and he'd embarked on a series of confidences I hadn't foreseen, and I realized at this moment that it was one thing to ask the guy what kind of planes he flew and something else entirely to go into his tiny room with him while he wept over his lost loves. Emotional intimacy has never been easy for me, much less with other men. Everything Laverde was going to tell me then, I thought, he could tell me the next day in the open air or in public places, without any vacuous camaraderie or tears on my shoulder, without any superficial masculine solidarity. The world's not going to end tomorrow, I thought. Nor is Laverde going to forget his life story.

So I wasn't too surprised to hear myself say, 'No really, Ricardo. It'll have to be another time.'

He remained quiet for an instant.

'OK then,' he said. If he was greatly disappointed, he didn't show it. He just turned his back and, closing the door behind him, muttered, 'Another time it'll have to be.'

Of course if I'd known then what I know now, if I could have foreseen the way that Ricardo Laverde would mark my life, I wouldn't have thought twice about it. Since then I've often wondered what would have happened if I'd accepted the invitation, what Laverde would have told me if I'd gone in for one last drink, which is never only just one, how that might have changed what came later.

But they're all useless questions. There is no more disastrous mania, no more dangerous whim, than the speculation over roads not taken.

It was a long while before I saw him again. I stopped in at the billiard club a couple of times over the following days, but my routines didn't coincide with his. Then, just when it occurred to me that I could go and visit him at his house, I found out that he'd gone away on a trip. I didn't know where, or with whom; but one afternoon Laverde had paid his tab of drinks and games, had announced he was going on vacation and the next day had vanished like a gambler's winning streak. So I also stopped frequenting the place, which, in the absence of Laverde, suddenly lost all interest. The university closed for the holidays, and the whole routine that spins around the department and exams was adjourned, and its spaces deserted (the voiceless halls, the offices without any hustle and bustle). It was during that interlude that Aura Rodríguez, a former student with whom I'd been going out more or less secretly, or at least cautiously, for a few months, told me she was pregnant.

Aura Rodríguez. Among her surnames were an Aljure and a Hadad, and that Lebanese blood showed in her deep eyes and in the bridge of her thick eyebrows and the narrowness of her forehead, a combination that might have given the impression of seriousness or even bad temper in someone less extroverted and affable. Her quick smile, eyes attentive to the point of impertinence, disarmed or neutralized features that, as beautiful as they might be (and yes, they were beautiful, they were very beautiful), could turn hard or even hostile with a slight knitting of her brow, with a certain way of parting her lips to breathe through her mouth at moments of greatest tension or anger. I liked Aura, at least in part, because her biography had so little in common with mine, beginning with the uprootedness of her childhood: Aura's parents, both from the Caribbean coast, had arrived in Bogotá with her a babe in arms, but they never managed to feel at home in this city of sly, shrewd people, and as the years went by ended up accepting an opportunity to work in Santo Domingo and then another in Mexico and then another very brief one in Santiago de Chile, so Aura left Bogotá when she was still very young and her adolescence was a sort of itinerant circus and, at the same time, a permanently inconclusive symphony. Aura's family returned to Bogotá at the beginning of 1994, weeks after

Pablo Escobar was killed; the difficult decade had just ended, and Aura would always be ignorant of what we who lived through it had seen and heard. Later, when the rootless young woman showed up at the university for her admissions interview, the dean of the faculty asked her the same question he asked all the applicants: why Law? Aura's answer swerved back and forth, but eventually arrived at a reason less related to the future than to the recent past: 'To be able to stay in a single place.' Lawyers can only practise where they've studied, said Aura, and she no longer felt able to postpone that kind of stability. She didn't say so at the time, but her parents had already begun to plan the next trip and Aura had decided she wouldn't be part of it.

So she stayed in Bogotá on her own, living with two girls from Barranquilla in an apartment with a few pieces of cheap furniture where everything, starting with the tenants, had a transitory quality. And she began to study Law. She was a student of mine in my first year as a professor, when I too was a novice; and we didn't really talk again after the course finished, in spite of sharing the same corridors, in spite of frequenting the same student cafés downtown, in spite of having said hello in the Legis or the Temis, the legal bookshops with their public-office air and bureaucratic white tiles smelling of detergent. One evening in March we met at a cinema on 24th Street; it struck us as funny that we were both going to see black-and-white movies on our own (there was a series of Buñuel films, that day they were showing *Simon of the Desert*, and I fell asleep fifteen minutes in). We exchanged phone numbers to meet for a coffee the next day, and the next day we left our coffees half finished when we realized, in the middle of a banal conversation, that we weren't interested in telling each other about our lives, but just wanted to be somewhere we could go to bed and spend the rest of the afternoon looking at the body we'd each been imagining since our paths had first crossed in the cold space of the classroom. I already knew the husky voice and the prominent collarbones; the freckles between her breasts surprised me (I'd imagined clear and smooth skin like that of her face) and her mouth surprised me too, as it was, for scientifically inexplicable reasons, always cold.

But then the surprises and explorations and discoveries gave way to another situation, perhaps more surprising, because it was so unexpected. Over the following days we went on seeing each other constantly and realizing that our respective worlds didn't change much after our clandestine encounters, that our relationship didn't affect the practical side of our lives for good or ill, but coexisted with it, like a parallel highway, like a story seen in the episodes of a television series. We realized how little we knew each other; I spent a long time discovering Aura, that peculiar woman who went to bed with me at night and came out with anecdotes about herself or others, and as she did so created for me an absolutely novel world where a friend's house smelled of headache, for example, or where a headache could quite easily taste of *guanábana* ice cream. 'It's like living with synaesthesia,' I told her. I'd never seen someone hold a gift to her nose before opening it, even though it was obviously a pair of shoes, or a stuffed animal, or a poor innocent ring. 'What does a ring smell like?' I said to Aura. 'It doesn't smell of anything, that's the truth. But there's no way to explain that to you.'

And so, I suspect, we could have gone on all our lives. But five days before Christmas Aura appeared dragging a red suitcase with tiny wheels, with pockets in every part of it. 'I'm six weeks pregnant,' she told me. 'I want us to spend the holidays together, and then we'll see what we do.' In one of those pockets there was a digital alarm clock and a case that didn't contain pencils, as I thought it did, but make-up; in another, a photo of Aura's parents, who by then were well settled in Buenos Aires. She took out the photo and placed it face down on one of the night-stands, and only turned it over when I said yes, we should spend the holidays together, that's a good idea. Then – the image is very much alive in my memory – she lay down on my bed, on top of my made bed, and closed her eyes and began to talk. 'People don't believe me,' she said. I thought she meant about her pregnancy and said, 'Who? Who've you told?' 'When I talk about my parents,' said Aura. 'They don't believe me.' I lay down beside her and crossed my arms behind my head and listened. 'They don't believe me, for example, when I say I don't understand why they had me, when they already had enough in each other. They still have enough. They're enough for each other, that's how it is. Have you ever felt that? Have you ever been with your parents and all of a sudden you feel superfluous? It happens to me a lot, or at least it did until I was old enough to move out, and it's weird, being with your folks and they start looking at each other with that look that you've already identified and they're laughing over something that's just between them and you have no idea what they're laughing at, and worse, you feel you have no right to ask. It's a look I learned by heart a long time ago, not complicity, it's something way beyond that, Antonio. More than once it happened to me as a little girl, in Mexico or in Chile, more than once. At a meal, with guests they didn't like much but invited anyway, or in the street when they met someone who said stupid things, suddenly I could fast forward five seconds and think: *here comes the look*, and sure enough, five seconds later their eyebrows moved, their eyes met, and I'd see on their faces that smile that no one else saw and that they used to make fun of people the way I've never seen anyone else make fun of other people. How do you smile without people seeing you smile? They could, Antonio, I swear I'm not exaggerating, I grew up with those smiles. Why did it bother me so much? It still bothers me. Why so much?'

There wasn't sadness in her words, but irritation or rather anger, the anger of someone who has suffered a deceit through inattention or neglect, yes, that was it, the anger of someone who's been led up the garden path. 'I've been remembering something,' she said then. 'I would have been about fourteen or fifteen, and we were just about to leave Mexico. It was a Friday, a school day, and I decided to go along with some friends who weren't really in the mood for geography or mathematics. We were walking across a park, it was San Lorenzo Park, but that doesn't matter. And then I saw a man who looked a lot like my dad, but in a car that wasn't my dad's. He stopped at the corner, facing down the avenue, and then a woman got into the car who looked a lot like my mother, but dressed in clothes that my mother wouldn't wear and with red hair, which my mother didn't have. That happened on the far side of the park, their only option was to turn the car around very slowly and drive right past us. I don't know what I was thinking when I signalled for them to stop, but the resemblance was too striking. So they stopped, me on the pavement and the car on the street, and up close I realized immediately that it was them, it was my parents. And I smiled at them, asked them what was going on, and that's when the fear started: they looked at me and spoke to me as if they didn't know me, as if they'd never seen me before. As if I was one of my friends. I later understood they were playing. A husband who picks up a pricey hooker on the street. They were playing and they couldn't let me ruin the game. And that night, everything was normal: we had dinner as a family, watched television, everything. They didn't say anything. And I spent a few days wondering what had happened, wondering without understanding and feeling something I'd never felt, feeling afraid, but afraid of what, isn't it absurd?' She took a gulp of air (her lips pressed against her teeth) and whispered, 'And now I'm going to have a child. And I don't know if I'm ready, Antonio. I don't know if I'm ready.'

'I think you are,' I told her.

Mine was also a whisper, as far as I remember. And then came another: 'Bring everything,' I told her. 'We're ready.'

In reply, Aura began to weep with a silent but sustained crying that only ended when she fell asleep.

The end of 1995 was typical of that time of year for Bogotá, with that intense blue sky of the Andean highlands, with those early mornings when the temperature goes down to zero and the dry air ruins the potato or cauliflower crops, and then the rest of the day is sunny and warm and the light is so clear that you end up with sunburn on your cheeks and the nape of your neck. I devoted that time to Aura with the constancy – no: the obsession – of a teenager. We spent the days walking at the doctor's recommendation and taking naps (her), reading deplorable research projects (me) or watching pirated films several days before they premiered in the meagre Bogotá listings (both of us). At night Aura accompanied me to novenas at the homes of my relatives or friends, and we danced and drank non-alcoholic beer and lit Catherine wheels and powder-keg volcanoes and launched rockets that exploded into rackets of colour in the yellowish night sky of the city, that darkness that's never really dark. And never, never did I wonder what Ricardo Laverde might be doing at that same instant, if he was praying the novenas too, if there were fireworks and if he was setting off rockets or lighting Catherine wheels, and if he was doing so on his own or in company.

The morning that followed one of those novenas, a cloudy, dark morning, Aura and I had our first ultrasound. Aura had been on the verge of cancelling it, and I would have done if that hadn't meant waiting another twenty days to find out about the child, with the risks that might entail. It wasn't just any old morning, it wasn't a 21 December like any other 21 December of any other year: since the early hours of the morning the radio and television and newspaper had been telling us that American Airlines Flight 965, which departed from Miami for Alfonso Bonilla Aragón International Airport in the city of Cali, had crashed into the west side of El Diluvio Mountain the previous night. It was carrying one hundred and fifty-five passengers, many of whom weren't even going to Cali, but were expecting to catch the last flight of the evening to Bogotá. At the time the news came out they'd found only four survivors, all with serious injuries, and the figure would not go any higher. I knew the inevitable details – that the plane was a 757, that the night was clear and starry, that they were starting to talk about human error – from the news broadcasts on all stations. I regretted the accident, felt all the sympathy I'm capable of for the people waiting for their relatives, and for those who, in their seats on the plane, understood from one moment to the next that they would not arrive, that they were living their last seconds. But it was an ephemeral and distracted sympathy, and I'm sure it had died out by the time we entered the narrow cubicle where Aura, lying down and half undressed, and I, standing by the screen, received the news that our little girl (Aura was magically sure it was a girl), who at that moment measured 7 millimetres, was in perfect health. On the screen was a sort of luminous universe, a confusing constellation in movement where, the woman in the white coat told us, our little girl was: that island in the sea – every one of her 7 millimetres – was her. Beneath the electric brightness of the screen I saw Aura smile, and I'm very afraid I won't forget that smile as long as I live. Then I saw her put a finger on her belly to smear it with the blue gel the nurse had used. And then I saw her put her finger to her nose, to smell it and classify it according to the rules of her world, and seeing that was absurdly satisfying, like finding a coin in the street.

I don't remember having thought of Ricardo Laverde there, during the ultrasound, while Aura and I, perfectly astonished, listened to the sound of an accelerated little heartbeat. I don't remember having thought of Ricardo Laverde later, while Aura and I listed girls' names on the same white envelope in which the hospital had given us the written report of the ultrasound. I don't remember having thought of Ricardo Laverde while reading this report out loud, discovering that our little girl was in a fundal intrauterine position and she was a normal oval shape, words that made Aura erupt into violent fits of laughter in the middle of the restaurant. I don't remember having thought of Ricardo Laverde even when I made a mental inventory of all the fathers of daughters that I knew, a little to see if the birth of a daughter had a predictable effect on people, or to start looking for sources of advice or possible support, as if I guessed that what I was heading into was the most intense, most mysterious, most unpredictable experience I'd ever live through. Actually, I don't remember with any certainty what thoughts passed through my head that day or the days that followed – while the world went through its slow and lazy passage from one year to the next – other than those of my impending paternity. I was expecting a daughter, at the age of twenty-six I was expecting a daughter, and faced with the vertigo of my youth the only thing that occurred to me was to think of my father, who at my age had already had me and my sister, and that was after my mother and he had already lost their first baby. I didn't yet know that an old Polish novelist had spoken a long time before of the shadow-line, that moment when a young man becomes the proprietor of his own life, but that was what I was feeling while my little girl was growing inside Aura's womb: I felt that I was about to become a new and unknown creature whose face I couldn't manage to see, whose powers I could not measure, and I also felt that after the metamorphosis there would be no turning back. To put it in other words and without so much mythology: I felt that something very important and also very fragile had become my responsibility, and I felt, improbably, that my abilities were equal to the challenge. It doesn't surprise me that I barely have any vague notion of living in the real world during those days, for my fickle memory has drained them of all meaning or relevance other than that related to Aura's pregnancy.

On 31 December, on our way to a New Year's Eve party, Aura was going through the list of names, a yellow sheet of paper with red horizontal lines and a green double margin, covered in underlinings and crossings-out and marginal comments, that we'd started carrying with us everywhere and would take out at those dead times – in bank queues, waiting rooms, Bogotá's famous traffic jams – when other people read magazines or imagine other people's lives or imagine improved versions of their own lives. Few names had survived from the long column of candidates, along with the future mother's corresponding note or prejudice.

Martina (but it's a tennis player's name)
Carlota (but it's an empress's name)

We were on the highway, driving north, under the 100th Street bridge. There was an accident up ahead and the traffic was almost completely stopped. None of that seemed to matter to Aura, involved as she was in considerations about the name of our daughter. Somewhere I could hear the ambulance's siren; I checked the rear-view mirror, trying to find the swirling red lights demanding a way through, making its way, but I couldn't see anything.

That was when Aura said, 'What about Leticia? I think one of my great-grandmothers or somebody was called Leticia.'

I repeated the name once or twice, its long vowels, its consonants that mixed vulnerability and strength.

'Leticia,' I said. 'Yes, sounds right.'

So I was a changed man the first working day of the year, when I arrived at the 14th Street billiard club and bumped into Ricardo Laverde, and I remember very well feeling surprised by my own emotions: sympathy for him and his wife, Señora Elena Fritts, and an intense desire, more intense than I ever would have expected, for their encounter during the holidays to have had the best possible consequences. He'd already started his game, on another table, and I started to play on my own. Laverde didn't look at me; he was treating me as if we'd just seen each other the previous night. At some point in the afternoon, I thought, the rest of the customers would start leaving, and the usual ones would end up finishing off the evening like in musical chairs. Ricardo Laverde and I would meet, play a little and then, with any luck, we'd resume the conversation we'd started before Christmas. But that didn't happen. When he finished his game I saw him return his cue to the rack, saw him start walking towards the door, saw him change his mind, and saw him walking over to the table where I had just finished my shot. In spite of the profuse sweat on his forehead, in spite of the tiredness bathing his face, there was nothing in his greeting that worried me. 'Happy New Year,' he said from a distance, 'how were your holidays?' But he didn't let me answer, or rather he interrupted my answer somehow, or there was something in his tone of voice or in his gestures that let me know the question was rhetorical, one of those vacuous courtesies always exchanged by *bogotanos,* with no expectation of a sincere or considered response. Laverde took an old-fashioned black cassette tape out of his pocket, with an orange sticker on it and on the sticker the letters *BASF.* He showed it to me without moving his arm very far from his body, like someone offering some illegal merchandise, emeralds in the plaza, a folded paper of drugs beside the criminal court.

'Hey, Yammara, I have to listen to this,' he told me. 'You wouldn't know anybody who could lend me a cassette player?'

'Doesn't Don José have one?'

'No, he hasn't got anything,' he said. 'And this is urgent.' He rapped on the plastic case a couple of times. 'And it's private as well.'

'Well,' I said, 'there is a place a couple of blocks away, couldn't hurt to ask.'

I was thinking of the Casa de Poesía, the only plausible option in the neighbourhood at that time of day. It was the former residence of the poet José Asunción Silva, now converted into a cultural centre where they hold readings and workshops. I used to go there quite often all through my degree. One of its rooms was a unique place in Bogotá: there, all sorts of word-struck people would go to sit on soft leather sofas, near fairly modern stereo equipment, and listen to now legendary recordings: Borges reading Borges, García Márquez reading García Márquez, León de Greiff reading León de Greiff. Silva and his work were on everybody's lips those days, for in that barely begun 1996 the centenary of his suicide was going to be commemorated. 'This year,' I'd read in an opinion piece by a well-known journalist, 'statues will be raised to him all over the city, and all the politicians will mention his name, and everyone will wander around reciting his "Nocturne", and everybody will take him flowers at the Casa de Poesía. And Silva, wherever he might be, will find this curious: this prudish society that humiliated him, that pointed their fingers at him every chance they got, paying homage to him now as if he were a head of state. The ruling class of our country, haughty charlatans, have always liked to appropriate culture. And that's what's going to happen with Silva: they are going to appropriate his memory. And his real readers are going to spend the whole year wondering why the hell they don't leave him alone.' It's not impossible that I had that column in mind (in some dark part of my mind, deep down, very deep, in the archive of useless things) at the moment I chose that place to take Laverde.

We walked the two blocks without saying a word, with our eyes on the broken paving stones or on the dark green hills that rose in the distance, bristling with eucalyptus and telephone poles like the scales on a Gila monster. When we got to the entrance and walked up the stone steps, Laverde let me go in first: he'd never been in such a place, and he acted with the misgivings, the suspicions, of an animal in a dangerous situation. There were two high-school students in the room with the sofas, a couple of teenagers listening to the same recording and every once in a while looking at each other and laughing indecently, and a man in a suit and tie, with a faded leather briefcase on his lap, snoring shamelessly. I explained the situation to the woman at the desk, who was no doubt used to exotic requests, and she looked me over through squinting eyes, seemed to recognize me or identify me as a person who'd been there many times before, and held out her hand.

'Let's see, then,' she said unenthusiastically. 'What is it you want to play?'

Laverde handed her the cassette like a soldier surrendering his weapon, with fingers visibly smudged with blue billiard chalk. He went to sit down, submissive as I'd never seen him before, in the armchair the woman pointed him to; he put on the headphones, leaned back and closed his eyes. Meanwhile, I was looking for something to occupy my time while I waited, and my hand picked up Silva's poems as it might have chosen any other recording (I must have given in to the superstition of anniversaries). I sat down in my chair, picked up the corresponding headphones, adjusted them over my ears with that feeling of putting myself beyond or closer to real life, of starting to live in another dimension. And when the 'Nocturne' began to play, when a voice I couldn't identify – a baritone that verged on melodrama – read that first line that every Colombian has pronounced aloud at least once, I noticed that Ricardo Laverde was crying. *One night all heavy with perfume*, said the baritone over a piano accompaniment, and a few steps away from me Ricardo Laverde, who wasn't listening to the lines I was listening to, wiped the back of his hand across his eyes, then his whole sleeve, *with murmurs and music of wings*. Ricardo Laverde's shoulders began to shake; he hung his head, brought his hands together like someone praying. *And your shadow, lean and languid*, said Silva in the voice of the melodramatic baritone, *And my shadow, cast by the moonbeams*. I didn't know whether to look at Laverde or not, whether to leave him alone in his sorrow or go and ask him what was wrong. I remember having thought that I could at least take off my headphones, a way like any other of opening a space between Laverde and me, of inviting him to speak to me; and I remember deciding against it, having chosen the safety and silence of my recording, where the melancholy of Silva's poem would sadden me without putting me at risk. I guessed that Laverde's sadness was full of risks, I was afraid of what that sadness might contain, but my intuition didn't go far enough to understand what had happened. I didn't remember the woman Laverde had been waiting for, I didn't remember her name, I didn't associate him with the accident at El Diluvio, but I stayed where I was, in my chair and with the headphones on, trying not to interrupt Ricardo Laverde's sadness, and I even closed my eyes so I wouldn't bother him with my indiscreet gaze, to allow him a certain privacy in the middle of that public place. In my head, and only in my head, Silva said: *And they were one single long shadow*. In my self-contained world, where all was full of the baritone voice and Silva's words and the decadent piano music that enveloped them, a time went by that lengthens in my memory. Those who listen to poetry know how this can happen, time kept by the lines of verse like a metronome and at the same time stretching and dispersing and confusing us like dreamtime.

When I opened my eyes Laverde was no longer there.

'Where did he go?' I said with the headphones still on. My voice reached me from afar, and my absurd reaction was to remove the headphones and repeat the question, as if the woman behind the desk wouldn't have heard it properly the first time.

'Who?' she asked.

'My friend,' I said. It was the first time I described him as such, and I suddenly felt ridiculous: no, Laverde was not my friend. 'The guy who was sitting there.'

'Oh, I don't know, he didn't say,' she replied. Then she turned away, checked the sound equipment; mistrustfully, as if I were complaining about something she'd done, she added, 'And I gave the cassette back to him, OK? You can ask him.'

I left the room and looked quickly through the building. The house where José Asunción Silva had spent his final days had a bright patio in the middle, separated from the corridors that framed it in narrow glass windows that wouldn't have existed in the poet's time and now protected the visitors from the rain: my footsteps, in those silent corridors, resounded without echoes. Laverde was not in the library, or sitting on the wooden benches, or in the conference room. He must have left. I walked towards the narrow front door to the house, past a security guard in a brown uniform (he wore a tilted cap, like a thug in a movie), past the room where the poet had shot himself in the chest a hundred years earlier, and as I came out onto 14th Street I saw that the sun was now hidden behind the buildings of 7th Avenue, saw that the yellow streetlights were timidly starting to come on, and saw Ricardo Laverde, in his long coat, his head down, walking two blocks from where I was, already almost at the billiard club. I thought: *And they were one single long shadow*, absurdly the line came back to mind; and in that same instant I saw a motorbike that had been still until now on the pavement. Maybe I saw it because its two riders had made a barely perceptible movement: the feet of the one on the back rising up onto the stirrups, his hand disappearing inside his jacket. Both of them were wearing helmets, of course; and the visors of both, of course, were dark, a large rectangular eye in the middle of the large head.

I shouted to Laverde, but not because I already knew what was going to happen to him, not because I wanted to warn him of anything: at that moment my only ambition was to catch up to him, ask him if he was all right, perhaps offer my help. But Laverde didn't hear me. I started to take bigger steps, avoiding people walking along the narrow pavement, which at that point is almost knee-high, stepping down onto the road if necessary to walk faster, and thinking unthinkingly: *And they were one single long shadow*, or rather tolerating the line like a jingle we can't get out of our head. At the corner of 4th Avenue, the dense afternoon traffic progressed slowly in a single lane, towards the exit onto Jiménez. I found a space to cross the street in front of a green bus, whose headlights, just turned on, had brought to life the dust of the street, the fumes from an exhaust pipe, an incipient drizzle. That's what I was thinking about, the rain I'd have to protect myself from in a little while, when I caught up to Laverde, or rather I got so close to him I could see how the rain was darkening the shoulders of his overcoat. 'Everything's going to be all right,' I said: a stupid thing to say, because I didn't know what everything was, much less whether or not it was going to be all right. Ricardo looked at me with his face contorted in pain. 'Elena was there,' he told me. 'Was where?' I asked. 'On the plane,' he answered. I think in a brief moment of confusion Aura had the name Elena, or I imagined Elena with Aura's face and pregnant body, and I think at that moment I experienced a new feeling that couldn't have been fear, not yet, but was quite similar to it. Then I saw the motorbike dropping down onto the road like a bucking horse, saw it accelerate to approach like a tourist looking for an address, and at the precise moment when I grabbed Laverde's arm, when my hand clutched at the sleeve of his coat by his left elbow, I saw the faceless heads looking at us and the pistol pointed towards us as naturally as a metal prosthesis, and saw two shots, and heard the explosions and felt the sudden tremor in the air. I remember having raised my arm to protect myself just before feeling the sudden weight of my body. My legs no longer held me up. Laverde fell to the ground and I fell with him, two bodies falling without a sound, and people started to shout and a continuous buzzing appeared in my ears. A man came over to Laverde's body to try to lift him up, and I remember the surprise I felt when another came over to help me. *I'm fine*, I said or remember having said, *there's nothing wrong with me*. From the ground I saw someone else jump out into the road waving his arms like a castaway and standing in front of a white pick-up truck that was turning the corner. I said Ricardo's name a couple of times; I noticed a warmth in my belly; the possibility occurred to me fleetingly that I'd wet myself, and I immediately discovered that it wasn't piss soaking through my grey T-shirt. A short while later I lost consciousness, but the last image that I have is still quite clear in my memory: it's that of my body lifted into the air and the effort of the men who put me into the back of the truck, who put me down beside Laverde like one shadow next to another, leaving on the bodywork a bloodstain, which at that hour, with so little light, was as black as the night sky.

2

Never One of My Dead

I KNOW, ALTHOUGH I don't remember, that the bullet passed through my gut without touching any organs but burning nerves and tendons and finally lodging itself in my hip bone a few inches from my spinal column. I know I lost a lot of blood and that, in spite of the supposed universality of my blood type, the stocks of it were low in the San José Hospital at the time, or its demand on the part of Bogotá's afflicted society was too high, and my father and my sister had to donate some to save my life. I know I was lucky. Everyone told me so as soon as it was possible, and besides, I know, I know in an instinctive way. The notion of my luck, this I remember, was one of the first manifestations of my recovered consciousness. I don't remember, however, the three days of surgery: they have disappeared completely, obliterated by the intermittent anaesthesia. I don't remember the hallucinations, but I do remember that I had them; I don't remember having fallen out of bed due to the abrupt movements that one of them provoked, and, although I don't remember that they tied me down in the bed to prevent that from happening again, I do remember quite well the violent claustrophobia, the terrible awareness of my vulnerability. I remember the fever, the sweat that soaked my whole body at night and obliged the nurses to change the sheets, the damage I did to my throat and the corners of my very dry lips when I tried to yank out the respirator tube; I remember the sound of my own voice when I screamed and I know, although I don't remember this either, that my screams disturbed the rest of the patients on the floor. The patients or their relatives complained, the nurses ended up moving me to another room, and in this new room, during a brief moment of lucidity, I asked about Ricardo Laverde and found out (I don't remember from whom) that he had died. I don't think I felt sad, or maybe I'm confusing, and always confused, the sadness at the news with the tears produced by pain, and anyway I know that there, busy as I was with the task of surviving, seeing the gravity of my own situation in the tattered expressions of those around me, I couldn't have thought much about the dead man. I don't remember, in any case, having blamed him for what had happened to me.

I did later. I cursed Ricardo Laverde, cursed the moment we met, and didn't for a second even consider that Laverde might not have been directly responsible for my misfortune. I was glad he'd died: I hoped, as compensation for my own pain, that he'd had a painful death. Between the mists of my faltering consciousness I responded in monosyllables to my parents' questions. You met him at the billiard club? Yes. You never knew what he did, if he was up to something fishy? No. Why was he killed? Don't know. Why was he killed, Antonio? I don't know, I don't know. Antonio, why was he killed? I don't know, I don't know, I don't know. The question was repeated insistently and my answer was always the same, and it soon became obvious that the question didn't require an answer: it was more like a lament. The same night Ricardo Laverde was gunned down another sixteen murders were committed in diverse parts of the city and using diverse methods, and the ones that have stuck in my mind are that of Neftalí Gutiérrez, a taxi driver, beaten to death with a wheel wrench, and that of Jairo Alejandro Niño, an automotive mechanic, who received nine machete blows in a vacant lot on the west side. The Laverde crime was one of many, and it was almost arrogant or pretentious to believe that we were due the luxury of an answer.

'But what had he done to get himself killed?' my father asked me.

'I don't know,' I told him. 'He hadn't done anything.'

'He must've done something,' he'd say.

'But what does it matter now,' my mother would say.

'Well, yes,' said my father. 'What does it matter now.'

As I began surfacing, my hatred for Laverde gave way to a hatred for my own body and what my body was feeling. And that hatred that had myself as its object transformed into a hatred for everyone else, and one day I decided I didn't want to see anybody, and I expelled my family from the hospital and forbade them from coming back to see me until my situation improved. 'But we worry,' said my mother, 'we want to take care of you.' 'But I don't. I don't want you to take care of me. I don't want anyone taking care of me. I want you all to go.' 'What if you need something? What if we can help you and we're not here?' 'I don't need anything. I need to be alone. I want to be alone.' I want to sample silence, I thought then: a line from León de Greiff, another of the poets I used to listen to at Silva's house (poetry accosts us at the most unexpected moments). *Quiero catar silencio, non curo de compaña,* I want to sample silence, I won't be cured by companionship. Leave me alone. Yes, that's what I said to my parents. Leave me alone.

A doctor came to explain the uses of the trigger I had in my hand: when I felt too much pain, he told me, I could press the button, and a spurt of intravenous morphine would soothe me immediately. But there were limits. The first day I used up my daily dose in a third of the time (I pressed the button like a child with a new video game), and the hours that followed are, in my memory, the closest I've been to hell. I'm telling this because that's how, between the hallucinations of the pain and those of the morphine, the days of my recovery went by. I fell asleep at any moment, without any apparent routine, like prisoners in stories; I opened my eyes to a landscape that was always strange, the most curious characteristic of which was that it never became familiar, I always seemed to be seeing it for the first time. At some moment I can't manage to pinpoint, Aura appeared in that landscape, sitting there on the brown sofa when I opened my eyes, looking at me with genuine pity. It was a new sensation (or it was new to be looked at and cared for by a woman who was expecting my child), but I don't recall having thought so at the time.

The nights. I remember the nights. The fear of the darkness began in those last days of my hospitalization, and only disappeared a year later: at six thirty in the evening, when night falls suddenly in Bogotá, my heart began to beat furiously, and at first it took the dialectic efforts of several doctors to convince me that I wasn't about to die of a heart attack. The long Bogotá night – it always lasts more than eleven hours, no matter the time of year and much less the mental state of those who suffer it – seemed almost unendurable to me in the hospital, with its nocturnal life marked by the permanently illuminated white corridors, by the neon gloom of the white rooms; but in the bedroom of my apartment the darkness was total, for the streetlights didn't reach my tenth floor, and the terror I felt at just imagining myself waking up in the dark obliged me to sleep with the light on, as I did when I was little. Aura put up with the illuminated nights better than I would have expected, sometimes resorting to those masks they give you on planes to create a personal darkness, sometimes giving up and turning on the television to watch an infomercial and amuse herself with machines that chop all kinds of fruit and lotions that dissolve all body fat. Her own body, of course, was transforming; a little girl called Leticia was growing in there, but I wasn't capable of giving her the attention she deserved. I was woken up on several nights by an absurd nightmare: I'd gone back to live at my parents' house, but with Aura, and suddenly the gas stove blew up and the whole family was dying and I realized there was nothing I could do. And, no matter what time it was, I ended up phoning my old house, just to make sure nothing had happened in reality and that the dream was just a dream. Aura tried to calm me down. She stared at me, I could feel her looking at me. 'It's nothing,' I told her. And only at the end of the night would I manage to sleep for a few hours, coiled up like a dog frightened by fireworks, wondering why Leticia wasn't in the dream, what had Leticia done to be banished from the dream.

In my memory, the months that followed were a time of large fears and small discomforts. On the street I was assailed by the unmistakable certainty I was being watched; the internal injuries caused by the bullet wound forced me to use crutches for several months. A pain I'd never felt before appeared in my left leg, similar to what people feel when they're about to have an appendicitis attack. The doctors told me how slowly nerves grow and the time it takes to recover a certain degree of autonomy, and I listened to them without understanding, or without understanding that they were talking about me; somewhere else, far from where I was, Aura listened to explanations from other doctors on very different subjects, and took folic acid tablets and received cortisone injections to help the baby's lungs mature (in Aura's family there was a history of premature deliveries). Her body was changing, but I didn't notice. Aura put my hand on one side of her prominent belly button. 'There, there she is. Did you feel?' 'But what does it feel like?' I asked. 'I don't know, like a butterfly, like tiny wings brushing against your skin. I don't know if you understand.' And I told her I did, that I understood perfectly, although it was a lie.

I didn't feel anything: I was distracted: the fear distracted me. I imagined the faces of the murderers, hidden behind the visors; the blast of the shots and the continuous whistle in my throbbing eardrums, the sudden apparition of blood. Not even now, as I write, can I manage to remember those details without the same cold fear easing into my body. The fear, in the fantastic language of the therapist who treated me after the first problems, was called post-traumatic stress, and according to him had a lot to do with the era of bombs that had ravaged us a few years earlier. 'So don't worry if you have problems of an intimate nature,' the man told me (he spoke those words, *intimate nature*). I didn't say anything to that. 'Your body is fighting something serious,' the doctor continued. 'It has to concentrate on this and eliminate what isn't strictly necessary. The libido is the first to go, you see? So don't worry. Any dysfunction is normal.' I didn't respond this time either. *Dysfunction*: the word seemed ugly to me, its sounds seemed to clash, disfiguring the atmosphere, and I thought I wouldn't talk about the matter with Aura. The doctor kept talking, there was no way to make him stop talking. Fear was the main ailment of *bogotanos* of my generation, he told me. My situation, he told me, was not at all unusual: it would eventually pass, as it had passed for all the others who had visited his office. All this he told me. He never managed to comprehend that I wasn't interested in the rational explanation or much less the statistical aspect of these violent palpitations, or the instantaneous sweating that in another context would have been comical, but in the magic words that would make the sweating and palpitations disappear, the mantra that would allow me to sleep through the night.

I got used to my nocturnal routines: after a noise or the illusion of a noise had frightened me out of sleep (and left me at the mercy of the pain in my leg), I reached for my crutches, went to the living room, sat in the recliner and stayed there, watching the movements of the night on the hills around Bogotá, the green and red lights of planes that could be seen when the sky was clear, the dew accumulating on the windows like a white shadow when the temperature dropped in the early hours. It wasn't only my nights that were disturbed but my waking hours as well. Months after what happened to Laverde, a backfiring exhaust pipe, a slamming door, or even a heavy book falling in a certain way onto a certain surface would be enough to set me off on an attack of anxiety and paranoia. At any moment, for no discernible reason, I might start to weep inconsolably. The tears would come upon me with no warning: at the dining-room table, in front of my parents or Aura, or with friends, and the feeling of being ill was joined by embarrassment. At first there was always someone who leapt up to hug me, there were the words one uses to comfort a child: 'It's all over now, Antonio, there there.' With time people, my people, got used to these bursts of tears, and the consoling words stopped, and the hugs disappeared, and the embarrassment was then greater, because it was obvious that I, rather than moving them to pity, seemed ridiculous. With strangers, who owed me no loyalty or compassion whatsoever, it was worse. During one of the first classes I taught after going back to work, a student asked me a question about Von Ihering's theories. 'Justice,' I began to say, 'has a double evolutionary base: the struggle of the individual to have his rights respected and that of the State to impose, among its associates, the necessary order.' 'So,' the student asked me, 'could we say that the man who reacts, feeling himself threatened or infringed, is the true creator of the law?' and I was going to tell him of the time when all law was incorporated within religion, those remote times when distinctions between morals and hygiene, public and private, were still non-existent, but I didn't manage to do so. I covered my eyes with my tie and burst into tears. The class was adjourned. On the way out, I heard the student say, 'Poor guy. He's not going to make it.'

It wasn't the last time I heard that diagnosis. One night Aura came home late from a get-together with her girlfriends that in my city is called by its English name, a baby shower, in which gifts rain down on the future mother. She slipped in quietly, undoubtedly hoping not to wake me, but I was still up and writing notes on Von Ihering's ideas, which had thrown me into crisis. 'Why don't you try to sleep,' she said, but it wasn't a question. 'I'm working,' I told her, 'I'll go to bed as soon as I finish.' I remember her then taking off her thin overcoat (no, it wasn't an overcoat, more like a trench coat), putting it over the back of the wicker chair, leaning on the doorframe with a hand resting on her enormous belly and running the other one through her hair, all a sort of elaborate prelude people enact when they don't want to say what they're going to say, when they hope some miracle is going to free them of that obligation. 'They're talking about us,' said Aura.

'Who?'

'At the university. I don't know, people, students.'

'Professors?'

'I don't know. The students at least. Come to bed and I'll tell you.'

'Not now,' I said. 'Tomorrow. I have to work now.'

'It's after midnight,' said Aura. 'We're both tired. You're tired.'

'I have work to do. I have to prepare this class.'

'But you're tired. And you don't sleep, and not sleeping is not a good way to prepare for class either.' She paused, looked at me in the yellow dining-room light and said, 'You didn't go out today, did you?'

I didn't answer.

'You haven't showered,' she continued. 'You didn't get dressed all day. You've spent the whole day stuck in here. People say the accident changed you, Antonio, and I tell them of course it did, not to be idiots, how could it not change you. But I don't like what I'm seeing, if you want me to tell you the truth.'

'Well don't,' I barked at her. 'Nobody's asked you to.'

The conversation could have ended there, but Aura noticed something, I saw on her face all the movements of someone just realizing something, and asked me one question, 'Were you waiting for me?'

I didn't answer this time either. 'Were you waiting for me to get home?' she insisted. 'Were you worried?'

'I was preparing my class,' I said, looking her in the eye. 'It seems I can't even do that now.'

'You were worried,' she said. 'That's why you stayed up.' And then, 'Antonio, Bogotá is not a war zone. There aren't bullets floating around out there, the same thing's not going to happen to all of us.'

You know nothing, I wanted to tell her, you grew up elsewhere. There is no common ground between us, I wanted to tell her as well, there's no way for you to understand, nobody's going to explain it to you, I can't explain it to you. But those words didn't come out of my mouth.

'Nobody thinks anything's going to happen to all of us,' I told her instead. I was surprised that it sounded so loud when it hadn't been my intention to raise my voice. 'Nobody was worried because you weren't home yet. Nobody thinks you're going to get blown up by a bomb like the one at Tres Elefantes, or the bomb at DAS, because you don't work at DAS, or the bomb at Centro 93, because you never shop at Centro 93. Besides, that era is over, isn't it? So nobody thinks that's going to happen to you, Aura, we'd be very unlucky, wouldn't we? And we're not unlucky, are we?'

'Don't be like that,' said Aura. 'I . . .'

'I am preparing my class,' I cut her off, 'is it too much to ask you to respect that? Instead of talking bollocks at two in the morning, is it too much to ask that you go to bed and stop pissing me off and let me finish this fucking thing?'

As far as I remember, she didn't start to move towards my bedroom at that moment, but went first to the kitchen, and I heard the fridge opening and closing and then a door, the door of one of those cupboards that close almost by themselves if you give them a tiny nudge. And in this series of domestic sounds (in which I could follow Aura's movements, imagine them one by one) there was an annoying familiarity, a sort of irritating intimacy, as if Aura, instead of having taken care of me for weeks and supervised my recovery, had invaded my space without any authorization whatsoever. I saw her leave the kitchen with a glass in her hand: it was some intensely coloured liquid, one of those fizzy drinks that she liked and I didn't. 'Do you know how much she weighs?' she asked me.

'Who?'

'Leticia,' she said. 'I got the test results, the baby's enormous. If she hasn't been born in a week, we're going to schedule a Caesarean.'

'In a week,' I said.

'The tests were all positive,' said Aura.

'Good,' I said.

'Don't you want to know how much she weighs?' she asked.

'Who?' I asked.

I remember her standing still in the middle of the living room, the same distance from the kitchen door as from the threshold to the hallway, in a sort of no man's land. 'Antonio,' she said, 'there's nothing wrong with worry. But yours is beginning to be unhealthy. You're sick with worry. And that makes me worry.' She left the drink she'd just poured herself on the dining-room table and locked herself in the bathroom. I heard her turn on the tap to fill the bathtub; I imagined her crying as she did so, covering her sobs with the sound of running water. When I got into bed, quite a while later, Aura was still in the tub, that place where her belly was not a burden, that happy, weightless world. I fell asleep straight away and the next morning left while she was still sleeping. I thought, I confess, that Aura wasn't really asleep, but pretending to be so she wouldn't have to say goodbye to me. I thought she was hating me at that moment. I thought, with something very closely resembling fear, that her hatred was justified.

I arrived at the university a few minutes before seven. On my shoulders and in my eyes I could feel the weight of the night, the few hours of sleep. I was in the habit of waiting outside the lecture hall until the students arrived, leaning on the stone banisters of the former cloister, and going in only when it was obvious that the majority of the students were already present; that morning, perhaps due to the weariness I felt in my abdomen, perhaps because when I was seated the crutches were less noticeable, I decided to wait for them sitting down. But I didn't even manage to get close to my chair: a drawing caught my attention from the blackboard, and turning my head I found myself in front of two stick figures in obscene positions. His penis was as long as his arm; her face had no features, it was just a chalk circle with long hair. Beneath the drawing was a printed caption:

Professor Yammara introduces her to law.

I felt faint, but I don't think anyone noticed. 'Who did this?' I said out loud, but I don't remember my voice coming out as loud as I'd intended. My students' faces were blank: they'd been emptied of all content; they were chalk circles like the woman on the blackboard. I began to walk towards the steps, as fast as my hobbled gait would allow, and as I started down them, just as I was passing the drawing of Francisco José de Caldas, I completely lost control. Legend has it that Caldas, one of the precursors of Colombian independence, was descending those stairs on his way to the scaffold when he bent down to pick up a piece of charcoal, and his executioners saw him draw on the whitewashed wall an oval crossed by a line: a long black bisected O, which patriots like to interpret as *Oh, long and dark departure*. Beside this implausible and absurd and undoubtedly apocryphal hieroglyphic I passed with my heart pounding and my hands, pale and sweaty, closed tightly around the grips of my crutches. My tie was torturing my neck. I left the university and kept walking, paying little attention to what streets I was crossing or the people I brushed past, until my arms started to ache. At the north corner of Santander Park, the mime who's always there began to follow me, to imitate my awkward gait and my clumsy movements, and even my panting. He wore a one-piece black suit covered in buttons, his face painted white but no other make-up of any other colour, and he moved his arms in the air with such talent that even I seemed to suddenly see his fictitious crutches. There, while that failed good actor made fun of me and provoked the laughter of passers-by, I thought for the first time that my life was falling apart, and that Leticia, ignorant little girl, could not have chosen a worse moment to come into the world.

Leticia was born one August morning. We had spent the night at the clinic, preparing for the surgery, and in the atmosphere of the room – Aura in the bed, me on the companion's sofa – there was a sort of macabre inversion of another room, of another time. When the nurses came to take her, Aura was already giddy with anaesthetic, and the last thing she said to me was, 'I think it was O. J. Simpson's glove.' I would have liked to hold her hand, not to have crutches and be able to hold her hand, and I told her so, but she was already unconscious. I went along beside her down corridors and in lifts while the nurses told me to relax, Papá, that everything was going to be fine, and I wondered what right these women had to call me Papá, much less to give me their opinion on the future. Later, in front of the huge swinging doors of the operating theatre, they showed me to a waiting room that was more like a way station with three chairs and a table with magazines on it. I left my crutches leaning in a corner, by the photograph or rather the poster of a pink baby smiling toothlessly, hugging a giant sunflower, against a blue sky in the background. I opened an old magazine, tried to distract myself with a crossword puzzle: *Threshing place. Brother of Onan. People slow to act, especially by pretence.* But I could only think of the woman who was sleeping inside there while a scalpel opened her skin and her flesh, of the gloved hands that were going to reach inside her body and take my daughter out. May those hands be careful ones, I thought, let them move with dexterity, and not touch what they shouldn't touch. Let them not hurt you, Leticia, and don't be scared, because there's nothing to fear. I was on my feet when a young man came out and, without taking his mask off, told me, 'Both your princesses are perfectly fine.' I didn't know when I had stood up, and my leg had started to ache, so I sat back down. I held my hands to my face out of shame, nobody likes to make a show of his tears. *People slow to act*, I thought, *especially by pretence*. And later, when I saw Leticia in a sort of bluish, translucent pool, when I saw her finally asleep and well wrapped up in little white blankets that even from a distance looked warm, I thought again of that ridiculous phrase. I concentrated on Leticia. From too far away I saw her eyes without lashes, I saw the tiniest mouth I'd ever seen, and regretted that they'd put her down with her hands hidden, because nothing seemed more urgent to me at that moment than seeing my daughter's hands. I knew I'd never love anyone like I loved Leticia in that instant, that nobody would ever be what, there and then, that new arrival, that complete stranger was to me.

I did not set foot on 14th Street again, much less in the billiard club (I stopped playing entirely: standing up for too long exacerbated the pain in my leg to the point of making it unbearable). So I lost one part of the city; or, to put it a better way, a part of my city was stolen from me. I imagined a city in which the streets, the pavements gradually closed themselves off to us, like the rooms of the house in Julio Cortázar's story, until eventually expelling us. 'We were fine, and little by little we began to live unthinkingly,' says the brother in that story after a mysterious presence has taken over another part of the house. And he adds, 'You can live without thinking.' It's true: you can. After 14th Street was stolen from me – and after months of physiotherapy, of enduring light-headedness and my stomach destroyed by medication – I began to despise the city, to fear it, to feel threatened by it. The world seemed to me a closed place, or my life a walled-in life; the doctor talked to me about my fear of going out on the street, he proffered the word *agoraphobia* as if it were a delicate object that mustn't be allowed to fall, and it was hard for me to explain that it was just the opposite, a violent claustrophobia was what was tormenting me. One day, during a session I don't remember anything else about, that doctor recommended I try a kind of personal therapy that, according to him, had worked well for several of his patients.

'Do you keep a diary, Antonio?'

I said no, that diaries had always seemed ridiculous to me, a vanity or an anachronism: the fiction that our life matters.

He replied, 'Well start one. I'm not suggesting a diary-diary, but a notebook to ask yourself questions.'

'Questions,' I repeated. 'Like what?'

'Like, for example: what dangers are real in Bogotá? What are the chances of what happened to you happening again? If you want I could pass you some statistics. Questions, Antonio, questions. Why what happened to you happened to you, and whose fault it was, if it was yours or not. If this would have happened to you in another country. If this would have happened to you in another time. If these questions have any pertinence. It's important to distinguish the pertinent questions from the ones that are not, Antonio, and one way to do that is to put them down in writing. When you've decided which ones are pertinent and which are silly attempts to find an explanation for what can't be explained, ask yourself other questions: how to get better, how to forget without kidding yourself, how to go back to having a life, to be good to the people who love you. What to do to not be afraid, or to have a reasonable amount of fear, like everyone has. What to do to carry on, Antonio. Lots of them will be things that have occurred to you before, sure, but a person sees the questions on paper and it's quite different. A diary. Keep one for the next two weeks and then we'll talk.'

It seemed an inane recommendation to me, more suited to a self-help book than to a professional with grey hair at his temples, headed notepaper on his desk and diplomas in several languages on his wall. I didn't say so to him, of course, nor was it necessary, because I soon saw him stand up and walk over to his bookshelves (the books leather-bound and homogeneous, the family photos, a childish drawing framed and signed illegibly). 'You're not going to do any such thing, I can see that,' he said as he opened a drawer. 'You think all these things I'm saying are stupid. Well, I suppose they might be. But do me a favour, take this.' He pulled a spiral notebook out of the drawer, like the ones I'd used in college, with those ridiculous covers that looked like denim; he tore four, five or six pages out of the front and looked at the last page, to make sure there weren't any notes there; he handed it to me, or rather he put it on the desk, in front of me. I picked it up and, for something to do, opened it and flipped through it as if it were a novel. The paper in the notebook was squared: I always hated grid-ruled notebooks. On the first page I could make out the pressure of the writing from the torn-out page, those phantom words. A date, an underlined word, the letter Y. 'Thanks,' I said, and left. That very night, in spite of my initial scepticism at the strategy, I locked the door to my room (an absurd security measure), opened the notebook and wrote: *Dear diary*. My sarcasm fell into the void. I turned the page and tried to begin:

What

Why

But that was it. And so, with my pen in mid-air and my gaze sunk in the isolated words, I remained for a few long seconds. Aura, who had been suffering from a slight but annoying cold all week, was sleeping with her mouth open. I looked at her, tried to make a sketch of her features and failed. I ran through a mental inventory of the next day's obligations, which included a vaccination for Leticia, who was sleeping quietly beside us in her cot. Then I closed the notebook, put it away in the nightstand and turned off the light.

Outside, in the depths of the night, a dog barked.

One day in 1998, shortly after the World Cup finished in France and shortly before Leticia's second birthday, I was waiting for a taxi somewhere around Parque Nacional. I don't remember where I was coming from but I know I was heading north, to one of those endless check-ups with which the doctors tried to reassure me, to tell me that my recovery was proceeding at a normal pace, that soon my leg would be what it used to be. No northbound taxis went by, but lots went by heading for the city centre. I had nothing to do in the centre, I thought absurdly, I hadn't lost anything down there. And then I thought: I'd lost everything there. So, without thinking too much about it, as an act of private courage that no one not in my situation would understand, I crossed the street and got into the first taxi that came by. A few minutes later I found myself, more than two years after the event, walking towards Plaza Rosario, entering the Café Pasaje, finding a free table and from there looking towards the corner where the attack happened, like a little boy peeking with as much fascination as prudence into the dark field where a bull is grazing at night.

My table, a brown disc with a single metal leg, was at the front: just a hand-span separated it from the window. I couldn't see the door of the billiard club from there, but I could see the route the murderers on the motorbike had taken. The sounds of the aluminium coffee machine blended with the traffic noise of the nearby avenue, with the clicking heels of passers-by; the aroma of the ground beans blended with the smell that emerged from the toilets every time someone pushed the swinging door. People inhabited the sad square of the plaza, crossing the avenues that framed it, skirted round the statue of the city's founder (his dark cuirass always spattered with white pigeon shit). The shoeshiners stationed in front of the university with their wooden crates, the huddles of emerald vendors: I looked at them and marvelled that they didn't know what had happened there, so close to that pavement where their footsteps resounded right now. It was maybe while looking at them that I thought of Laverde and realized I was doing so without anxiety or fear.

I ordered a coffee, then I ordered another. The woman who brought my second one wiped the table with a melancholy, stinking rag and then put the new cup on top of a new saucer. 'Anything else, sir?' she asked. I saw her dry knuckles, crisscrossed by gritty lines; a spectre of steam rose from the blackish liquid. 'No thanks,' I said, and tried to find a name in my memory, unsuccessfully. All my student days coming to this café, and I was unable to remember the name of the woman who, in turn, had spent her whole life serving these tables. 'Can I ask you something?'

'If you must.'

'Do you know who Ricardo Laverde was?'

'That depends,' she said, drying her hands on her apron, impatient and bored. 'Was he a customer?'

'No,' I said. 'Or maybe, but I don't think so. He was killed there, on the other side of the plaza.'

'Oh,' said the woman. 'How long ago?'

'Two years,' I said. 'Two and a half.'

'Two and a half,' she repeated. 'No, I don't remember anyone dying there two and a half years ago. I'm very sorry.'

I thought she was lying. I didn't have any proof of that, of course, nor did I have the meagre imagination to invent a reason for her to lie, but it didn't seem possible to me that someone could have forgotten such a recent crime. Or maybe Laverde had died and I had gone through agony and fever and hallucinations without the events becoming fixed in the world, in the past or in the memory of my city. This, for some reason, bothered me. I think that at that moment I decided something, or felt capable of something, although I don't remember the words I used to formulate the decision. I left the café and turned right, taking the long way around to avoid the corner, and ended up crossing La Candelaria towards the place where Laverde had been living until the day he was shot and died.

Bogotá, like all Latin American capitals, is a mobile and changing city, an unstable element of seven or eight million inhabitants: here you close your eyes for too long and you might very well open them to find yourself surrounded by another world (the hardware store where yesterday they sold felt hats, the alcove where a cobbler sold lottery tickets), as if the whole city was the set of one of those practical-joke shows where the victim goes to the men's room of a restaurant and comes back and finds himself not in a restaurant but in a hotel room. But in all Latin American cities there's one place or sometimes several places that live outside of time, that seem immutable while the rest is transformed. That's what La Candelaria is like. On Ricardo Laverde's street, the corner print shop was still there, with the same sign by the doorframe and even the same wedding invitations and the same visiting cards that had served as an advertisement in December 1995; the walls that in 1995 were covered in cheap paper posters were still covered, two and a half years later, with other posters on the same kind of paper and in the same format, yellowing rectangles announcing funerals or a bullfight or a Council candidate where the only difference was the proper names. Everything was still the same here. Here reality adjusted – as it doesn't often do – to the memory we have of it.

Laverde's house was also identical to the memory I had of it. The line of tiles was broken in two places, like teeth missing in an old man's mouth; the paint on the door was peeling off at foot level and the wood was splintering: the exact spot where a person kicks it when arriving overburdened so the door won't close. But everything else was the same, or that's how it seemed to me as I listened to my knock echo through the inside of the house. When nobody answered, I took two steps backwards and looked up, hoping for a sign of human life on the roof. I didn't find any: I saw a cat frolicking near a television aerial and a patch of moss growing near the base of the antenna, and that was all. I had started to give up when I heard some movement from the other side of the door. A woman opened. 'What can I do for you?' she said. And the only thing I could find to say was a marvel of awkwardness: 'The thing is, I was a friend of Ricardo Laverde's.'

I saw an expression of uncertainty or suspicion. The woman spoke to me now with hostility but not surprise, as if she'd been expecting me.

'I don't have anything to say any more,' she said. 'All that happened a while ago, I already told everything to the journalists.'

'What journalists?'

'That was back then, I already told them everything.'

'But I'm not a journalist,' I said. 'I was a friend . . .'

'I already told everything,' the woman said. 'You people already got all that filth out of me, don't think I've forgotten.'

At that moment, a boy appeared behind her, a boy who looked a bit old to have such a dirty face. 'What's up, Consu? Is this gentleman bothering you?' He leaned a little closer to the door and into the daylight: it wasn't dirt around his mouth, but the shadow of incipient fuzz. 'Says he was a friend of Ricardo's,' said Consu in a low voice. She looked me up and down, and I did the same to her: she was short and fat, had her hair up in a bun that didn't look grey but rather divided into black and white locks like a board game, and was covered in a black dress of some elasticized material that clung to her bulges so that the knitted woollen belt was devoured by the loose flesh of her abdomen, and what one saw was a sort of thick white worm coming out of her belly button. She remembered something, or looked like she remembered something, and on her face – in the folds of her face, pink and sweaty as if Consu had just done some physical labour – a pout formed. The woman in her sixties then turned into an immense little girl who someone has refused a sweet. 'Excuse me, señor,' said Consu, and began to close the door.

'Don't close the door,' I begged. 'Let me explain.'

'Get lost, brother,' said the young man. 'You've got no business here.'

'I knew him,' I said.

'I don't believe you,' said Consu.

'I was with him when he was killed,' I said then. I lifted up my shirt and showed the woman the scar on my belly. 'One of the bullets hit me,' I said.

Scars can be eloquent.

* * *

For the next few hours I talked to Consu about that day, about meeting Laverde at the billiard club, about the Casa de Poesía and about what happened afterwards. I told her what Laverde had told me and that I still didn't understand why he'd told me that. I also told her about the recording, about the distress that had swept over Laverde while he listened to it, about the speculations that crossed my mind at that moment about its possible contents, about what could be said to produce that effect on a more or less hardened adult. 'I can't imagine,' I told her. 'And I've tried, I swear, but I can't figure it out. I just can't.' 'You can't, can you?' she said. 'No,' I said. By this point we were in the kitchen, Consu sitting in a white plastic chair and me on a wooden stool with a broken rung, so close to the gas cylinder that we could have touched it by simply stretching out an arm. The inside of the house was just as I'd imagined it: the patio, the wooden beams visible on the ceiling, the green doors of the rented rooms. Consu listened to me and nodded, put her hands between her knees and clamped her legs together as if she didn't want her hands to escape. After a while, she offered me a black coffee, which she made by putting the ground coffee beans into a piece of a nylon stocking and then putting the stocking into a little brass pot covered in grey dents, and when I finished it she offered me another and repeated the procedure, and each time the air became impregnated with the smell of gas and then of the burnt match. I asked Consu which was Laverde's room, and she pursed her lips and pointed with them, moving her head like an uncomfortable colt. 'That one there,' she said. 'Now it's occupied by a musician, such a nice guy, you should see him, he plays guitar at the Camarín del Carmen.' She fell quiet, looking at her hands, and eventually said, 'He had a combination lock, because Ricardo didn't like carrying keychains around with him. I had to break it when he was killed.'

The police had arrived, by chance, at the same time Ricardo Laverde usually came home, and Consu, thinking it was him, opened the door before they knocked. She found herself facing two officers, one with grey hair who lisped when he spoke and another who stayed two steps behind and didn't say a single word. 'You could see the grey hair was premature, who knows what that man had seen,' said Consu. 'They showed me an ID card and asked me if I recognized the individual, that's how he put it, the individual, what a strange word for a dead man. And the truth is, I didn't recognize him,' said Consu, crossing herself. 'The thing is he'd really changed. I had to read the card to tell them yes, the man was called Ricardo Laverde and he'd been living here since whatever month. First I thought: he's got himself into trouble. They're going to put him away again. I felt sorry for him, because Ricardo complied with all that stuff since he got out.'

'What stuff?'

'Things convicts have to do. When they get out of prison.'

'So you knew,' I said.

'Of course, dear. Everybody knew.'

'And did you know what he'd done, too?'

'No, not that,' said Consu. 'Well, I never tried to find out. That would have messed up our relationship, don't you think? What the eye doesn't see, the heart doesn't grieve over, that's what I say.'

The police followed her to Laverde's room. Using a hammer as a lever, Consu shattered the aluminium semicircle, and the lock landed in one of the little ditches in the central patio. When she opened the door she found a monk's cell: the perfect rectangle of the mattress, the impeccable sheet, the pillow in its unwrinkled pillowcase, without the curves and avenues that a head leaves over the course of the nights. Beside the mattress, an untreated wooden board on top of two bricks; on the board a glass of water that looked cloudy. The next day that image, that of the mattress and the improvised bedside table, came out in the tabloids beside the smear of blood on the pavement of 14th Street. 'Since that day no journalist sets foot in this house,' said Consu. 'Those people have no respect.'

'Who killed him?'

'Oh, if only I knew. I don't know, I don't know who killed him, when he was so nice. One of the nicest people I've known, I swear. Even if he might have done bad things.'

'What things?'

'That I don't know,' said Consu. 'He must've done something.'

'He must've done something,' I repeated.

'Anyway, what does it matter now,' said Consu. 'Or is finding out going to bring him back?'

'Well, no,' I said. 'Where is he buried?'

'Why do you want to know?'

'I don't know. To pay a visit. Take him flowers. What was the funeral like?'

'Small. I organized it, of course. I was the closest thing Ricardo had to a relative.'

'Of course,' I said. 'His wife had just been killed.'

'Ah,' Consu said. 'You know a few things too, who would have thought.'

'She was coming to spend Christmas with him. He'd had this absurd picture taken to give to her.'

'Absurd? Why absurd? I thought it was sweet.'

'It was an absurd picture.'

'The picture with the pigeons,' said Consu.

'Yes,' I said. 'The picture with the pigeons.' And then, 'It must have had to do with that.'

'What did?'

'What he was listening to. I've always thought that what he was listening to had something to do with her, with his wife. I imagine maybe a recorded letter, I don't know, a poem she liked.'

For the first time, Consu smiled. 'You imagined that?'

'I don't know, something like that.' And then, I don't know why, I lied or exaggerated. 'I've spent two and a half years thinking about that, it's funny how a dead person can take up so much space even when we didn't even know them. Two and a half years thinking about Elena de Laverde. Or Elena Fritts, or whatever her name was. Two and a half years,' I said. I felt good saying it.

I don't know what Consu saw in my face, but her expression changed, and even her way of sitting changed.

'Tell me one thing,' she said, 'but tell me the truth. Did you like him?'

'What?'

'Were you fond of him?'

'Yes,' I said. 'I was very fond of him.'

That wasn't true either, of course. Life hadn't given us the time for affection, and what was driving me was neither sentiment nor emotion, but the intuition we sometimes have that some events have shaped our lives more than they should or appear to have. But I've learned very well that these subtleties don't cut any ice in the real world, and must often be sacrificed, tell the other person what the other person wants to hear, don't get too honest (honesty is inefficient, it gets you nowhere). I looked at Consu and I saw a lonely woman, as lonely as I am. 'Very much,' I repeated. 'I was very fond of him.'

'OK,' she said, standing up. 'Wait here, I'm going to show you something.'

She disappeared for a few moments. I could follow her movements by their sounds, the shuffling of her flip-flops, the brief exchange with her tenant – 'It's late, *papito*'; 'Ay, Doña Consu, don't stick your nose into what's none of your business' – and for a moment I thought our chat had finished and the next thing would be the boy with the sparse moustache asking me to leave with some affected phrase, *I'll see you to the door* or *Thank you for your visit, señor.* But then I saw her coming back looking distracted, glancing at the nails of her left hand: once again the little girl I'd seen at the door to her house. In the other hand (her fingers made themselves delicate to hold it, as if it were a sick pet) she was carrying a football too small to be a football and that very soon revealed itself to be an old radio in the shape of a football. Two of the black hexagons were speakers; in the top part was a little window showing the cassette player; in the cassette player was a black cassette. A black cassette with an orange label. On the label, a single word: *BASF*.

'It's just side A,' Consu told me. 'When you finish listening to it, leave it all beside the stove. There where the matches are. And make sure the door's closed properly when you leave.'

'Just a moment, one moment,' I said. Questions were flooding my mouth. 'You have this?'

'I have this.'

'How did you get it? Aren't you going to listen to it with me?'

'It's what they call personal effects,' she said. 'The police brought me everything Ricardo had in his pockets. And no, I'm not going to listen to it. I know it off by heart, and I don't want to hear it any more, this cassette has nothing to do with Ricardo. And really it has nothing to do with me either. Strange, isn't it? One of my most cherished possessions, and it's got nothing to do with my life.'

'One of your most cherished possessions,' I repeated.

'You know how people get asked what they'd take from their house if it was on fire. Well, I'd take this cassette. It must be because I never had children, and there aren't any photo albums here or anything like that.'

'The boy I met at the door?'

'What about him?'

'He's not family?'

'He's a tenant,' said Consu, 'like any other.' She thought for a moment and added, 'My tenants are my family.'

With those words (and with a perfect sense of melodrama) she went out the front door and left me alone.

What was on the recording was a dialogue in English between two men: talking about weather conditions, which were good, and then talking about work. One of the men explained to the other the regulation about the number of hours they were allowed to fly before their obligatory rest. The microphone (if it was a microphone) picked up a constant buzzing and, over the white noise of the buzzing, a shuffling of papers.

'I got this chart,' said the first man.

'Well, you see what you come up with,' said the second. I'll watch the plane and the radio. OK?'

'OK. All I see on this little chart they handed out is duty-on time, but it doesn't say anything about rest period.'

'That's another very confusing thing.'

I remember very well having listened to the conversation for several minutes – all my attention focused on finding a reference to Laverde – before establishing, half disconcerted and half perturbed, that the people talking had nothing at all to do with Ricardo Laverde's death, and, what's more, that Ricardo Laverde wasn't mentioned there at any moment. One of the men started to talk about the 136 miles to go to the VOR, of the 32,000 feet they had to descend, and they had to slow down as well, so they might as well get started. At that moment the other man says the words that change everything: 'Bogotá, American nine six five request descent.' And it seemed unbelievable that it had taken me so long to comprehend that in a few minutes this flight would crash into El Diluvio, and that among the dead would be the woman who was coming to spend the holidays with Ricardo Laverde.

'American Airlines operations at Cali, this is American nine six five, do you read?'

'Go ahead, American nine six five, this is Cali ops.'

'All right, Cali. We will be there in just about twenty-five minutes from now.'

This was what Ricardo Laverde had been listening to shortly before being murdered: the black box recording of the flight on which his wife had died. I suffered the revelation like a punch, with the same loss of balance, the same upheaval of my immediate world. But how had he got hold of it? I then wondered. Was that possible, requesting the recording of a crashed flight and obtaining it like you might obtain, I don't know, a document from the Land Registry? Did Laverde speak English, or at least did he understand enough to listen to and understand and regret – yes, especially regret – that conversation? Or maybe it wasn't necessary to understand any of it to regret it, because nothing in the conversation referred to Laverde's wife: was not the awareness, the terrible awareness, of the proximity between these two pilots speaking and one of their passengers regrettable enough? Two and a half years later, those questions remained unanswered. Now the captain asked about the arrival gate (it was number two), and now the runway (it was zero one), now he put on the headlights because there was a lot of visual traffic in the area, now they were talking about a position 47 miles north of Rio Negro and looking for it on the flight plan . . . And now, finally, came the announcement over the loudspeaker: 'Ladies and gentlemen, this is your captain speaking. We have begun our descent.'

They've begun the descent. One of those ladies is Elena Fritts, who's coming from seeing her sick mother in Miami, or from her grandmother's funeral, or simply from visiting her friends (from spending Thanksgiving with them). No, it's her mother, her sick mother. Elena Fritts is perhaps thinking of her sick mother, worrying about having left her, wondering if leaving had been the right thing to do. She's also thinking about Ricardo Laverde, her husband. Is she thinking about her husband? She's thinking about her husband, who's been released from prison. 'I'd like to wish everyone a very, very happy holiday and a healthy and prosperous 1996. Thank you for flying with us.' Elena Fritts thinks about Ricardo Laverde. She thinks that now they can pick up their life where they left off. Meanwhile, in the cabin, the captain offers the first officer some peanuts. 'No thank you,' says the first officer. The captain says, 'Pretty night, huh?' And the first officer, 'Yeah it is, looking nice out here.' Then they address the control tower, request permission to descend to a lower altitude, the tower tells them to descend to flight level two zero zero, and then the captain says, with a heavy American accent, '*Feliz Navidad, señorita.*'

What is Elena Fritts thinking about back in her seat? I imagine her, I don't know why, sitting in a window seat.

I've imagined that moment a thousand times, a thousand times I've reconstructed it like a stage designer constructs a scene, and I've filled it with speculations about everything: from what Elena Fritts might be wearing – a pale blue light blouse and shoes without stockings – to her opinions and prejudices. In the image I've formed and that's imposed itself on me, the window is on her left; to her right, a sleeping passenger (hairy arms, jagged snoring). The seatback table is open; Elena Fritts had wanted to put it up when the captain announced the descent, but no one's come past yet to collect her little plastic glass. Elena Fritts looks out the window and sees a clear sky; she doesn't know her plane is going down to 20,000 feet; it doesn't matter that she doesn't know. She's tired: it's past nine at night, and Elena Fritts has been travelling since early morning, because her mother's house is not in Miami itself, but in a suburb. Or even in some completely other place, Fort Lauderdale, for example, or Coral Springs, one of those small cities in Florida that are more like gigantic geriatric homes, where the old people from all across the country move to spend their final years far from the cold and the stress and the resentful eyes of their children. So Elena Fritts had to get up early this morning; a neighbour who had to go to Miami anyway has given her a lift to the airport, and Elena has had to cover one or two or three hours with him on those straight highways famous the world over for their anaesthetic powers. Now she's only thinking about getting to Cali, catching her connection on time, getting to Bogotá as tired as passengers who take this flight to catch this connection have always arrived, but happier than the other passengers, because a man who loves her is waiting for her there. She thinks of that and then of taking a nice shower and going to bed. Down below, in Cali, a voice says, 'American nine six five, distance now?'

'Uh, what did you want, sir?'

'Distance DME.'

'OK,' says the captain, 'the distance from, uh, Cali is, uh, 38.'

'Where are we?' asks the first officer. 'We're going out to . . .'

'Let's go right to, uh, Tuluá first of all, OK?'

'Yeah. Where we headed?'

'I don't know. What's this? What happened here?'

The Boeing 757 has descended to 13,000 feet turning to the right first and then to the left, but Elena Fritts doesn't notice. It's night-time, a dark though clear night, and below the contours of the mountains can already be seen. In the little plastic window Elena sees the reflection of her face, wonders what she's doing here, if it had been a mistake to come to Colombia, if her marriage can really be repaired or if what her mother said in her tone of an apocalyptic fortune-teller was true, 'Going back to him will be the last of your idealisms.' Elena Fritts is prepared to accept her idealistic character, but that, she thinks, is no reason to condemn an entire life of mistaken decisions: idealists also get it right occasionally. The lights go out, the face in the window disappears, and Elena Fritts thinks that she doesn't care what her mother says: not for anything in the world would she have forced Ricardo to spend his first Christmas Eve in freedom on his own.

'Just doesn't look right on mine,' says the captain. 'I don't know why.'

'Left turn. So you want a left turn back around?'

'Naw . . . Hell no, let's press on to . . .'

'Where to?'

'Tuluá.'

'That's a right.'

'Where're we going? Come to the right now. Let's go to Cali first of all. We got fucked up here, didn't we?'

'Yeah.'

'How did we get fucked up here? Come to the right, right now, to the right, right now.'

Elena Fritts, sitting in her economy-class seat, doesn't know that something's going wrong. If she had any aeronautical knowledge she might find the changes in the route suspicious, she could have recognized that the pilots have deviated from the established course. But no: Elena Fritts does not know anything about aeronautics, and doesn't imagine that descending to less than 10,000 feet in mountainous terrain can entail risks if one doesn't know the zone. What is she thinking about then?

What is Elena Fritts thinking about a minute before her death?

The cockpit alarm sounds: 'Terrain, terrain,' says an electronic voice. But Elena Fritts doesn't hear it: the alarms don't sound where she is seated, nor does she sense the dangerous proximity of the mountain. The crew turns up the power, but doesn't disengage the brakes. The plane lifts its nose briefly. None of this is enough.

'Oh shit,' says the pilot. 'Pull up, baby.'

What is Elena Fritts thinking about? Is she thinking about Ricardo Laverde? Is she thinking about the looming holiday season? Is she thinking about her children? 'Shit,' says the captain in the cockpit, but Elena Fritts can't hear him. Do Elena Fritts and Ricardo Laverde have children? Where are those children, if they exist, and how had their lives been changed after their father's absence? Do they know the reasons for that absence, have they grown up wrapped in a web of family lies, sophisticated myths, scrambled chronologies?

'Up,' says the captain.

'It's OK,' says the first officer.

'Pull up,' says the captain. 'Easy does it, easy.' The automatic pilot has been disconnected. The stick shift begins to shake in the hands of the pilot, a sign that the plane's speed is not enough to keep it up in the air. 'More, more,' says the captain.

'OK,' says the first officer.

And the captain, 'Up, up, up.'

The siren sounds again.

'*Pull up*,' says the electronic voice.

There is a faltering scream, or something that sounds like a scream. There is a sound that I cannot or have never been able to identify: a sound that's not human or is more than human, the sound of lives being extinguished but also the sound of material things breaking. It's the sound of things falling from on high, an interrupted and somehow also eternal sound, a sound that didn't ever end, that kept ringing in my head from that very afternoon and still shows no sign of wanting to leave it, that is forever suspended in my memory, hanging in it like a towel on a hook.

That sound is the last thing heard in the cockpit of Flight 965.

The noise sounds, and then the recording stops.

It took me a long time to recover. There's nothing as obscene as spying on a man's last seconds: they should be secret, inviolable, they should die with the man who dies, and nevertheless, there in that kitchen in that old house in La Candelaria, the final words of the dead pilots came to form part of my experience, in spite of the fact that I didn't know and still don't know who those unfortunate men were, what they were called, what they saw when they looked in the mirror; those men, for their part, never knew of me, and yet their final moments now belong to me and will continue to belong to me. What right do I have? Their wives, their mothers, fathers and children haven't heard these words that I've heard, and have perhaps lived through the last two and a half years wondering what their husband, or father or son had said before crashing into El Diluvio Mountain. I, who had no right to know, now know; they, to whom those voices belong by right, do not know. And I thought that I, deep down, *had no right to listen to that death*, because those men who died in the plane are strangers to me, and the woman who was travelling behind them *is not, will never be, one of my dead*.

However, those sounds now form part of my auditory memory. Once the tape fell silent, once the noises of the tragedy gave way to static, I knew I would have preferred not to have listened to it, and I knew at the same moment that in my memory I would go on hearing it for ever. No, those are not my dead, I had no right to hear those words (just as I probably have no right to reproduce them in this story, undoubtedly with some inaccuracies), but the words and the voices of the dead had already swallowed me like a whirlpool in a river swallows a tired animal. The recording also had the power to modify the past, for now Laverde's tears were not the same, couldn't be the same ones I'd witnessed in the Casa de Poesía: now they had a density they'd previously lacked, owing to the simple fact that I'd heard what he, sitting in that soft leather armchair, heard that afternoon. Experience, or what we call experience, is not the inventory of our pains, but rather the learned sympathy towards the pain of others.

With time I have found out more about black boxes. I know, for example, that they're not black, but orange. I know that aeroplanes carry them in the empennage – the structure we profane people call the tail – because they have a better chance of surviving an accident there. And yes, I know that black boxes survive: they can withstand 2,250 kilograms of pressure and temperatures of 1,100 degrees Celsius. When they fall into the sea, a transmitter is activated; the black box then begins to pulsate for thirty days. That's how long the authorities have to find it, to discover the reasons for an accident, to ensure that nothing similar happens again, but I don't think anyone considers that a black box might have other fates, to fall into hands that were not part of its plan. However, that's what happened to me with Flight 965's black box, which, having survived the accident, was magically transformed into a black cassette with an orange label and went through two owners before coming to form part of my memories. And that's how this apparatus, invented to be the electronic memory of planes, has ended up turning into a definitive part of my memory. There it is, and there's nothing I can do. Forgetting it is not possible.

I waited quite a while before leaving the house in La Candelaria, not just to listen to the recording again (which I did, not once, but twice more), but also because seeing Consu again had suddenly become urgent for me. What else did she know about Ricardo Laverde? Perhaps it had been in order not to find herself obliged to make revelations, not to be suddenly at the mercy of my interrogations, that she had left me alone in her house with her most precious possession. It was starting to get dark. I looked outside: the streetlights were already on, the white walls of the houses were changing colour. It was cold. I looked down the street to the corner, then to the other one. Consu was not around, I couldn't see her anywhere, so I went back into the kitchen and inside a bigger bag I found a small paper bag the size of a half-bottle of *aguardiente*. My pen didn't write very well on its surface, but I would have to make do.

Dear Consu,

I waited for almost an hour. Thank you for letting me hear the recording. I wanted to tell you in person, but it just wasn't possible.

Beneath these scribbled lines I wrote my complete name, that surname that's so unusual in Colombia and that still provokes a certain timidity when I write it depending on the people, for there are many who distrust a person in my country if it's necessary to spell out their surname. Then I smoothed out the bag with my hands and left it on top of the tape recorder, with one of its corners trapped by the cassette door. And I went out into the city with a mixture of sensations in my chest and a single certainty: I didn't want to go home; I wanted to keep to myself what had just happened to me, the secret and its revelation that I'd just witnessed. I thought that I was never going to be as close to Ricardo Laverde's life as I had been there, in his house, during the minutes the black box recording had lasted, and I didn't want that curious exaltation to dissipate, so I went down 7th Avenue and began to walk around downtown Bogotá, passing through Bolivár Plaza and continuing north, mingling with the people on the always packed pavement and letting myself be pushed by those in the most hurry and bumping into those coming towards me, and looking for less busy smaller streets and even going into the craft market on 10th Street, I think it's 10th, and during all that time thinking that I didn't want to go home, that Aura and Leticia were part of a different world from the world inhabited by the memory of Ricardo Laverde and of course different from the world in which Flight 965 had crashed. No, I couldn't go home yet. That's what I was thinking as I arrived at 22nd Street, how to delay my arrival home in order to keep living in the black box, with the black box, and then my body made the decision for me and I ended up going into a porn cinema where a naked woman with long, very fair hair in the middle of a fully equipped kitchen lifted up her leg until the heel of her shoe got caught in the burners on top of the stove, and maintained this delicate balancing act while a fully dressed man penetrated her and gave her incomprehensible orders at the same time, the movements of his mouth never corresponding to the words his mouth was pronouncing.

The Thursday before Easter in 1999, nine months after my encounter with Ricardo Laverde's landlady and eight before the end of the millennium, I arrived at my apartment and found a woman's voice and a phone number on the answering machine. 'This is a message for Antonio Yammara,' said the voice, a young but melancholy voice, a voice that was both tired and sensual, the voice of one of those women who has had to grow up prematurely. 'Señora Consuelo Sandoval gave me your name. I looked up your number. I hope I'm not bothering you, but you're in the phone book. Please call me. I need to speak with you.' I dialled the number immediately. 'I was waiting for your call,' said the woman.

'With whom am I speaking?' I asked.

'I'm sorry to trouble you,' the woman said. 'My name is Maya Fritts. I'm not sure if my surname means anything to you. Well, it's not my original surname, it's my mother's, my real one is Laverde.' And since I remained silent, the woman added what was by then unnecessary: 'I'm the daughter of Ricardo Laverde. I need to ask you some things.' I think I said something then, but it's possible I simply repeated the name, the two names, her name and that of her father. Maya Fritts, Ricardo Laverde's daughter, kept talking. 'But listen, I live far away and I can't go to Bogotá. It's a long story. So the favour is a double favour, because I want to invite you to spend the day here, at my house, with me. I want you to come and talk to me about my father, to tell me everything you know. It's a big favour, I know, but it's warm here and the food's good, I promise you won't regret coming. So, it's up to you, Señor Yammara. If you have a pencil and paper, I'll tell you right now how to get here.'

3

The Gaze of Absent Ones

AT SEVEN THE NEXT morning I found myself driving down 80th Street, having had nothing but a black coffee for breakfast, heading for the city's western exit routes. It was an overcast and cold morning, and the traffic at that hour was already dense and even aggressive; but it didn't take me too long to get to the outskirts of the city, where the urban landscapes change and the lungs perceive a sudden absence of contamination. The exit had changed over the years, wide, recently paved roads flaunting the brilliant white of their signposts, zebra crossings and intermittent lines on the tarmac. I don't know how many times I made similar trips as a child, how many times I went up the mountains that surround the city to then make that precipitous descent, and thus pass in a matter of three hours from our cold and rainy 2,600 metres down into the Magdalena Valley, where the temperatures can approach 40 degrees Celsius in some ill-fated spots. That was the case in La Dorada, the city that marks the halfway point between Bogotá and Medellín and that often serves as a stop or meeting point for those who make that trip, or occasionally even as a place for a swim. On the outskirts of La Dorada, somewhere that sounded quite separate from the city, from the hustle and bustle of its roads and heavy traffic, lived Maya Fritts. But now, instead of thinking of her and the strange circumstances that had brought us together, I spent the four hours of the trip thinking of Aura or, more specifically, about what had happened with Aura the previous night.

After taking down Maya Fritts's directions and ending up with a badly drawn map on the back of a piece of paper (on the other side were notes for one of my upcoming classes: we would discuss what right Antigone had to break the law in order to bury her brother), I had gone through the evening routine with Aura in the most peaceable way possible, the two of us making dinner while Leticia watched a movie, telling each other about our respective days, laughing, touching as we crossed paths in the narrow kitchen. *Peter Pan*, Leticia was very fond of that movie, and also *The Jungle Book*, and Aura had bought her two or three videos of *The Muppets*, less for our little girl's pleasure than to satisfy her own private nostalgia, her affection for Count von Count, her glib contempt for Miss Piggy. But no, it wasn't the Muppets that we could hear that evening from the television in our room, but one of those films. *Peter Pan*, yes: it was *Peter Pan* that was playing – 'All of this has happened before, and it will all happen again,' said the anonymous narrator – when Aura, wrapped in a red apron with an anachronistic image of Santa Claus, said without looking me in the eye, 'I bought something. Remind me to show you later.'

'What kind of something?'

'Something,' said Aura.

She was stirring a saucepan on the stove, the extractor fan was on full blast and forced us to raise our voices, and the light from the hood bathed her face in a coppery tone. 'You're so lovely,' I said. 'I'll never get used to it.' She smiled, was about to say something, but at that moment Leticia appeared at the door, silent and discreet, with her chestnut hair still wet from her bath up in a ponytail. I picked her up from the floor, asked her if she was hungry, and the same coppery light shone on her face: her features were mine, not Aura's, and that had always moved and disappointed me at the same time. That idea was strangely stuck in my head while we ate: that Leticia should be able to resemble Aura, she should have been able to inherit Aura's beauty, and instead had inherited my rough features, my thick bones, my prominent ears. Maybe that's why I was looking at her so closely as I took her to bed. I stayed with her a while in the darkness of her room, broken only by the small round nightlight that gives off a weak pastel-coloured light that changes its tone over the course of the night, so Leticia's room is blue when she calls me because she's had a nightmare, and can quite easily be pink or pale green when she calls me because she's run out of water in her little bottle. Anyway: there in the coloured shadows, while Leticia fell asleep and the whisper of her breathing changed, I spied on her features and the genetic games in her face, all those proteins moving mysteriously to imprint my chin on hers, my hair colour in my little girl's hair colour. And that's what I was doing when the door opened a little and a sliver of light appeared and then Aura's silhouette and her hand calling me.

'Is she asleep?'

'Yes.'

'Sure?'

'Yes.'

She pulled me by the hand to the living room and we sat on the sofa. The table was already cleared and the dishwasher running in the kitchen, sounding like an old dying pigeon. (We didn't usually spend time in the living room after dinner: we preferred to get into bed and watch some old American sitcom, something light and cheerful and soothing. Aura had got used to missing the evening news, and could joke about my boycott, but understood how seriously I took it. I didn't watch the news, it was as simple as that. It would take me a long time to be able to endure it again, to allow my country's news to invade my life again.) 'Well, look,' Aura said. Her hands disappeared behind the edge of the sofa and reappeared with a small package wrapped up in a sheet of newspaper. 'For me?' I said. 'No, it's not a present,' she said. 'Or it is, but for both of us. Shit, I don't know, I don't know how to do things like this.' Embarrassment was not a feeling that often bothered Aura, but that's what this was, embarrassment, that's what her gestures were full of. The next thing was her voice (her nervous voice) explaining where she had bought the vibrator, how much it had cost, how she'd paid cash for it so there would be no record of this purchase anywhere, how she'd despised at that moment her many years of religious education that had made her feel, as she entered the shop on 19th Avenue, that very bad things were going to happen to her as punishment, that with this purchase she would end up earning a permanent place in hell. It was a purple apparatus with a creased texture, with more buttons and possibilities than I would have imagined, but it wasn't the shape I'd assigned it in my overly literal imagination. I looked at it (there, sleeping in my hand) and Aura looked at me looking at it. I couldn't keep the word *consolador*, which is also sometimes used for this object, from appearing in my mind: Aura as a woman in need of consoling, or Aura as a disconsolate woman. 'What is it?' I said. A question as stupid as questions get.

'Well, it is what it is,' said Aura. 'It's for us.'

'No,' I said, 'it's not for us.'

I stood up and dropped it on the glass-topped table and the apparatus bounced slightly (after all, it was made out of something springy). At another moment I would probably have been amused by the sound, but not there, not then. Aura grabbed my arm.

'There's nothing wrong with it, Antonio, it's for us.'

'It's not for us.'

'You had an accident, that's all, I love you,' said Aura. 'There's nothing wrong, we're together.'

The purple vibrator sat there half lost among the ashtrays and coasters and coffee-table books, all chosen by Aura: *Colombia from the Air*, a big book on José Celestino Mutis and another recent one by an Argentine photographer about Paris (that one Aura hadn't chosen, but had been given). I felt embarrassed, an absurd and childish embarrassment. 'Do you need consoling?' I said to Aura. My tone even surprised me.

'What?'

'That's a *consolador*. Do you need consoling?'

'Don't do this, Antonio. We're together. You had an accident and we're together.'

'The accident happened to me, don't be an idiot,' I said. 'I was the one who was shot.' I calmed down a little. 'Sorry,' I said. And then, 'The doctor told me.'

'But it was three years ago.'

'That I shouldn't worry, that the body knows how to do its things.'

'Three years ago, Antonio. What's happening now is something else. I love you and we're together.'

I didn't say anything.

'We can find a way,' said Aura.

I didn't say anything.

'There are so many couples,' said Aura. 'We're not the only ones.'

But I didn't say anything. A light bulb somewhere must have blown at that moment, because the living room was suddenly a little darker, the sofa and the two chairs and the only painting – a couple of billiard players by Saturnino Ramírez who are playing, for reasons I've never managed to discover, in dark glasses – had lost their contours. I felt tired and in need of a painkiller. Aura had sat back down on the sofa and was now holding her face in her hands, but I don't think she was crying. 'I thought you would be pleased,' she said. 'I thought I was doing a good thing.' I turned around and left her alone, maybe even mid-sentence, and I locked myself in our bathroom. In the narrow blue cupboard I looked for my pills, the little white plastic bottle and its red lid that Leticia had once chewed on till it broke, to our great alarm (it turned out she hadn't found the pills hidden under the cotton, but a two- or three-year-old child is at risk all the time, the whole world is a danger to her). With water straight from the tap I took three pills, a bigger dose than recommended or advisable, but my size and weight allow me these excesses when the pain is very bad. Then I took a long shower, which always makes me feel better; by the time I returned to our room Aura was asleep or pretending to be asleep, and I endeavoured not to wake her or to maintain the convenient fiction. I undressed, lay down beside her but with my back to her, and then I don't know anything else: I fell asleep immediately.

It was very early, especially for a Good Friday, when I left the next morning. The light was not yet filling the air of the apartment. I wanted to think that was why, because of the general somnolence floating in the world, I didn't wake anyone up to say goodbye. The vibrator was still on the table in the living room, coloured and plastic like a toy Leticia had lost there.

Up by the Alto del Trigo a thick fog descended over the road, unexpectedly as if a cloud had lost its way, and the almost complete lack of visibility forced me to slow down so much that farmworkers on bicycles were overtaking me. The fog accumulated on the glass like dew, making it necessary to turn on the windscreen wipers even though it wasn't raining, and shapes – the car in front, a couple of soldiers flanking the roadway with machine guns across their chests, a cargo mule – emerged gradually from that milky soup that let no light through. I thought of low-flying planes: 'Up, up, up.' I thought of the fog and remembered the famous accident at El Tablazo, way back in the 1940s, but I didn't remember whether the visibility at these treacherous altitudes had been to blame. 'Up, up, up,' I said to myself. And then, as I descended towards Guaduas, the fog lifted the same way it had fallen, and the sky suddenly opened and a wave of heat transformed the day: there was a burst of vegetation, a burst of fragrances, fruit stalls appeared at the side of the road. I began to sweat. When I opened the window at some point, to buy one of the cans of beer slowly warming up on top of a crate full of ice, my sunglasses misted up from the blast of heat. But the sweat was what bothered me most. My body's pores were, suddenly, at the centre of my consciousness.

I didn't arrive in the area until past midday. After a traffic jam of almost an hour and a half near Guarinocito (a truck with a broken axle can be lethal on a two-lane highway with no hard shoulder), after the headlands arose on the horizon and my car entered the region of cattle ranches, I saw the rudimentary little school I was supposed to see, continued for the distance indicated beside a big white pipe bordering the road and turned right, towards the Magdalena River. I passed a metallic structure where once there had been a billboard, but that now, seen from far away, resembled a sort of giant abandoned corset (a few turkey vultures, perched on the struts, guarded the plot of land); I passed a trough where two cows were drinking, their bodies very close together, pushing and getting in each other's way, their heads protected from the sun by a squalid aluminium roof. At the end of 300 metres of unpaved road, I found myself passing several groups of boys in shorts who shouted and laughed and raised a great cloud of dust as they ran. One of them stuck out a small brown hand with his thumb extended. I stopped, pulled the car onto the shoulder; now still, I felt again on my face and body the violent slap of the midday heat. I felt the humidity again; I sensed the smells. The child spoke first.

'I'm going where you're going, sir.'

'I'm going to Las Acacias,' I said. 'If you know where it is, I'll take you that far.'

'Oh well, that's no good to me then, sir,' the boy said without his smile disappearing for a second. 'It's just down there, you see. That dog's from there. He doesn't bite, don't worry.'

It was a black, tired-looking German shepherd with a white mark on his tail. He noticed my presence, raised his ears and looked at me without interest; then he walked a couple of times around a mango tree, his nose to the ground and tail stuck to his ribs like a feather duster, and finally lay down beside the trunk and began licking a paw. I felt sorry for him: his fur was not designed for this climate. I drove a bit further, beneath the trees whose dense foliage didn't let any light through, until I arrived in front of a gate of solid columns and a wooden crossbeam from which hung a board that looked recently rubbed with furniture oil, and on the board appeared, etched and singed, the graceless and bland name of the property. I had to get out to open the gate, the original bolt of which seemed to have been stuck in its place since the beginning of time; I continued on quite a way along a track across an open field made simply by driving across it, two strips of earth separated by a crest of stiff grass; and finally, beyond a post where a small vulture perched, I arrived in front of a one-storey white house.

I called out but nobody appeared. The door was open: a glass-topped dining table and a living room with light-coloured armchairs, all dominated by ceiling fans whose blades seemed animated by a sort of inner life of their own, a private mission against high temperatures. On the terrace hung three brightly coloured hammocks, and under one of them someone had left a half-eaten guava that was now being devoured by ants. I was about to ask at the top of my lungs if there was anybody at home when I heard a whistle, and then another, and it took me a couple of seconds to discover, beyond the bougainvillea bushes that flanked the house, beyond the *guanábana* trees that grew behind the bougainvilleas, the silhouette moving its arms as if asking for help. There was something monstrous in that overly white figure with too big a head and legs too thick; but I couldn't look closely as I walked towards her, because all my attention was concentrated on not breaking my ankle on the stones or uneven ground, on not getting my face scratched by the low branches of the trees. Behind the house sparkled the rectangle of a swimming pool that didn't look well cared for: a blue slide with the paint bleached by the sun, a round table with its parasol folded down, the skimmer net leaning against a tree as if it had never been used. That's what I was thinking when I arrived beside the white monster, but by that time the head had turned into a veiled mask, and the hand into a glove with thick fingers. The woman took off the mask, passed a hand quickly through her hair (light brown, cut with intentional clumsiness, styled with genuine carelessness), greeted me without smiling and explained that she'd had to interrupt the inspection of her hives to come and receive me. Now she had to get back to work. 'It's stupid for you to have to go get bored in the house waiting for me,' she said, pronouncing every letter, almost one at a time, as if her life depended on it. 'Have you ever seen a honeycomb up close?'

I immediately realized she was about the same age as me, more or less, although I couldn't say what secret generational communication there was between the two of us, or if such a thing really exists: an ensemble of gestures or words or a certain tone of voice, a way of saying hello or thanks or of moving or crossing our legs when we sit down, that we share with other members of our litter. She had the palest green eyes I'd ever seen and on her face a girl's skin met a mature and careworn woman's expression: her face was like a party that everyone had left. There were no adornments, except for two sparks of diamonds (I think they were diamonds) barely visible on her slender earlobes. Dressed in her beekeeper's suit that hid her shape, Maya Fritts took me to a shed that might once have been a manger: a room that smelled of manure with two masks and a pair of white overalls hanging on the wall.

'Put these on,' she ordered me. 'My bees don't like bright colours.'

I wouldn't have called the blue of my shirt a bright blue, but I didn't argue. 'I didn't know bees saw in colour,'

I said, but she was already putting a white hat on my head and explaining how to secure the nylon veil of the mask. As she passed the cords under my armpits to tie them behind my back, she hugged me like a passenger on a motorbike; I liked the proximity of her body (I thought I felt the phantom pressure of her breasts against my back) but also the sureness with which her hands acted, the firmness or lack of embarrassment as they touched my body. From somewhere she took out another pair of white shoelaces, went down on one knee, used them to tie closed the bottom of the trouser legs and said, looking me in the eye without the least embarrassment, 'So they don't go stinging you in sensitive places.' Then she grabbed a kind of metal bottle with golden bellows and asked me to carry it, and she stuck a red brush and a steel crowbar in her pockets.

I asked her how long she'd had this hobby.

'It's not a hobby,' she told me. 'I make my living from this, my dear. The best honey in the region, if I do say so myself.'

'Well, congratulations. And how long have you been producing the best honey in the region?'

She explained on the way to the hives. She explained other things too. And so I learned how she had come to set up home on this property, which was her only inheritance. 'My parents bought the land when I was born, more or less,' she said. So, I commented, this was all that was left of them. 'There was money left too,' said Maya, 'but I spent it on lawyers.' 'Lawyers are expensive,' I said. 'No,' she said, 'they're like dogs: they smell fear and attack. I was very inexpert when it all started. I should say that someone less honest could have taken everything.' As soon as she came of age and could take charge of her own life, she started planning a way of leaving Bogotá, and she hadn't turned twenty when she did so definitively, dropping out of university and falling out with her mother over it. When the final inheritance settlement came down, Maya had already been settled here for a good decade. 'And I've never regretted having left Bogotá,' she told me. 'I couldn't take it any more. I detest that city. I've never been back. I wouldn't know what it's like now, maybe you can tell me. You live in Bogotá?'

'Yes.'

'You've never left?'

'Never,' I said. 'Not even during the worst years.'

'Me neither. I was there for all of it.'

'Who did you live with?'

'With my mother, of course,' said Maya. 'A strange life, now that I think of it, the two of us alone. Then each of us chose her own path, you know how those things go.'

In 1992 she set up the first rustic hives at Las Acacias, a curious decision at the very least in a person who, according to her own confession, didn't know any more about apiculture at that moment than I do now. But those hives barely lasted a few months: Maya couldn't stand having to destroy the combs and kill the bees every time she collected the honey and wax, and in secret she imagined the surviving bees were escaping with a message to the whole region and one day, when she was taking her siesta in the hammock by the pool, a cloud of vengeful stingers would fall upon her. She exchanged the four rustic hives for three with removable honeycombs and never had to kill another bee.

'But that was seven years ago,' I said. 'You haven't been back to Bogotá in all those years?'

'Well, yes. To see the lawyers. To look for that woman, Consuelo Sandoval. But I've never stayed overnight in Bogotá, or even till sundown. I can't stand it, I can't endure more than a few hours there.'

'And that's why you prefer the rest of us to come and see you.'

'No one comes to see me. But yes, that's it. That's why I preferred you to come here.'

'I understand.'

Maya looked up.

'Yes, I think you do understand,' she said. 'People our age usually do. We have an abnormal relationship to Bogotá. Being there through the '80s will do that to you.'

The last syllables of her sentence were drowned out by a strident buzzing. We were a few steps from the apiary. The terrain was slightly sloping, and through the veil it wasn't easy to see where I was placing my feet, but even so I was able to witness the best spectacle in the world: a person doing their job well. Maya Fritts took me by the arm so we would approach the hives from the side, not the front, and signalled for me to give her the bottle that I'd been carrying the whole time. She lifted it up as high as her face and squeezed the bellows once, to check the mechanism, and a ghost of white smoke came out of the spout and dissolved in the air. Maya stuck the spout into an opening in the first hive and squeezed the golden bellows again, once, twice, three times, filling the hive with smoke, and then took the lid off to spray the whole interior at once. I stepped back and brought my arm up to my face out of pure instinct; but where I'd thought I'd find a swarm of hysterical bees coming out to sting anything in their path, I saw the exact opposite: the bees were quiet and calm, and their bodies were overlapping. The buzzing died down then: it was almost possible to see the wings stopping, the black and yellow rings ceasing to vibrate as if their batteries had run out.

'What did you spray on them?' I asked. 'What's in that bottle?'

'Dry wood and cow dung,' said Maya.

'And the smoke puts them to sleep? What does it do to them?'

She didn't answer. With both hands she lifted the first frame and gave it a brisk shake, and the drugged or sleeping or stunned bees fell back into the hive. 'Pass me the brush,' said Maya Fritts, and she used it to delicately sweep off the few stubborn ones who stayed stuck to the honey. Some bees climbed up her fingers, wandered through the soft bristles of the brush, a bit curious or perhaps drunk, and Maya pushed them off her with a smooth gesture, the stroke of a paintbrush. 'No, sweetie,' she said to one, 'you're staying home.' Or, to another, 'Down you get, we're not playing today.' The same procedure – the extraction of the combs, sweeping off the bees, the affectionate chitchat – was repeated at the rest of the hives, and Maya Fritts watched everything with her eyes wide open and was probably making mental notes of things that I, in my ignorance, was incapable of seeing. She turned over the wooden frames, looked at them straight on and from the back, a couple of times she used the smoke from the bottle again, as if she feared some unruly bee would wake up at the wrong moment, and I took the opportunity to take off one glove and stick my hand in the cloud, just to find out a little more about that cold smelly smoke. The smell, more wood than manure, stayed on my skin until well into the night. And it would remain forever associated with my long conversation with Maya Fritts.

After checking all the hives, after returning smokers and brushes and little crowbars to their places in the shed, Maya took me back to the house and surprised me with a suckling pig that her staff had been cooking all morning for us. Having acclimatized to the midday heat unawares, the first thing I felt on entering was instant relief, and as I received that sudden hit of shade and cool air I finally realized how much I'd been suffering inside the overall, gloves and mask. My back was drenched with sweat and my shirt stuck to my chest, and my body was screaming for any sort of comfort. Two fans, one over the living room and the other over the dining table, were spinning furiously. Before we sat down to eat, Maya Fritts got a box from somewhere and brought it into the dining-room. It was made of woven wicker, the size of a small suitcase, with a stiff lid and reinforced bottom, and on each end was a handle or a woven grip to make it easier to pick up and carry. Maya put it at the head of the table, like a guest, and sat opposite it. Then, while she served the salad from a wooden bowl, she asked me what I had come to know about Ricardo Laverde, if I had got to know him well.

'Not really,' I said. 'It was just a few months.'

'Do you mind remembering those things? Because of your accident, I mean?'

'Not any more,' I said. 'But, like I said, I don't know much. I know he loved your mother very much. I know about the flight from Miami. But I didn't know about you.'

'Nothing? He never talked about me?'

'Never. Only about your mother. Elena, wasn't it?'

'Elaine. Her name was Elaine, the Colombians changed it to Elena and she let them. Or she got used to it.'

'But Elena doesn't mean Elaine.'

'If you only knew,' she said, 'how many times I'd heard her explain that.'

'Elaine Fritts,' I said. 'She should be a stranger to me, but she isn't. It's odd. Do you know about the black box?'

'The cassette?'

'Yes. I had no way of knowing I'd be here today, Maya. I would have tried to keep that tape. I don't think it would have been so difficult.'

'Oh, don't worry about that,' said Maya. 'I've got it.'

'What?'

'Of course, what did you expect? It's the plane my mother died on, Antonio. It took me a little longer than you. To find the tape, I mean, Ricardo's house and the tape. You had an advantage, you were with him at the end, but anyway, I looked and finally got there. It's not my fault either.'

'And Consu gave you the tape.'

'Yes, she gave it to me. And I've got it. The first time I heard it I was devastated. I had to let whole days go by before listening to it again, and in spite of that I think I've been very brave, most other people would have put it away and never listened to it again. But I did, I listened to it again and since then I haven't stopped. I don't know how many times I've heard it now, twenty or thirty. At first I thought I played it again to find something in it. Then I realized that I keep playing it precisely because I know I'm not going to find anything. Dad just heard it the once, right?'

'As far as I know.'

'I can't even imagine what he felt.' Maya paused. 'He adored her. He adored my mother. Like any good couple, of course, but with him it was special. Because of what happened.'

'I don't understand.'

'Well, because he went away and she stayed the same as before. She remained sort of paralysed in his memory, in a way.'

She took off her glasses, and pinched her tear ducts: the universal gesture of those who do not want to cry. I wondered where in our genetic code these things are imprinted, these gestures repeated in all parts of the world, in all races, in all cultures, or almost all of them. Or maybe it wasn't like that, but cinema had made us think so. Yes, that was possible too. 'Sorry,' said Maya Fritts. 'It still happens.' On the pale skin of her nose a blush appeared, a sudden cold.

'Maya,' I said, 'can I ask you something?'

'Maybe.'

'What's in there?'

I didn't have to clarify what I was talking about. I didn't look at the wicker box, I didn't point at it in any way (not even with my mouth, as some do: pursing the lips and moving one's head like a horse). Maya Fritts, however, looked across the table and answered me while staring at the empty place.

'Well, that's what I asked you to come for,' she said. 'Let's see if I can explain it properly.' She paused, encircled her glass of beer with her fingers but didn't go so far as to take a sip. 'I want you to talk to me about my father.' Another pause. 'Sorry, I already told you that.' Yet another pause. 'Look, I didn't ever . . . I was very young when he . . . The thing is, I want you to tell me about his final days, you lived through them with him, and I want you to tell me in as much detail as possible.'

Then she stood up and brought the wicker crate, which must have weighed quite a lot because Maya had to lean it against her belly and hold it with both handles like a washerwoman from another century. 'Look, Antonio, it's like this,' she said. 'This box is full of things about my father. Photos, letters written to him, letters he wrote and that I've collected. All this material I've acquired, it's not like I've found it in the street, it's cost me a lot of effort. Señora Sandoval had a lot of things, for example. She had this photo, see.' I recognized it immediately, of course, and I would have recognized it even if someone had cropped it or removed the figure of Ricardo Laverde.

There were the pigeons of Bolívar Plaza, there was the corn cart, there was the Capitolio, there was the grey background of my grey city. 'It was for your mother,' I said. 'It was for Elaine Fritts.'

'I know,' said Maya. 'Had you seen it before?'

'He showed it to me. The day after he'd had it taken.'

'And did he show you other things? Did he ever give you anything, a letter, a document?'

I thought of the night I refused to go into Laverde's boarding house. 'No, nothing,' I said. 'What else have you got?'

'Stuff,' said Maya, 'unimportant stuff, stuff that doesn't mean anything. But having them makes me feel calmer. They're the proof. Look,' she said, and she showed me a stamped piece of paper. It was a bill: at the top, on the left, was a hotel logo, a circle of some undefined or indefinable colour (time had taken its toll on the paper) above which were distributed the words *Hotel*, *Escorial* and *Manizales*. To the right of the logo, the following inscrutable text:

> *Accounts are charged on the Friday of every month and must be settled immediately. All rooms include meals. Anyone occupying a room will be charged by the hotel for the minimum stay of one day.*

Then there was the date, 29 September 1970, the hour of the guest's arrival, 3:30 p.m., and the room number, 225; above the square that followed, handwritten, the date of departure (30 September, she'd just stayed one night) and the word *Paid*. The guest was called Elena de Laverde – I imagined her giving her married name to avoid any potential harassment – and during her brief stay at the hotel she'd made one phone call and eaten one dinner and breakfast, but she hadn't used the cablegram, laundry, press or car service. A paper without importance and at the same time a window into another world, I thought. And this crate was full of similar windows.

'Proof of what?' I asked.

'Pardon?'

'You said before that these papers are the proof.'

'Yes.'

'Well, proof of what?'

But Maya didn't answer. Instead she kept going through documents with her hand and spoke without looking at me. 'All this I acquired not long ago,' she told me. 'I found out some names, wrote to the United States telling them who I was, I negotiated by letter and by phone. And one day a package arrived with the letters Mom wrote when she first arrived in Colombia, back in '69. That's how it's been with all this, a historian's work. Many people think it's absurd. And I don't know, I don't really know how to justify it. I'm not even thirty yet and I live way out here, far from everything, like an old maid, and this has become important to me. Constructing my father's life, finding out who he was. That's what I'm trying to do. Of course, I wouldn't have got into anything like this if I hadn't been left like this, alone, with nobody, and so suddenly. It all started with what happened to my mother. It was so absurd . . . The news reached me here, I was in this hammock where I am now, when I heard that the plane had crashed. I knew she was on that plane. And three weeks later, my father.'

'How did you find out?'

'Reading *El Espacio*,' she said. 'It came out in *El Espacio*, with photos and everything.'

'Photos?'

'Of the pool of blood. Of two or three witnesses. Of Señora Sandoval, the one who told me about you. Of his room, and that was very painful. A sensationalist tabloid I'd always despised; I'd always despised its topless women and even its crossword puzzles, which are too easy. And I have to see the most important news of my life there. Tell me it's not ironic. That's how it was, I went to buy something in La Dorada and there was the paper, hanging up next to the beach balls and toy masks and kites for tourists. Then, one day, I realize. It might have been a Saturday (I was having breakfast here on the terrace, and I only do that on weekends), yeah, let's say one Saturday, I realized I was all alone. Months had passed and I had grieved a lot and I didn't know why I suffered so much, since we'd been apart for a long time, each living our own lives. We didn't have a life in common or anything like that. And that's what happened to me: I was alone, I'd been left alone, there was no longer anyone between me and my own death. That's what being orphaned is: there's no one ahead, you become next in line. It's your turn. Nothing changed in my life, Antonio, I'd spent many years without them, but now they're nowhere. They're not just not with me: they're nowhere. It was as if they'd absented themselves. And as if they were watching me, too, this is difficult to explain, but they watched me, Elaine and Ricardo were watching me. It's tough, the gaze of absent ones. Anyway, you can imagine what happened next.'

'It always seemed strange to me,' I said.

'What did?'

'Well, that a pilot's wife should die in a plane crash.'

'Oh. Well, that's not so strange when you know certain things.'

'Like what?'

'Have you got time?' Maya asked me. 'Do you want to read something that has nothing to do with my father and at the same time everything to do with him?'

From the crate she took out a copy of *Cromos* magazine with a design I didn't recognize – the name in white letters in a red box – and a colour photo of a woman in a swimming costume, her hands delicately placed on a sceptre, the crown balanced on her puffed-up hair: a beauty queen. The magazine was from May 1968, and the woman, as I immediately discovered, was Margarita María Reyes Zawadzky, Miss Colombia that year. The cover had various headlines, yellow letters over the blue background of the Caribbean Sea, but I didn't have time to read them, because Maya's fingers were already opening the magazine to the page marked with a yellow post-it note. 'You have to handle it gently,' Maya told me. 'Paper doesn't last at all in this humidity. I don't know how this has held together all these years. OK, here it is.' *THE SANTA ANA TRAGEDY*, was the headline in block capitals. And then a few lines to claim: 'Thirty years after the air accident that scarred Colombia, *Cromos* recovers the exclusive testimony of a survivor.' The article appeared beside an ad for *Club del Clan*, and it struck me as funny because I remembered having heard my parents talk about that television programme on several occasions. The drawing of a young woman playing guitar above the words *Televisión limitada*. 'A message to the youth of Colombia,' boasted the ad, 'is not complete if it doesn't include the *Clan Club*.'

I was about to ask what the article was about when my eyes fell on the surname Laverde, scattered across the page like a dog's dirty paw prints.

'Who is this Julio?'

'My grandfather,' said Maya. 'Who at the time of those events wasn't my grandfather yet. Nowhere near being my grandfather, he was fifteen years old.'

'Nineteen thirty eight,' I said.

'Yes.'

'Ricardo isn't in this piece.'

'No.'

'He hadn't been born yet.'

'Not for a good few years,' said Maya.

'So then?'

'So, that's why I asked you: have you got time? Because if you're in a hurry I'd understand. But if you really want to know who Ricardo Laverde was, start there.'

'Who wrote it?'

'That doesn't matter. I don't know. It doesn't matter.'

'What do you mean it doesn't matter?'

'The staff,' said Maya impatiently. 'Someone on the editorial staff wrote it, some journalist, a reporter, I don't know. Some nameless guy who showed up at my grandparents' house one day and started asking questions. And then sold the article and then wrote others. What does it matter, Antonio? What does it matter who wrote it?'

'But I don't understand,' I said. 'What is this?'

Maya sighed: it was a ridiculous sigh, like that of a bad actor, but in her it seemed genuine, just as genuine as her impatience. 'This is the story of one day,' she said. 'My great-grandfather takes my grandfather to an exhibition of planes. Captain Laverde takes his son Julio to see planes. His son Julio is fifteen. Later he will grow up and get married and have a son he'll name Ricardo. And Ricardo will grow up and then he'll have me. I don't know what's so hard to understand. This is the first gift my father gave my mother, a long time before they were married. I read it now and I understand perfectly well.'

'What?'

'Why he gave this to her. To her it seemed a brazen gesture and even a little pretentious: look what they wrote about my family, my family's in the press, and so on. But later she started to realize. She was a stray *gringa* who was going out with a Colombian without understanding very much about Colombia or that Colombian. When a person is new in a city, the first thing to find is a guide, right? Well, that's what this 1968 magazine article about a day of thirty years earlier was. My father was offering my mother a guide. Yes, a guide, why not think of it like that. A guide to Ricardo Laverde. A guide to his emotions with all the routes well marked, and everything.'

I left a silence and she added, 'Well, see for yourself. Shall I get you a beer?'

I said yes please, a beer, thanks. And I started to read. There was a short section title: *A Holiday in Bogotá*. And then the story began:

That Sunday of 1938 they were commemorating four hundred years since its founding, and the city was full of flags. The anniversary was not that exact day, but a little later; but the flags were already up all over the city, for the people of Bogotá back then liked to do things in good time. Many years later, remembering that ill-fated day, Julio Laverde would talk about the flags more than anything else. He remembered walking with his father from their family home to the Campo de Marte, in the neighbourhood of Santa Ana, which at that time was less a neighbourhood than an area of empty ground and was quite separate from the city. But with Captain Laverde there was not the slightest possibility of catching a bus or accepting a lift; walking was a noble and honourable activity and moving on wheels was something for the nouveau riche. According to Julio, Captain Laverde spent the entire walk talking about the flags, repeating that a true *bogotano* needed to know the significance of the city's flag and constantly testing his son on civic history.

'Don't they teach you these things at school?' he'd say. 'It's a disgrace. Where is this city headed in the hands of such citizens?'

And then he'd force him to recite that the red was a symbol of liberty, charity and health, and the yellow of justice, virtue and clemency. And Julio repeated uncomplainingly, 'Justice, virtue and clemency. Liberty, charity and health.'

Captain Laverde was a decorated hero of the war against Peru. He'd flown with Gómez Niño and Herbert Boy, among other legends, and had been commended for his conduct in the Tarapacá operation and in the taking of Güepí. Gómez, Boy and Laverde, those were the three names that were always mentioned later when people talked about the Colombian Air Force's role in the victory. The three musketeers of the air: one for all and all for one. Although they weren't always the same musketeers. Sometimes it was Boy, Laverde and Andrés Díaz; or Laverde, Gil and Van Oertzen. It depended on who was telling the story. But Captain Laverde was always one of them.

Going to See a Hero

On that Sunday morning, at the Campo de Marte, there was to be a military fly-past to celebrate the anniversary of the founding of Bogotá. It was as lavish an event as a Roman emperor might have organized. Captain Laverde had arranged to meet three veterans there, friends he hadn't seen since the armistice because none of them lived in Bogotá, but he had other reasons for attending the review as well. On the one hand, he'd been invited to the presidential grandstand by President López Pumarejo himself. Or almost: General Alfredo De León, who was very close to the president, had told him that the president would be very pleased to count on his illustrious presence.

'Imagine,' he'd said to him, 'a figure like yourself who has defended our colours against the enemy aggressor, a man like you to whom we owe the liberty of our nation and the integrity of our borders.'

The honour of the presidential invitation was one of the other reasons. But there was an added reason, less honourable but more urgent. Among the pilots who were going to be flying was Captain Abadía.

César Abadía was not yet thirty, but Captain Laverde had already predicted that this young man from the provinces, skinny and smiling who had already clocked up fifteen hundred flying hours despite his youth, was going to become the best pilot of light aircraft in Colombian history. Laverde had seen him fly during the war with Peru, when the captain was not a captain but a lieutenant, a young man from Tunja who gave lessons in bravery and control to the most experienced German pilots. And Laverde admired him from a position of sympathy and experience: the sympathy of knowing that one is also admired and the experience of knowing that one has what the other lacks.

But what mattered to Laverde was not to see Captain Abadía's reputed aerial feats himself. What he sought and desired was *that his son should see them*. That was why he was taking Julio to the Campo de Marte. That was why he had made him cross Bogotá on foot, through the flags. That was why he had explained they were going to see three types of plane, the Junkers, the Falcons of the observation squadron and the Hawks of the attack squadron. Captain Abadía would be flying a Hawk 812, one of the most agile and fastest machines ever invented by man for the tough and cruel tasks of warfare.

'Hawk means *halcón* in English,' the captain told young Julio, as he mussed the boy's short hair. 'You know what a hawk is, right?'

Julio said that he knew very well, and politely thanked his father for the explanation. But he spoke without enthusiasm. He was looking down at the ground as he walked, or maybe looking at the shoes of the people in the crowd, the fifty thousand people among whom they were now mingling. The coats brushing against him, wooden walking sticks and closed umbrellas banging into each other or getting tangled up, ponchos leaving a smell of wool in their wake, dress uniforms of soldiers, their chests covered in medals, police on duty strolling slowly among the crowd or observing from above, astride tall, ill-fed horses leaving a hazardous trail of stinking excrement in unpredictable places . . . Julio had never seen so many people in one place together for the same purpose.

An Uncomfortable Foreboding

Suddenly he wasn't feeling well. Maybe it was the noise the people made, their enthusiastic greetings, their shouted conversations, or maybe the mixture of smells coming off their clothes and their breath. Whatever the case, Julio suddenly felt as if he were stuck on a merry-go-round that was spinning too fast.

'I feel woozy,' he said to Captain Laverde.

But Laverde didn't pay any attention to him. Or rather, he did pay attention, but not to worry about how he was feeling but to introduce him to a man who was now approaching. He was tall, had a Rudolph Valentino-style moustache and was wearing a military uniform.

'General De León, this is my son,' said the captain. And then he spoke to Julio. 'The general is the General Prefect of Security.'

'General Prefect General,' said the general. 'I wish they'd change the name of the rank. Captain Laverde, the president has sent me to see you to your place. It's so easy to get lost in this throng.'

That was Laverde: a captain who generals came to look for on behalf of the president. And that's how the captain and his son found themselves walking towards the presidential grandstand a couple of steps behind General De León, trying to follow him, not to lose sight of him and to pay attention to the extraordinary world of the celebrations at the same time. It had rained the previous night and there were still puddles here and there, and if there wasn't a puddle there were patches of mud where the heels of the women's shoes were getting stuck. This happened to a young lady with a pink scarf: she lost a shoe, a cream-coloured one, and Julio bent down to retrieve it while she stood smiling, paralysed like a flamingo. Julio recognized her. He was sure he'd seen her in the society pages: she was a foreigner, he thought, the daughter of a businessman or an industrialist. He tried to find the name in his memory, but he didn't have time, because Captain Laverde was now grabbing him by the arm and making him climb the creaking wooden steps that led up to the presidential grandstand, and over his shoulder Julio managed to see how the pink scarf and cream-coloured shoes were starting to climb another set of steps, those up to the diplomatic grandstand. They were two identical structures and they were separated by a strip of land as wide as an avenue, like two-tiered cabins constructed on thick piles, placed side by side but both facing the empty ground above which the planes would pass. Identical, yes, except for one detail: in the middle of the presidential grandstand stood an 18-metre-tall pole from which waved the Colombian flag. Years later, talking about what happened that day, Julio would say that the flag, placed in that precise space, had made him wary from the start. But it's easy to say such things after it's all over.

The Show Begins

The atmosphere was festive. The air smelled of fried food. People carried drinks in their hands that they were finishing before going up. Every plank of the two sets of steps was filled with people who hadn't fitted into the grandstands, and so was the strip of ground in between the two sets of steps. Julio felt queasy and he said so, but Captain Laverde didn't hear him. Walking between the guests was difficult: he had to greet his acquaintances at the same time as spurning social climbers, to be very careful not to snub somebody who was due a greeting while being equally careful not to honour someone who wasn't. Making their way through the people, without getting separated for a moment, the captain and his son reached the railing. From there Julio saw two men with receding hairlines speaking with a circumspect air a few metres from the flagpole, and those he did recognize immediately: it was President López, wearing a light-coloured suit, dark tie and round-framed glasses, and President-elect Santos, wearing a dark suit, light waistcoat and round-framed glasses as well. The man on his way out and the man on his way in: the country's destiny settled on two square metres of carpentry. A small crowd of distinguished people – the Lozanos, the Turbays, the Pastranas – divided the presidents' box from the back part of the grandstand, the upper level, where the Laverdes were. From the distance, the captain saluted López, López returned the greeting with a smile that didn't show his teeth, and the two of them made mute signals to each other about meeting later because the thing was starting now. Santos turned to see to whom López was gesturing; recognized Laverde, nodded slightly, and at that moment the triple-engine Junkers appeared in the sky and dragged everyone's gaze in their slipstream.

Julio was absorbed. He had never seen such complex manoeuvres up so close. The Junkers were heavy, and their streaky bodies made them look like big prehistoric fish, but they moved with dignity. Each time they passed, the air they displaced arrived at the stand in waves, ruining the hairdos of the women not wearing hats. The cloudy Bogotá sky, that dirty sheet that seemed to have covered the city since its foundation, was the perfect screen for the projection of this film. Against a background of clouds the triple-engine planes flew past and now the six Falcons, as if from one side to the other of a giant theatre. The formation was perfectly symmetrical. Julio forgot the bitter taste in his mouth for a moment and his dizziness disappeared. His attention wandered over to the hills east of the city, their misty silhouette that extended back, long and dark like a sleeping lizard. It was raining over the hills: the rain, he thought, would soon be here. The Falcons flew past again and again he felt the tremor in the air. The thunder of the engines didn't manage to drown out the shouts of admiration from the stands. The translucent discs of the spinning propellers threw off brief sparkles of light when the plane banked to turn. Then the fighter planes appeared. They came out of nowhere, immediately assuming a V-formation, and it was suddenly difficult to remember that they weren't living creatures, that there was someone in command. 'There's Abadía,' said a woman's voice. Julio turned to see who had spoken, but then the same words were being repeated from another side of the stand: the star pilot's name moved among the people like a nasty rumour. President López raised a martial arm and pointed at the sky.

'Here we go,' said Captain Laverde. 'Here comes the real thing.'

Beside Julio there was a couple in their fifties, a man in a polka-dot bow tie and his wife, whose mousy face didn't hide the fact that she'd once been beautiful. Julio heard the man say that he was going to go and get the car. And he also heard the wife. 'But don't be silly. Stay here and we'll go afterwards. You're going to miss the best part.'

At that moment, the squadron flew past at a low altitude in front of the stand and then in a straight line to the south. Applause broke out, and Julio clapped too. Captain Laverde had forgotten him: his eyes were fixed on what was happening in the sky, the dangerous designs that were taking place up there, and then Julio understood that his father had never seen anything like this before either. 'I didn't know such things could be done with a plane,' he would say much later, when the episode was relived in social get-togethers, or family dinners. 'It was as though Abadía had suspended the laws of gravity.' Returning from the south, Captain Abadía's Hawk fighter left the formation, or rather the rest of the Hawks peeled away from his. Julio didn't know when Abadía had been left alone, or where the other eight pilots had gone, having disappeared all of a sudden as if the cloud had swallowed them. Then the solitary aircraft flew past in front of the stand doing a roll that drew shouts and applause. Heads followed it and saw it twist and turn over and return, this time flying lower and faster, tracing another roll with the mountains as background, then disappear once again into the northern skies, then reappear in them, as if looming out of nowhere, and heading towards the grandstands.

'What's he doing?' said someone.

Abadía's Hawk was flying straight towards the spectators.

'But what's that crazy man doing?' said someone else.

This time the voice came from below, from one of the men with President López. Without knowing why, Julio looked at the president at that moment and saw him clutching the wooden railing with both hands, as if he wasn't standing on a construction well planted on the ground, but at the rails of a ship on the high sea. Again Julio sensed the acrid taste in his mouth, the dizziness and also a sudden sharp pain in his forehead behind his eyes. And that was when Captain Laverde said, in a low voice to no one specifically, or just to himself, with a mixture of admiration and envy, as if watching someone else resolve an enigma, 'Good God. He wants to grab the flag.'

What happened next occurred for Julio as if outside of time, like a hallucination produced by the migraine. Captain Abadía's fighter plane approached the presidential grandstand at 400 kilometres per hour, but it seemed to be floating in one place in the cool air; and a few metres away performed a roll in the air and then another one – loop the loop, Captain Laverde called it – and all in the middle of a deathly silence. Julio remembered that he had time to look around, to see faces paralysed by fear and astonishment, and mouths open as if they were screaming. But there were no screams: the world was hushed. In one instant Julio realized that his father was right: Captain Abadía had planned to finish his double roll so close to the waving flag that he could grasp the fabric in his hand, an impossible pirouette dedicated to President López the way a toreador dedicates a bull. All this he understood, and he still had time to wonder if the rest had understood too. And then he felt the shadow of the plane in his eyes, an impossibility since the sun was not shining, and he felt a gust of something that smelled burnt, and he had the presence of mind to see how Abadía's fighter plane did a strange leap in the air, bent as if it were rubber and hastened to the ground, destroying as it did the wooden roofs of the diplomatic stand, taking the stairs of the presidential grandstand down with it and shattering into bits as it crashed against the field.

The world exploded. There was an explosion of noise: shouts, heels against wood floors, the sound bodies make when they flee. A black cloud that didn't look like smoke, but like dense ash, exploded down there where the plane had fallen, and remained in place for longer than it should have. From the area of impact came a wave of brutal heat that killed those who were closest to it in seconds, and the rest felt like they were being charred alive. The luckiest ones thought they were dying of asphyxiation, because the heat was consuming all the oxygen in the air. It was like being inside an oven, one of those present would say later. When the set of steps was detached from the stand, the boards and rails gave way and both the Laverdes fell to the ground, and that was when, Julio would say much later, the pain began.

'Papá,' he called, and saw Captain Laverde stand up to try to help a woman who had been trapped beneath the wood of the steps, but it was obvious the woman was beyond all help. 'Papá, something's wrong with me.'

Julio heard the voice of a man calling a woman. 'Elvia,' he shouted, 'Elvia.' And Julio recognized the guy with the polka-dot bow tie who'd gone to fetch the car, walking among the fallen bodies, stepping on some of them or tripping over them. There was that burnt smell, and Julio identified it: it was the smell of meat. Captain Laverde turned around and Julio saw, reflected on his face, the disaster of what had happened. Captain Laverde took him by the hand and began to walk to get away from the catastrophe, looking for a way to get to a hospital as quickly as possible. Julio had now begun to cry, less from the pain than from the fear, when they walked past the diplomatic stand and he saw two dead bodies, and recognized the cream-coloured shoes on one of them. Then he passed out. He woke up hours later, in pain and surrounded by worried faces, in a bed in the San José Hospital.

Lucky to Survive

No one ever knew how it happened, if the plane broke up in the air or if it came from the crash, but the fact is that Julio received a gob of motor oil full in the face, and the oil burned his skin and his flesh and it was lucky it didn't kill him, as it did so many others. There were fifty-five dead after the accident: first among them was Captain Abadía. It was explained that the manoeuvre had produced a ball of air; that the plane, after the double roll, had entered a void; that all that caused the loss of altitude and control and the inevitable downfall. In the hospitals, the injured people received that news with indifference or amazement, and heard that the Treasury would pay for the funerals of the dead, that the poorest families would receive assistance from the city and that the president had visited all the injured the first night. He had certainly visited young Julio Laverde, at least. But he was not awake at the time and was unaware of the visit. His parents told him about it in great detail.

The next day, his mother stayed with him while his father attended the funerals of Abadía, Captain Jorge Pardo and two cavalry soldiers stationed at Santa Ana, all buried at the Central Cemetery after a procession that included several representatives of the government and the cream of the military Air and Ground Forces. Julio, lying on the good side of his face, received morphine injections. He saw the world as if from inside an aquarium. He touched the sterilized dressing and was dying to scratch, but he couldn't scratch. At the moments of greatest pain he hated Captain Laverde and then he said an Our Father and asked forgiveness for his evil thoughts. He also prayed that his injury wouldn't become infected, because he had been told that it might. And then he saw the foreign girl and started talking to her. He saw himself with his burnt face. Sometimes her face was burnt too and sometimes it wasn't, but she always had the pink scarf and the cream-coloured shoes. In those hallucinations the young woman spoke to him sometimes. She asked him how he was. She asked him if he was in pain.

And sometimes she asked him, 'Do you like planes?'

Night was falling. Maya Fritts lit a scented candle to frighten off the mosquitoes. 'They all come out at this hour,' she said. She handed me a stick of repellent and told me to put it everywhere, but especially on my ankles, and when I tried to read the label I realized how ferociously dark it was getting. I also realized that there was now no possibility whatsoever of my returning to Bogotá, and I realized that Maya Fritts had realized that too, as if we'd both been working on the assumption until now that I would spend the night here, with her, like a guest of honour, two strangers sharing a roof because they weren't such strangers, after all: they had a dead man in common. I looked at the sky, marine blue like one of those skies of Magritte's, and before it got completely dark I saw the first bats, their black silhouettes outlined against the background. Maya stood up, put a wooden chair in between the two hammocks, and on top of the chair arranged a lit candle, a small polystyrene cooler filled with chunks of ice, a bottle of rum and a bottle of Coke. She went back to lie down in her hammock (a skilful manoeuvre of opening it and getting in with a single movement). My leg hurt. In a matter of minutes the musical scandal of crickets and cicadas burst out and a few minutes later had calmed down again, and only a few soloists chimed up here and there, interrupted every once in a while by the croak of a lost frog. The bats fluttered 3 metres above our heads, coming in and out of their refuges in the wooden roof, and the yellow light moved with the puffs of a gentle breeze, and the air was warm and the rum was going down nicely. 'Well, someone's not going to be sleeping in Bogotá tonight,' said Maya Fritts. 'If you want to call, there's a telephone in my room.'

I thought of Leticia, of her little sleeping face. I thought of Aura. I thought of a vibrator the colour of ripe mulberries.

'No,' I said, 'I don't have to phone anybody.'

'One less problem,' she said.

'But I don't have any clothes either.'

'Well,' she said, 'that we can fix.'

I looked at her: her bare arms, her breasts, her square chin, her small ears with narrow lobes where a spark of light flashed every time she moved her head. Maya took a sip, rested her glass on her belly, and I did the same. 'Look, Antonio, this is the thing,' she said then, 'I need you to tell me about my father, about the end of his life, about the day of his death. Nobody else saw the things that you saw. If all this is a puzzle, then you have a piece that nobody else has, if you see what I mean. Can you help me?' I didn't answer immediately. 'Can you help me?' Maya insisted, but I didn't answer. She leaned on one elbow, anyone who's been in a hammock knows how difficult it is to lean on one elbow, you lose your balance and get tired pretty fast. I sunk into my hammock so that I was wrapped in the material that smelled of humidity and past sweat, of a history of men and women lying here after swimming in the pool or working on the property. I stopped looking at Maya Fritts. 'And if I tell you what you want to know,' I said, 'are you going to do the same?' I was suddenly thinking about my virgin diary, about that solitary and lost question mark, and some words sketched themselves out in my head: *I want to know*. Maya didn't reply, but in the shadows I saw her settled down into her hammock the same way I was in mine, and that was all I needed. I started to talk, I told Maya all that I knew and thought I knew about Ricardo Laverde, all that I remembered and what I feared I'd forgotten, all that Laverde had told me and also all that I'd found out after his death, and that's how we stayed until after midnight, each wrapped in our hammock, each scrutinizing the roof where the bats moved, filling with words the silence of the warm night, but without ever looking at each other, like a priest and sinner in the sacrament of confession.

4

We're All Fugitives

IT WAS STARTING TO get light when, exhausted and half drunk and almost hoarse, I let Maya Fritts guide me to the guest room, or what she, at that moment, called the guest room. There was no bed, just two simple and rather fragile-looking camp beds (mine let out a crack when I dropped like a dead man onto the mattress, without pulling back the thin white sheet). A fan whirred furiously above my head, and I think I had a fleeting drunken bout of paranoia when I chose the bed that wasn't directly under the blades, in case the contraption came loose as I slept and fell on top of me. But I also remember having received certain instructions, through the fog of sleepiness and rum. Not to leave the windows open without the screens, not to leave Coke cans anywhere (the house fills up with ants), not to throw paper down the toilet. 'That's really important, people from the city always forget,' she said, or I think she said. 'Going to the toilet is one of the most automatic things in the world, nobody thinks when they're sitting there. And I'd rather not tell you about the problems later with the septic tank.' The discussion of my bodily functions by a complete stranger didn't make me uncomfortable. Maya Fritts was the most natural person I'd ever met, so different from most *bogotanos* whose puritanism meant they were quite capable of going through life pretending never to shit. I think I agreed, don't know if I said anything. My leg was hurting more than usual, my hip hurt. I put it down to the humidity and exhaustion after so many hours on an unpredictable and dangerous highway.

I woke up disoriented. It was the midday heat that woke me up: I was sweating and the sheet was soaked, like the sheets at the San José Hospital under the sweats of my hallucinations, and when I looked at the ceiling I realized the fan had stopped spinning. The aggressive daylight filtered through the wooden blinds and formed puddles of light on the white floor tiles. Beside the closed door, on a wicker chair, there was something like a change of clothes: two short-sleeved checked shirts, a green towel. The house was silent. In the distance I could hear voices, the voices of people working, and the sounds of their tools as they worked: I didn't know who they were, what they were doing at that hour, in that heat, and just as I was wondering, the noises stopped, and I thought: they will have gone for a siesta. I opened the blinds and the window and peered out with my nose practically pressed against the mosquito screen, and didn't see anybody: I saw the luminous rectangle of the pool, saw the solitary slide, I saw a ceiba tree like the ones I'd seen along the highway, specially designed to give shade to the poor creatures who inhabited this world of harsh sunshine. Beneath the ceiba was the German shepherd I'd seen on my way in. Behind the ceiba stretched the plain, and behind the plain somewhere flowed the Magdalena River, the sound of which I could easily imagine or conjecture, because I'd heard it as a child, though at other parts of its course, far from Las Acacias. Maya Fritts was not around, so I took a cold shower (I had to kill a considerable-sized spider who held out for quite a while in a corner) and I put on the bigger of the two shirts. It was a man's shirt; I allowed myself to pretend it had belonged to Ricardo Laverde, imagined him with the shirt on; in the image I conjured up, for some reason, he looked like me. As soon as I went out into the hall a young woman approached wearing red Bermuda shorts with blue pockets and a sleeveless shirt on the front of which a butterfly and a sunflower were kissing. She had a tray in her hands and on the tray a tall glass of orange juice. In the living room as well the ceiling fans were still.

'Señorita Maya left the things for you on the terrace,' she told me. 'She'll see you for lunch.' She smiled at me, and waited for me to take the glass from the tray.

'Can't we turn on the fans?'

'The power's gone out,' said the woman. 'Would you like some coffee, sir?'

'First a telephone. To call Bogotá, if it's no trouble.'

'Well, the telephone's in there,' she said. 'But that's something for you to sort out with the señorita.'

It was one of those old, all-in-one phones from the late 1970s that I remembered from my childhood: a sort of small, chubby, long-necked bird with the dial on the underside and a red button. To get a dial tone you just picked it up. I dialled my number and marvelled at feeling a childish impatience while waiting for the dial to turn back before being able to start the next number. Aura answered before the second ring. 'Where are you?' she said. 'Are you OK?'

'Of course. Why wouldn't I be?'

Her tone changed, sounding cold and dense and heavy. 'Where are you?' she said.

'In La Dorada. Visiting someone.'

'The woman who left the message?'

'What?'

'The one who left the message on the answering machine?'

I wasn't surprised by her clairvoyance (she'd shown signs of it since the beginning of our relationship). I explained the situation without going into details: Ricardo Laverde's daughter, the documents she possessed and images stored in her memory, the possibility for me to understand so many things. I want to know, I thought, but didn't say. While I was speaking I heard a series of short, perhaps guttural sounds, and then Aura was suddenly crying. 'You are a son of a bitch,' she said. She didn't run all the words together in a more efficient and natural way, but separated them out and pronounced each letter of every word. 'I haven't slept a wink, Antonio. I haven't checked the hospitals because I don't have anyone to leave Leticia with. I don't understand you. I don't understand any of this,' Aura said between sobs, and the way she was crying seemed almost aggressive, I'd never heard her cry like that: it was the tension, without a doubt, the tension built up throughout the night. 'Who is that woman?'

'No one,' I said. 'At least not what you're imagining.'

'You don't know what I'm imagining. Who is she?'

'She's the daughter of Ricardo Laverde,' I said. 'The guy who was . . .'

I heard a huff. 'I know who he was,' said Aura. 'Don't insult me any more, please.'

'She wants me to tell her, and I want her to tell me too. That's all.'

'And is she pretty? I mean, is she hot?'

'Aura, don't do this.'

'But, I just don't understand,' said Aura again. 'I don't see why you didn't call yesterday. Would that have been so difficult? Couldn't you have picked up that phone yesterday? You spent the night there, right?'

'Yes,' I said.

'Yes what? Yes you could have picked up that phone or yes you spent the night?'

'Yes I spent the night here. Yes I could have used this phone.'

'So then?'

'So nothing,' I said.

'What did you do? What did the two of you do?'

'Talked. All night. I woke up late, that's why I didn't call till now.'

'Oh, that's why.'

'Yes.'

'I see,' said Aura. And then, 'You're a son of a bitch, Antonio.'

'But there's information here,' I said, 'I can find things out here.'

'An inconsiderate son of a bitch,' said Aura. 'You can't do this to your family. Awake all night, scared to death, thinking the worst things. What a son of a bitch. The worst things. All of Friday stuck in here, waiting for news, without going anywhere in case you called just at that moment. And lying awake all night, scared to death. Didn't you think of that? Didn't it matter to you? What if it had been the other way round? Then it would, right? Imagine if I went away for the whole day and night with Leticia and you didn't know where we were. You who live in fear, who thinks I'm going to fool around on you all the time. You, who wants me to phone you when I get anywhere so you know I got there. You, who wants me to call you when I'm leaving, so you know what time I left. Why are you doing this, Antonio? What's going on? What do you want?'

'I don't know,' I told her then, 'I don't know what I want.'

In the seconds of silence that followed I managed to hear and recognize Leticia's movements, that sonorous trace that resembles a little cat's bell that parents learn to notice without realizing: Leticia walking or running on the carpeted floor, Leticia talking to her toys or getting her toys to talk to each other, Leticia rearranging things in the house (things she wasn't allowed to touch, forbidden ashtrays, the forbidden broom she liked to bring out of the kitchen to sweep the carpet: all the subtle displacements of air her little body produced). I missed her; realized I'd never spent a night away from her before, so far away from her; and I felt, as I'd felt so many times, anxiety for her vulnerability and the intuition that accidents (lying in wait for her in every room, in every street) were more likely in my absence. 'Is Leticia all right?' I asked.

Aura hesitated a heartbeat before answering. 'Yes, she's fine. She ate a good breakfast.'

'Put her on.'

'What?'

'Put her on the phone, please. Tell her I want to talk to her.'

Silence. 'Antonio, it's been more than three years. Why don't you want to get over it? Why do you want to keep living in your accident? I don't know why you'd want that. I don't see what good it can do. What is going on?'

'I want to speak to Leticia. Give her the telephone. Call her and hand her the phone.'

Aura huffed with something that sounded like annoyance or desperation, or maybe open irritation, the irritation of someone who feels powerless: they are emotions that are hard to distinguish over the phone, you need to see the person's face to interpret them correctly. In my tenth-floor apartment, in my city stuck up there at 2,600 metres above sea level, my two girls were moving and talking and I was listening to them and loving them, yes, I loved them both and didn't want to hurt them. That's what I was thinking when Leticia spoke. 'Hello?' she said. It's a word children learn that nobody has to teach them. 'Hello, sweetheart,' I said.

'It's Papá,' she said.

Then I heard Aura's distant voice. 'Yes,' she told her. 'But listen, listen to hear what he says.'

'Hello?' Leticia said again.

'Hello,' I said. 'Who am I?'

'Papá,' she said, pronouncing the second P forcefully, taking her time over it.

'No,' I said, 'I'm the big bad wolf.'

'The big bad wolf?'

'I'm Peter Pan.'

'Peter Pan?'

'Who am I, Leticia?'

She thought for a moment. Then she said, 'Papá.'

'Exactly,' I said. I heard her laugh: a short little laugh, the wing beat of a hummingbird. And then I said, 'Are you looking after Mamá?'

'Aha,' said Leticia.

'You have to take good care of Mamá. Are you looking after her?'

'Aha,' said Leticia. 'Here she is.'

'No, wait,' I tried to say, but it was too late, she'd got rid of the phone and left me in Aura's hands, my voice in Aura's hands, and my nostalgia hanging in the warm air: the nostalgia for things that weren't yet lost. 'OK, go and play,' I heard Aura say in her sweetest tone of voice, speaking to her almost in whispers, a lullaby in five syllables. Then she spoke to me and the contrast was violent: there was sadness in her voice, as close as she sounded to me; there was disenchantment and also a veiled reproach. 'Hello,' said Aura.

'Hello,' I said. 'Thank you.'

'What for?'

'For putting Leticia on the phone.'

'She's scared of the hallway,' said Aura.

'Leticia?'

'She says there are things in the hallway. Yesterday she didn't want to go from the kitchen to her bedroom by herself. I had to go with her.'

'It's just a phase,' I said. 'All her fears will pass.'

'She wanted to sleep with the light on.'

'It's a phase.'

'Yes,' said Aura.

'The paediatrician told us.'

'Yes.'

'She's just at the nightmare age.'

'The thing I don't want is . . .' said Aura. 'I don't want us to go on like this, Antonio.' Before I could answer she added, 'It's not good for anyone. It's not good for Leticia, it's not good for anyone.'

So that was it. 'I get it now,' I said. 'So it's my fault.'

'Nobody said anything about anyone's fault.'

'It's my fault Leticia's afraid of the hallway.'

'Nobody said that.'

'Oh please, what nonsense. As if fear was hereditary.'

'Not hereditary,' said Aura, 'contagious.' And then immediately, 'I didn't mean to say that.' And then, 'You know what I mean.'

My hands were sweating, especially the one holding the phone, and I had an absurd fear: I thought the receiver could slip out of my sweaty fist and fall to the floor, and the call would be cut off against my will. By accident: accidents do happen. Aura was talking to me about our past, about the plans we'd had before a bullet that didn't have my name on it hit me by chance, and I was listening to her carefully, I swear I was, but no memory formed in my mind. *In the mind's eye*, as is sometimes said. My mind's eye tried to see Aura before the death of Ricardo Laverde; it tried to see myself; but it was in vain. 'I have to hang up,' I heard myself say, 'I'm on a borrowed phone.' Aura – this I remember well – was saying that she loved me, that we could get through this together, that we were going to work to achieve it. 'I have to hang up,' I said.

'When are you coming back?'

'I don't know,' I said. 'There's information here, there are things I want to know.'

There was silence on the line.

'Antonio,' Aura said then, 'are you coming back?'

'What kind of question is that?' I said. 'Of course I'm coming back, I don't know where you think I am.'

'I don't think anything. Tell me when.'

'I don't know. As soon as I can.'

'When, Antonio?'

'As soon as I can,' I said. 'But don't cry, it's not a big deal.'

'I'm not crying.'

'It's not what you think. Leticia's going to get worried.'

'Leticia, Leticia,' Aura repeated. 'Go to hell, Antonio.'

'Aura, please.'

'Go to hell,' she said. 'We'll see you when you can make it.'

After hanging up I went out to the terrace. There, resting beneath the hammock like a pet, was the wicker box; there, on the paper, were the lives of Elaine Fritts and Ricardo Laverde, letters they wrote to each other, letters they'd written to other people. The air was

perfectly still. I settled into the hammock that Maya Fritts had used the night before and there, with my head on a cushion with a white, embroidered cover, I took out the first folder and set it on my stomach, and from the folder took out the first letter. It was a piece of greenish, almost see-through paper. 'Dear Grandpa & Grandma,' it opened. And then the first line, independent and on its own, leaning on the paragraph that followed like a suicidal person on a cornice.

Nobody warned me Bogotá was going to be like this.

I forgot the humid heat, forgot the orange juice, forgot how uncomfortable I was in that position (and, of course, didn't imagine the agonizing stiff neck it would cause). Lying in Maya's hammock I forgot myself. Later I tried to remember the last time I had experienced something like that, unceremoniously blocking out the real world, my consciousness absolutely sequestered, and came to the conclusion that nothing similar had happened to me since childhood. But that reasoning, that effort, would come much later, during the hours I spent talking to Maya to fill the voids left by the letters, so she could tell me everything the letters didn't tell but only hinted at; all that they didn't reveal, but hid or kept quiet. That would be later, as I said, that conversation could only take place later, when I had already been through the documents and their revelations. There, in the hammock, while I read them, I felt other things, some of them inexplicable and an especially confusing one: the discomfort of knowing that this story in which

my name did not appear spoke of me in each and every one of its lines. All this I felt, and in the end all my feelings were reduced to a tremendous solitude, a solitude without a visible cause and therefore without remedy. The solitude of a child.

The story, as far as I could reconstruct it and as it exists in my memory, began in August of 1969, eight years after President John Fitzgerald Kennedy signed the executive order creating the Peace Corps, when after five weeks' training at Florida State University, Elaine Fritts, future volunteer number 139372, landed in Bogotá ready to carry out various clichés: to have an enriching experience, leave her mark, do her share, no matter how small. The journey didn't start too well, for the gusts of wind shaking the aircraft, an old Avianca DC-4, forced her to put out her cigarette and to do something she hadn't done since she was fifteen: cross herself. (But it was a quick blessing, just a careless sketch across her unmade-up face and chest with two strings of wooden beads. No one saw.) Before she left, her grandmother had talked to her about a passenger plane that had crashed the previous year as it arrived in Bogotá from Miami, and there, while hers began its descent towards the greenish grey of the mountains, while it emerged from the low clouds in the midst of gusts of wind and with its windows marked by highways of thick rain, Elaine tried to remember if all the passengers on the plane that crashed had died. She hung on to her knees – the wrinkled, sweaty trace of her hands on her trouser legs – and closed her eyes when the plane, with a shudder of

crunching tin, touched down. It still seemed miraculous to her that she'd survived the landing, and she thought she'd write her first letter to her grandparents as soon as she could sit down at a table somewhere warm. I've arrived, I'm well, the people are very friendly. There is lots of work to be done. Everything's going to be great.

Elaine's mother had died in childbirth, and she had been raised by her grandparents since her father, on a reconnaissance mission near Old Baldy, stepped on an anti-personnel mine and returned from Korea with his right leg amputated at the hip and lost to life. He hadn't been back for a whole year yet when he went out to buy cigarettes and never came back. They never heard from him again. Elaine was a baby when that happened, so she didn't really notice the absence, and her grandparents took charge of her education and also of her happiness as meticulously as they had with their own children, but with much more experience. So the adults in Elaine's life were these two figures from another time, and she herself grew up with notions of responsibility unlike those of most other children. On social occasions she would hear opinions from her grandfather that filled her with pride and sadness at the same time: 'This is how my daughter should have turned out.' When Elaine decided to postpone her journalism degree to volunteer for the Peace Corps, her grandfather, who had worn black for nine months after Kennedy's assassination, was her biggest supporter. 'With one condition,' he said. 'That you don't stay down there, like so many others. It's good to lend a hand, but your country needs you more.' She agreed.

The Embassy staff, Elaine Fritts said in her letter, found her a room in a two-storey house out near the racetrack, half an hour north of Bogotá, in a collection of badly paved streets that turned to mud whenever it rained. The world where she would spend the next twelve weeks was a grey place still under construction: most of the houses didn't have roofs because the roof was the most expensive part and was left for last, and the daily traffic was made of big orange mixers as noisy as bees in a nightmare, dump trucks that emptied mountains of gravel in any old place, workers with sponge cake in one hand and a soda pop in the other who whistled obscenely at her as soon as she walked out of the house. Elaine Fritts – the palest green eyes that had ever been seen in this place, her long, straight, chestnut-coloured hair sweeping like a curtain down to her waist, her nipples standing out under her flowered blouse in the morning chill – kept her eyes fixed on the puddles, on the reflection of the grey skies, and only raised her head when she got to the open field that separated the neighbourhood from the Autopista Norte, more than anything to make sure the two cows that grazed there were a comfortable distance away. Then she had to climb aboard a small yellow bus with unpredictable timetables and no predetermined stops and start, from the first moment, to elbow her way through the thick soup of passengers. 'The rest was very simple,' she wrote. 'You just have to get off in time.' In the half-hour of the journey, Elaine had to get from the aluminium turnstile at the front door (which she learned to move by bumping it with her hips, without needing to use her hands) to the back door, and get off the bus without knocking off the two or three passengers who were hanging on with one foot in the air. All this required an apprenticeship, of course, and during the first week it was normal to go a mile or two beyond the place she needed to get off and arrive at the CEUCA several minutes after her eight o'clock class had already started, soaked through by the persistent drizzle, walking down unknown streets.

The Centro de Estudios Universitarios Colombo-Americano, or Colombian-American University Study Centre: a long pretentious name for a few rooms full of people Elaine found familiar, too familiar. Her colleagues, at this stage of training, were white, in their twenties as was she, and like her they were tired of their own country, tired of Vietnam, tired of Cuba, tired of Santo Domingo, tired of mornings catching them off guard, making small talk with their parents or their friends, and going to bed knowing they'd just witnessed a unique and regrettable day, a day that would immediately go down in the universal history of infamy: the day a sawed-off shotgun killed Malcolm X, a car-bomb killed Wharlest Jackson, a bomb in the post office killed Fred Conlon, police gunfire killed Benjamin Brown. And at the same time the coffins kept arriving from every inoffensively or picturesquely named Vietnamese operation, Deckhouse Five, Cedar Falls, Junction City. The My Lai revelations began to start popping up and soon they'd be talking about Thanh Phong, one barbarous act replaced and displaced another, rapes became interchangeable. Yes, that's how it was: in her country, a person woke up and didn't know what to expect, what cruel joke history might be about to play, what would be spat in her face that day. When had this happened to the United States of America? That question, which Elaine asked herself in a thousand confusing ways every day, floated in the air of the classrooms, above all the white, twenty-year-old heads, and also occupied their spare time, lunches in the cafeteria, the trips from the CEUCA to the shantytowns where the apprentice volunteers did their field work. The United States of America: who was ruining it, who was responsible for the demolition of the dream? There, in the classroom, Elaine was thinking: *that's what we've fled*. She thought: *we're all fugitives*.

The mornings were devoted to learning Spanish. For four hours, four arduous hours and with a stevedore's tension in her shoulders, Elaine unravelled the mysteries of the new language in front of a teacher in riding boots and turtleneck sweaters, a thin, haggard woman who often brought her three-year-old son to class because she had no one to leave him with at home. To each slip-up with the subjunctive, to each mistakenly gendered word, Señora Amalia responded with a speech. 'How are you going to work with the poor people of this country if you can't understand them?' she would say to them leaning on her two closed fists on her wooden desk. 'And if you can't get them to understand you, how do you expect to win the confidence of the community leaders? In three or four months, some of you will be going out to the coast or up to the coffee-growing region. Do you think the Acción Comunal people are going to wait while you look up words in the dictionary? Do you think the *campesinos* are going to sit in their villages while you lot try to figure out how to say *La leche es mejor que el aguapanela*?' But in the afternoons, during the hours taught in English that appeared in the official programme as *American Studies* and *World Affairs*, Elaine and her classmates listened to lectures from Peace Corps veterans who for one reason or another had stayed in Colombia, and from them they learned that the important phrases weren't the ones to do with sugar-water or milk, but rather some quite different ones, the common ingredient being the word *No: No, I'm not from the Alliance for Progress*, *No, I'm not in the CIA*, and, especially, *No, I'm very sorry, I don't have any dollars.*

In October, Elaine wrote a long letter to her grandparents to say happy birthday to her grandmother, thank them both for the cuttings from *Time*, and ask her grandfather if he'd seen the new Paul Newman and Robert Redford movie, which people were already talking about in Bogotá (though the film itself would take a little longer to arrive). Then, suddenly solemn, she asked them what they knew about the crimes in Beverly Hills. 'Everybody has an opinion here, you can't sit down to lunch without talking about the subject. The photos are horrific. Sharon Tate was pregnant, I don't know how anyone could do something like that. This world's a scary place these days. Grandpa, you've seen worse things, haven't you? Please tell me the world has always been like this.' And then she changed the subject. 'I think I already told you about the squatter neighbourhoods,' she wrote. She explained that every class of the CEUCA is divided up into groups, and each group has its neighbourhood, that the other three members of her group are Californians: all men, very good at putting up walls and talking to the leaders of the local council (Elaine explained), and also very good at getting hold of very high-quality marijuana from La Guajira or Santa Marta at a good price for downtown Bogotá (this she didn't explain). So anyway, she went up the mountains around Bogotá with them once a week along muddy roads where it's not unusual to step on a dead rat, between houses made of cardboard and rotten wood, beside septic tanks open to all eyes (and noses). 'We have a lot to do,' Elaine wrote. 'But I don't want to tell you any more about the work right now, I'll save that for the next letter. I want to tell you that I had a lucky break.'

This is what happened. One afternoon, after a long session with the neighbourhood council – talking about contaminated water, declaring the absolute necessity of building an aqueduct, agreeing there was no money to do so – Elaine's group ended up drinking beer in a windowless shop. After a couple of rounds (the brown glass bottles accumulating on the narrow table) Dale Cartwright lowered his voice and asked Elaine if she could keep a secret for a few days. 'Do you know who Antonia Drubinski is?' he asked. Elaine, like everyone else, knew who Antonia Drubinski was: not only because she was one of the most senior volunteers, or because she'd already been arrested twice for civil disorder offences in the public highway – where *disorder* should be read as *protests against the Vietnam War*, and *public highway* should be read as *in front of the US Embassy* – but because Antonia Drubinski's whereabouts were unknown, and had been for several days.

'Anything but unknown,' said Dale Cartwright. 'They know where she is, the thing is they don't want it to become news.'

'Who doesn't want that?'

'The Embassy. The CEUCA.'

'And why not? Where is she?'

Dale Cartwright looked around and dropped his head.

'She's gone to the mountains,' he whispered. 'She's gone to join the revolution, it seems. Anyway, that's not important. The important thing is that her room is free.'

'Her room?' said Elaine. '*That* room?'

'*That* room, yes. The very one that's the envy of the whole class. And I thought maybe you'd like to get it. You know, live ten minutes away from the CEUCA, shower with hot water.'

Elaine thought for a minute.

'I didn't come here for material comforts,' she finally said.

'Hot showers,' Dale said again. 'Not having to manoeuvre like a quarterback to get off the bus.'

'But the thing is the family . . .' said Elaine.

'What about the family?'

'I pay them 750 pesos rent,' said Elaine. 'It's a third of their earnings.'

'And what's that got to do with it?'

'Well, I wouldn't want to deprive them of that money.'

'But who do you think you are, Elaine Fritts?' said Dale with a theatrical sigh. 'Do you think you're unique and irreplaceable? That's incredible. Elaine, dear, fifteen new volunteers are arriving in Bogotá today. There's another flight from New York on Saturday. All over the country there are hundreds, maybe thousands of *gringos* like you and me, and lots of them are coming to Bogotá to work. Believe me, your room will be taken before you finish packing.'

Elaine took a sip of her beer. Much later, when everything had happened, she'd remember that beer, the gloomy atmosphere in the shop, the reflection of the last rays of twilight in the panes of the aluminium-topped counter. That's where it all started, she would think. But at that moment, at Dale Cartwright's transparent offer, she did a quick calculation in her head. She smiled.

'And how do you know I make quarterback manoeuvres to get off the bus?' she finally said.

'All is known in the Peace Corps, my dear,' he said. 'All is known.'

And that's how three days later Elaine Fritts travelled for the last time from out near the racetrack, but this time weighed down with luggage. She would have liked it if the family had seemed a little sad, she couldn't deny it, she would have liked a sincere hug, perhaps a going-away present like the one she'd given them, a musical box that began to spew out the notes of Scott Joplin's *The Entertainer* when it was opened. There was none of that: they asked her for the key and saw her to the door, more out of mistrust than courtesy. The father left in a hurry, so it was just the mother, a woman whose figure filled the doorframe and who watched her go down the stairs and out to the street without offering any help with her luggage. At that moment the little boy appeared (he was an only child, his shirt was untucked and he was carrying a blue-and-red wooden toy truck), and asked something she didn't really understand. The last thing Elaine heard before turning round was her hostess's reply.

'She's leaving, son, she's going to live in a rich folks' house,' said the woman. 'Ungrateful *gringa*.'

A rich folks' house. It wasn't true, because rich folks didn't take in Peace Corps volunteers, but at that moment Elaine didn't have the arguments to embark on a debate about the economy of her second family. Her new accommodation, she had to confess, had luxuries that would have seemed unimaginable to Elaine a few weeks earlier: it was a comfortable construction on Caracas Avenue, with a narrow façade, but very long inside, with a little garden at the back and a fruit tree in a corner of the garden, beside a tiled wall. The façade was white, the wooden window frames painted green, and to get in you had to open an iron gate that separated the front garden from the pavement and that let out a squeal whenever someone arrived. The main door led into a dark but pleasant corridor. On the left-hand side were French doors that opened onto the living room, and further along was the dining room, and further along the corridor skirted the narrow interior patio where the geraniums grew in hanging planters; on the right, the bottom of the staircase was the first thing one saw. Elaine understood it all at a glimpse of the wooden steps: the red carpet had once been a fine one, but was now worn from use (on certain steps the grey threads of the base weave were beginning to show through); the copper rods that kept the carpet in place had lost their rings, or rather the rings had broken free of the wooden floor, and sometimes, when you went up quickly, you'd feel a slip and hear the brief jingle of loose metal. The staircase, for Elaine, was like a memorandum or a witness to what this family had been and no longer was. 'A respectable family who'd come down in the world', the man at the Embassy had said when Elaine went to complete the paperwork for the move. Come down in the world: Elaine thought a lot about those words, tried to translate them literally, failed in the attempt. Only when she noticed the carpet on the staircase did she understand, but she understood instinctively, without organizing it into coherent phrases, without making a scientific diagnosis in her head. In time it would all make sense, because Elaine had seen similar cases several times in her life: families with fine pasts who one day notice that the past doesn't bring in money.

The family was called Laverde. The mother was a woman with plucked eyebrows and sad eyes whose abundant red hair – exotic in this country, or perhaps it was dyed – was eternally fixed in a perfect coiffure that smelled of freshly applied hairspray. Doña Gloria was a housewife who never wore an apron: Elaine never saw her wielding a duster, and nevertheless the dressing tables, the bedside tables, the porcelain ashtrays, never had a trace of the yellow dust one breathed out in the street: everything cared for with the obsession of those who depend entirely on appearances. Don Julio, the father, had a scar on his face, not straight and thin as a cut would have left, but extended and asymmetrical (Elaine thought, mistakenly, of some skin ailment). Actually it wasn't just the cheek: the damage extended down beneath the line of his beard, it was like a stain trickling over his jaw and bathing his neck, and it was very difficult not to stare at it. Don Julio was an actuary by profession, and one of the first conversations in the dining room, under the bluish light of the chandelier, was devoted to telling their guest about insurance policies and probabilities and statistics.

'How do you know what kind of life insurance a man should buy?' the father said. 'The insurers need to know these types of things, of course, it's not fair that a man in his thirties in good health should pay the same as an old man who's already had two heart attacks. That's where I come in, Señorita Fritts: to look into the future. I'm the one who says when this man will die, when this other one will die, what is the probability that this car will crash on these highways. I work with the future, Señorita Fritts, I'm the one who knows what is going to happen. It's a question of numbers: the future is in the numbers. Numbers tell us everything. Numbers tell me, for example, if the world considers that I'll die before I'm fifty. And you, Señorita Fritts, do you know when you're going to die? I can tell you. If you give me some time, a pencil and paper and a margin of error, I can tell you when it's most likely that you'll die, and how. Our societies are obsessed with the past. But you *gringos* aren't interested in the past at all, you look forward, you're only interested in the future. You've understood it better than us, better than the Europeans: the future is what we have to focus on. Well, that's what I do, Señorita Fritts: I earn my living by keeping my eye on the future, I support my family by telling people what's going to happen. Today these people are insurers, of course, but one fine day there will be other people interested in this talent, it's impossible there won't be. In the United States they understand better than anyone. That's why you people are going forwards, Señorita Fritts, and that's why we're so far behind. Tell me if you think I'm mistaken.'

Elaine didn't say anything. From the other side of the table the couple's younger son was looking at her, a sideways mocking smile, long thick eyelashes that gave his black eyes a vaguely feminine quality. He'd looked at her like this from the start, with an insolence that, for some reason, she felt flattered by. Nobody in Colombia had looked at her like that: months after her arrival, Elaine still hadn't slept with anyone who wasn't North American, who didn't have orgasms in English.

'Ricardo doesn't believe in the future,' said Don Julio.

'Of course I do,' said the son. 'But in my future I won't be asking to borrow money.'

'Now then, let's not start that,' said Doña Gloria with a smile. 'What's our guest going to think, having just arrived, and all.'

Ricardo Laverde: too many Rs for Elaine's obstinate accent. 'OK, Elena, say my name,' Ricardo had ordered her while showing her the bathroom that went with the room she'd be staying in, pastel-coloured bedside table and the dresser with three drawers and the canopied bed that had been his older sister's until she got married (there was a studio photo of the girl: her hair with a straight centre parting, her gaze lost in the distance, the photographer's baroque signature). The guest room: legions of *gringos* like her had passed through there. 'Say my name three times and I'll give you an extra blanket,' this Ricardo Laverde said to her. It was a game, but a hostile one. Uncomfortably, Elaine entered into the game.

'Ricardo,' she said with her tongue tangled up. 'Laverde.'

'Bad, very bad,' said Ricardo. 'But it doesn't matter, Elena, your mouth looks pretty saying it.'

'My name's not Elena,' said Elaine.

'I don't understand, Elena,' he said. 'You're going to have to practise, I'll help you if you want.'

Ricardo was a couple of years younger than her, but he acted as if he had far more experience of the world. At first they would meet at dusk, when Elaine got back from her classes at the CEUCA, and they'd exchange a few phrases in the sitting room on the second floor, almost under Paco the canary's cage: *How are you, How did you get on, What did you learn today, Say my name three times without getting tongue-tied.* '*Bogotanos* are very good at talking without saying anything,' Elaine wrote to her grandparents. 'I'm drowning in small talk.' But one afternoon they met on 7th Avenue, and it struck them as such a remarkable coincidence that they had both just spent the morning shouting slogans outside the US Embassy, calling Nixon a criminal and singing, 'End it Now, End it Now, End it Now!'

A long time later Elaine would find out that the encounter had not been coincidental in the slightest: Ricardo Laverde had waited for her to come out of the CEUCA and had followed her for hours, spying on her from afar, hiding among the people on the street and behind the signs saying *Calley = Murderer* and *Proud To Be A Draft Dodger* and *Why Are We There, Anyway?* and soaking up all the songs a couple of metres behind the spot Elaine had stationed herself, while rehearsing different versions, various intonations, of the words he eventually said to her: 'Well now, this is a coincidence, isn't it? Come on, let me buy you a drink, and you can tell me all your complaints about my parents.'

Away from the Laverde house, far from the carefully arranged porcelain and the gaze of a military officer in oils and the canary's irritating whistle, her relationship with the son of her hosts was transformed or started from scratch. There, sitting with a hot chocolate in her hands, Elaine told him things and listened to what Ricardo told her. So she found out that Ricardo had graduated from a Jesuit-run high school, that he'd started to study Economics – a sort of bequest or imposition of his father's – and a few months earlier he'd dropped out to pursue the only thing he was actually interested in: flying planes. 'My father doesn't like it, of course,' Ricardo would tell her much later, when they could confess such things to each other. 'He's always been resistant. But my grandfather's on my side. I can count on my grandfather. And Papá can't do anything. It's not easy to contradict a war hero. Even if it was just a little war, an amateur war compared to the one that came before and the one that followed in the world, an inter-war war. But anyway, a war is a war and all wars have their heroes, right? The worth of the actor does not depend on the size of the theatre, my grandfather said. And of course, for me it was lucky. My grandfather supported me when it came to planes. When I started to get interested in learning how to fly, my grandfather was the only one who didn't call me crazy, immature, deranged. He supported me, supported me openly, even confronting my father, and it's not easy to say no to a hero of the air war. My father tried, that I remember perfectly, but without success. That happened a few years ago, but I remember it as if it were yesterday. Sitting right here, my grandfather where you are, under the cage, my father where I am. My grandfather passing a hand over Dad's scar on his face and telling him not to make me catch his fears. A lot of time would have to pass before I understood all the cruelty that gesture contained, a tired old man, although he didn't seem so, patting the face of a strong young man, although he didn't seem so. Not just that, of course, but the scar as well, the fact that it was the scar that received the pats . . . You'll say that it would be quite difficult to pat my father's face without touching his scar in some way, and yes, that may be, and more so because my grandfather was right-handed. And of course, the pats of a right hand fall on the left cheek of the person receiving them, on my father's left cheek, his disfigured cheek.'

The conversation about the origin of the disfigured cheek would come much later, when they were already lovers and the curiosity for each other's bodies had led to a curiosity for each other's lives. Neither was surprised when they started having sex, which was like a piece of furniture that had been there the whole time without either of them noticing. Every night, after dinner, host and guest would keep talking for a while, then they'd say goodnight and climb the stairs together, and when they got to the second floor Elaine went to the end of the hall and into the bathroom, locked the door and minutes later came back out in a white nightgown and with her hair tied up in a long ponytail. One rainy Friday night – the water was crashing against the skylight and drowning out any other noises – Elaine came out of the bathroom as she always did, but, instead of finding the corridor dark and the glow of the streetlights shining through the skylights of the interior patio, she saw the silhouette of Ricardo Laverde leaning against the banister. Against the light she couldn't see his face very well, but Elaine read the desire in his pose and in his tone of voice.

'Are you going to sleep?' Ricardo asked.

'Not yet,' she said. 'Come in and tell me about planes.'

It was cold, the wood of the bed creaked with every single movement of their bodies, and also it was a little girl's bed, too narrow and short for these games, so Elaine ended up pulling off the bedspread with one tug and spreading it out on top of the carpet, beside her felt slippers. There, on the woollen bedspread, freezing to death, they had a quick and to-the-point encounter. Elaine thought her breasts seemed smaller in Ricardo Laverde's hands, but she didn't tell him that. She put her nightgown back on to go out to the bathroom, and there, sitting on the toilet, thought she'd give Ricardo time to go back to his own room. She also thought she'd enjoyed being with him, that she'd do it again if the occasion arose, and that what had just happened must be forbidden in the statutes of the Peace Corps. She washed in the bidet, looked in the mirror and smiled, turned off the bathroom light before opening the door, and returning to her bedroom in the dark, walking slowly so she wouldn't trip, she found that Ricardo had not left, but had rather remade the bed and was waiting for her there, lying on his side, resting on his elbow, leaning his head on his hand like the leading man of some terrible Hollywood movie.

'I want to sleep alone,' said Elaine.

'I don't want to sleep, I want to talk,' he said.

'OK,' she said. 'And what shall we talk about?'

'Whatever you want, Elena Fritts. You suggest a topic and I'll follow.'

They talked about everything except themselves. They were naked and Ricardo let his hand wander over Elaine's belly, his fingers through her straight hair, and they talked of intentions and projects, convinced, as only new lovers can be, that saying what you wanted was the same as saying who you were. Elaine talked about her mission in the world, about youth as a weapon of progress, of the obligation to confront worldly powers. And she asked Ricardo questions: Did he like being Colombian? Would he like to live in another part of the world? Did he hate the United States? Had he read any of the New Journalists? But it took another seven couplings over the next two weeks before Elaine dared to ask the question that had intrigued her since the first day: 'What happened to your father's face?' 'How prudent the señorita is,' said Ricardo. 'It's never taken anybody so long to ask me that question.' They were going up to Monserrate in the cable car when Elaine asked: Ricardo had waited for her to come out of the CEUCA and told her it was time for some tourism, that a person couldn't come to Colombia just to work, that she should stop behaving like such a Protestant, for the love of God. And now Elaine was holding onto Ricardo (her head glued to his chest, her hands clenched around his elbows) every time a gust of wind shook the cabin on its cable and the tourists all gasped at the same time. And over the course of the afternoon, suspended in the air or sitting in the pews of the church, wandering in circles around the gardens of the sanctuary or seeing Bogotá from an altitude of 3,000 metres, Elaine began to listen to the story of an aerial exhibition in a year as distant as 1938, she heard talk of pilots and acrobatics and of an accident and the half a hundred dead the accident left. And when she woke up the next morning a package was waiting for her next to her recently served breakfast. Elaine tore off the wrapping paper and found a magazine in Spanish with a leather bookmark stuck between the pages. She started to think the bookmark was the gift, but then she opened the magazine and saw the surname of her hosts and a note from Ricardo: *So you'll understand.*

Elaine devoted herself to understanding. She asked questions and Ricardo answered them. His father's burnt face, Ricardo explained over the course of several conversations, that map of skin darker and rougher and more jagged than the desert of Villa de Leyva, had formed part of the landscape that surrounded him his whole life; but not even as a child, when one asks everything and assumes nothing, did Ricardo Laverde take an interest in the causes of what he saw, the difference between his father's face and everyone else's. Although it was also possible (Laverde said) that his family hadn't even given him time to feel that curiosity, for the tale of the accident at Santa Ana had floated among them ever since it happened and never evaporated, being repeated in the most diverse situations and thanks to the widest range of narrators, and Laverde remembered versions heard at Christmas novenas, versions from Friday-afternoon tea parties and others on Sundays at the football stadium, versions on the way to bed in the evening and others on the way to school in the mornings. They talked about the accident, yes, and they did so in every tone of voice and with all sorts of intentions, to demonstrate that planes were dangerous, unpredictable things like rabid dogs (according to his father), or that planes were like Greek gods, always putting people in their place and never tolerating men's arrogance (according to his grandfather). And many years later he, Ricardo Laverde, would tell of the accident as well, adorning and adulterating it until he realized that it wasn't necessary. At school, for example, telling the origins of his father's burnt face was the best way to capture his classmates' attention. 'I tried with my grandfather's war exploits,' said Laverde. 'Then I realized no one wants to hear heroic stories, but everyone likes to be told about someone else's misery.' And that's what he would remember, the faces of his classmates when he told them about the accident at Santa Ana and then showed them pictures of his father and his scarred face so they'd see he wasn't lying.

'Now I'm sure,' said Laverde. 'If nowadays I want to be a pilot, if there's nothing else that interests me in the world, it's Santa Ana's fault. If I end up killing myself in a plane, it'll be Santa Ana's fault.'

That story is to blame, said Laverde. It was that story's fault that he'd accepted his grandfather's first invitations. It was that story's fault that he'd started to go to the runways of the Guaymaral Aeroclub to fly with the heroic veteran and to feel alive, more alive than ever. He walked between the Canadian Sabres and managed to get to sit in the cockpits (his surname opened them all), and then managed (again his surname) to get the best flying instructors at the Aeroclub to devote more hours than they'd been paid for to him: the story of Santa Ana was to blame for all that. He would never feel so much like a dauphin as he'd felt during those times, would never again know what it's like to have a little inherited power. 'I've made good use of it, Elena, I swear,' he said. 'I've learned well, been a good student.' His grandfather always said he had the makings of a good pilot. His instructors were veterans too: mostly of the war with Peru, but some who'd flown in Korea and been decorated by the *gringos*, or at least that's what was said. And they all agreed that this boy was good, that he had a rare instinct and golden hands and, what was most important, that the planes respected him. And the planes were never wrong.

'And so that's how it's been till now,' said Laverde. 'It kills my father, but I'm now the boss of my own life, with one hundred flying hours you become boss of your own life. He spends his days guessing the future, but it's other people's future, Elena, my father doesn't know what's in mine, and his formulas and statistics can't tell him either. I've wasted a lot of time trying to find out, and only now, in the last few days, have I come to understand the relationship between my life and my dad's face, between the accident at Santa Ana and this person you see before you, who is going to do great things in life, a grandson of a hero. I'm going to get out of this mediocre life, Elena Fritts. I'm not afraid, I'm going to restore the name Laverde to its rightful place in aviation history. I'm going to be better than Captain Abadía and my family's going to be proud of me. I'm going to leave this mediocre life and get out of this house where we suffer every time another family invites us for dinner because we'll have to invite them over in return. I'm going to stop counting centavos as my mother does every morning. I'm not going to have to offer a bed to a *gringo* so my family will have enough to eat, sorry, no offence, I didn't mean to offend you. What do you want, Elena Fritts, I'm the grandson of a hero, I'm made for better things. Great things, that's how it is, I say it and I mean it. No matter whether people like it or not.'

They were on their way down in the cable car, the same way they'd gone up. The sun was setting, and the sky over Bogotá had turned into a gigantic violet blanket. Below them, in the fading light, the pilgrims who'd walked up and were walking down looked like coloured drawing pins on the stone steps. 'What strange light this city has,' said Elaine Fritts. 'You close your eyes for a second and it's already night by the time you open them.' A gust of wind shook the cabin, but this time the tourists didn't cry out. It was cold. The wind sighed as it blew through the cabin. Elaine, her arm around Ricardo Laverde, leaning on the horizontal bar that protected the window, found herself suddenly in the dark. The heads of the other passengers were vague silhouettes against the background of the sky, black on black. Ricardo's breathing reached her in waves, a smell of tobacco and clean water, and there, floating over the eastern hills, watching the city light itself up for the night, Elaine wished the cabin would never reach the bottom. She thought, perhaps for the first time, that a person like her could live in a country like this. In more than one sense, she thought, this country was still just starting, barely discovering its place in the world, and she wanted to be part of that discovery.

The deputy director of Peace Corps Colombia was a small, thin, distant man with thick-framed glasses like Henry Kissinger's and a knitted tie. He received Elaine in his shirtsleeves, which would not have been odd if the man hadn't been wearing a short-sleeved shirt as if he were in the unbearable heat of Barranquilla or Girardot instead of freezing to death up on this plateau. He used so much brilliantine in his black hair that the light from the neon strip lighting could produce the illusion of premature greying at his temples or white roots in his parting as straight as that of any military officer. She couldn't tell if he was North American or local, or an American son of locals, or a local son of Americans; there were no clues, no posters on the walls or music playing anywhere or books on the shelves that might allow someone to guess at his life, his origins. He spoke perfect

English, but his surname – the long surname that looked up at Elaine from the desk, carved in a brass sign that looked solid – was Latin American or at least Spanish, Elaine didn't know if there was any difference. The interview was routine: all the Peace Corps volunteers had passed or would pass through this dark office, sit in this uncomfortable chair where Elaine now half-rose to smooth her long aquamarine skirt with her hands. Here, before the lean and aloof Mr Valenzuela, all those who'd been trained in the CEUCA sat sooner or later and listened to a short speech on how the training was approaching its end, how the volunteers would soon be travelling to the places where they would fulfil their mission, speeches on generosity and responsibility and the opportunity to make a difference. They listened to the words *permanent site placement* and then immediately the same question: 'Do you have any preference?' And the volunteers pronounced recently acquired names of unknown content: Bolívar, Valledupar, Magdalena, Guajira. Or Quindío (which they'd pronounce *Kwindio*). Or Cauca (pronounced *Coka*). Then they'd be transferred to a place near their final destination, a sort of intermediate stop where they'd spend three weeks at the side of a volunteer with more experience. Field training, it was called. All this was decided in a half-hour interview.

'So, what's it gonna be?' said Valenzuela. 'Cartagena is out, so's Santa Marta. They're already full. Everyone wants to go there, to be on the Caribbean.'

'I don't want to go to a city,' said Elaine Fritts.

'No?'

'I think I can learn more in the countryside. The spirit of a people is in its *campesinos*.'

'The spirit,' said Valenzuela.

'And a person can help more,' said Elaine.

'Well, that too. Let's see, tropical or temperate?'

'Wherever I can be more helpful.'

'Help is needed all over, miss. This country is still only half-baked. Think about what you know as well, the things you do well.'

'Things I know?'

'Of course. You're not going to go plant potatoes if you've never even seen a photo of a hoe.' Valenzuela opened a brown folder that had been beneath his hand the whole time, turned a page, looked up. 'George Washington University, journalism major, right?'

Elaine nodded. 'But I have seen hoes,' she said. 'And I learn fast.'

Valenzuela grimaced with impatience.

'Well, you've got three weeks,' he said. 'That, or become a burden and make a fool of yourself.'

'I'm not going to be a burden,' said Elaine. 'I . . .'

Valenzuela shuffled some papers, took out a new folder. 'Look, in three days I'm meeting with the regional leaders. I'll find out there who needs what, and I'll find out where you can do your field training. But what I know for sure is that there's a place near La Dorada, do you know where I mean? The Magdalena Valley, Miss Fritts. It's far away, but it's not another world. In this place it's not quite as hot as in La Dorada, because it's a little way up the mountain.

You go by train from Bogotá, it's easy to get to and get back from, you'll have noticed that the buses here are a public menace. Anyway, it's a good place and not much in demand. It'd help to know how to ride a horse. It'd help to have a strong stomach. There's a lot of work to be done with the people from Acción Comunal, community development, you know, literacy, nutrition, things like that. It's just three weeks. If you don't like it, it won't be too late to change your mind.'

Elaine thought of Ricardo Laverde. Suddenly, having Ricardo a few hours away by train seemed like a good idea. She thought of the name of the place, La Dorada, and translated it in her head: The Golden One.

'La Dorada,' said Elaine Fritts, 'sounds good.'

'First the other place, then La Dorada.'

'Yes, that place too. Thanks.'

'OK,' said Valenzuela. He opened a metal drawer and took out a piece of paper. 'Look, before I forget. This is for you to fill in and return to the secretary.'

It was a questionnaire, or rather a carbon copy of a questionnaire. The heading was just one question, typed in capital letters: *What are some of the things which you have found different about your home in Bogotá?* Below the question were several subheadings separated by generous spaces, ostensibly to be filled in by the volunteers with as much detail as possible. Elaine answered the questionnaire in a motel in Chapinero, lying on her stomach on an unmade bed that smelled of sex, using a telephone directory to support the page and covering her bum with the sheet to protect it from Ricardo's hand, its risqué roving, its obscene incursions. Under the subheading *Physical Discomforts and Inconveniences*, she wrote: 'The men of the household never lift the seat when they use the toilet.' Ricardo told her she was a spoilt, fussy girl. Under *Restrictions on Guests' Freedom* she wrote: 'The door is barred at nine, and I always have to wake up my señora.' Ricardo told her she was too much of a night-owl. Under *Communication Problems* she wrote: 'I don't understand why they speak so formally with their children, calling them *usted* instead of *tú*.' Ricardo told her she still had a lot to learn. Under *Behaviour of Family Members* she wrote: 'The son likes to bite my nipples when he comes.' Ricardo didn't say anything.

The whole family accompanied her to catch the train at Sabana Station. It was a large solemn building with fluted columns and a carved stone condor on the high point of the façade, wings extended as if it were about to take off in flight and carry away the attic in its talons. Doña Gloria had given Elaine a bouquet of white roses, and now, as she crossed the foyer with her suitcase in one hand and her handbag across her chest, the flowers had turned into a hateful nuisance, a sort of duster that crashed against other travellers leaving a trail of sad petals on the stone floor, and the thorns stabbed Elaine every time she tried to get a better grip on the stems and protect them from the hostility of the environment. The father, for his part, had waited until they arrived at the platform before presenting his gift, and now, in the midst of the hustle and bustle of people and the cries of the shoeshine boys and the importuning of beggars, he explained that it was a book by a journalist that had come out a couple of years ago but was still selling, that the guy was uncouth but the book, from what he'd heard, wasn't bad. Elaine tore off the wrapping paper, saw a design of nine blue frames with trimmed corners, and inside the frames saw bells, suns, Phrygian caps, floral sketches, moons with women's faces, skulls and crossbones and dancing demons, and it all seemed a bit absurd and gratuitous, and the title, *Cien años de soledad*, exaggerated and melodramatic. Don Julio put a long fingernail over the E of the last word, which was backwards. 'I didn't notice till I'd already bought it,' he apologized. 'If you want we can try to exchange it.' Elaine said it didn't matter, that she wasn't going to get on the train with nothing to read because of a silly typo. And days later, in a letter to her grandparents, she wrote: 'Send me something to read, please, I get bored at night. The only thing I have here is a book the señor gave me as a going-away present, and I've tried to read it, I swear I've tried, but the Spanish is very difficult and everybody has the same name. It's the most tedious thing I've read in a long time, and there's even a typo on the cover. It's incredible, it's in its fourteenth printing and they haven't corrected it. When I think of you reading the latest Graham Greene, it doesn't seem fair.'

The letter goes on:

> Well, let me tell you a bit about where I am and where I'm going to be for the next two weeks. There are three mountain ranges in Colombia: the Eastern Cordillera, the Central and (you guessed it) the Western Cordillera. Bogotá is 8,500 feet up in the first. What my train did

was descend the mountain down to the Magdalena River, the largest in the country. The river runs through a beautiful valley, one of the prettiest landscapes I've ever seen in my life, a real paradise. The journey here was also impressive. I've never before seen so many birds and so many flowers. How I envied Uncle Philip! I envied his knowledge, of course, but also his binoculars. He'd love it here! Tell him I send my best regards.

So, let me tell you about the river. In times gone by passenger steamships would come down from the Mississippi and even from London, that's how important the river was. And there are still ships here that look straight out of *Huckleberry Finn*, I'm not exaggerating. My train arrived in a town called La Dorada, which is where I'm going to be stationed permanently. But according to the Peace Corps' arrangements the volunteers have to do three weeks of field training in a different place from our permanent site, in the company of another volunteer. Theoretically the other volunteer should have more experience, but that's not always the case. I've been lucky. They placed me in a municipality a few miles from the river, in the foothills of the Cordillera. It's called Caparrapí, a name that seems designed to make me look ridiculous trying to pronounce it. It's hot and very humid, but liveable. And the volunteer I've been assigned to is a terribly nice guy and knows a lot of things, particularly things I'm entirely ignorant of. His name's Mike Barbieri, he's a University of Chicago drop-out. One of those guys who makes you feel at ease immediately, two seconds and you feel like you've known him your whole life. There are some people who are just naturally charismatic. Life in other countries is easier for them, I've noticed. These are the people who eat up the world, who aren't going to have any problems surviving. If only I could be more like that.

Barbieri had already been in the Peace Corps in Colombia for two years, but before that he'd spent another two in Mexico, working with *campesinos* between Ixtapa and Puerto Vallarta and before Mexico he'd spent several months in the poor neighbourhoods of Managua. He was tall, wiry, fair but tanned, and it wasn't unusual to find him shirtless (a wooden crucifix hanging invariably round his neck), wearing Bermuda shorts and leather sandals and nothing else. He'd welcomed Elaine with a beer in one hand and in the other a plate of small *arepas* of a texture that was new to her. Elaine had never met anyone so talkative and at the same time so sincere, and in a few minutes she found out he was about to turn twenty-seven, his team was the Cubs, he hated *aguardiente* and that that was a problem here, that he was afraid, no, absolutely terrified of scorpions and he advised Elaine to buy open shoes and check them carefully every morning before putting them on. 'Are there a lot of scorpions here?' asked Elaine. 'There can be, Elaine,' said Barbieri in the voice of a fortune-teller. 'There can be.'

The apartment had two bedrooms, a living room and hardly any furniture, and was on the second floor of a house with sky-blue walls. On the first floor there was a shop with two aluminium tables and a counter – caramel candies, corn cakes, Pielroja cigarettes – and behind the shop, where as if by magic the world became a domestic one, lived the couple who ran it. Their surname was Villamil; their age was somewhere above sixty. 'My señores,' said Barbieri when he introduced them to Elaine, and, realizing that his señores hadn't understood the name of the new tenant, he told them in good Spanish: 'She's a *gringa*, like me, but she's called Elena.' And that's how the Villamils referred to her: that's what they called her to ask if she had enough water, or to get her to come and say hello to the drunks. Elaine put up with it stoically, missed the Laverdes' house, was ashamed of her spoilt little girl thoughts. In any case, she avoided the Villamils whenever possible. A concrete stairway on the exterior wall of the building allowed her to leave without being seen. Barbieri, affable to the point of impertinence, never used it: there was never a day he didn't stop in at the shop to tell them about his day, his achievements and failures, to hear the anecdotes the Villamils and even their customers had to tell, and to try to explain to those old *campesinos* the situation of the blacks in the United States or the theme of a song by The Mamas & the Papas. Elaine, in spite of herself, watched him do this and admired him. She took longer than she should have to discover why: in a way, this extroverted and curious man, who looked at her brazenly and talked as if the world owed him something, reminded her of Ricardo Laverde.

For twenty days, the twenty hot days that her rural apprenticeship lasted, Elaine worked shoulder to shoulder with Mike Barbieri, but also beside the local leader of

Acción Comunal, a short, quiet man whose moustache covered his harelip. He had a simple name, for a change: he was called Carlos, just Carlos, and there was something hermetic or menacing in that simplicity, in that lack of a surname, in the phantasmal way he'd appear to collect them in the mornings and disappear again in the afternoons, after dropping them off. Elaine and Barbieri, out of some sort of previous agreement, had lunch at Carlos's house, an interregnum between two intensive work sessions with the *campesinos* in the surrounding villages, interviews with local politicians, ever fruitless negotiations with landowners. Elaine discovered that all the work in the countryside was done by talking: to teach the *campesinos* to raise chickens with tender flesh (keeping them in enclosures instead of letting them run around wild), to convince the politicians to build a school using local resources (since nobody expected anything of the central government) or to try to get the rich to see them as more than simply anticommunist crusaders, they first had to sit round a table and drink, drink until they didn't understand the words any more. 'So I spend my days on the backs of decrepit horses or talking to half-drunk people,' Elaine wrote to her grandparents. 'But I think I'm learning, although without really noticing. Mike explained that in Colombian Spanish this is called *cogerle el tiro* of something. Understanding how things work, knowing how to get them done, all that. Getting the hang of things, we might say. That's what I'm doing. Oh, one little thing: don't write to me here any more, send the next letter to Bogotá. I'm going back to Bogotá soon and will spend a month there on the final details of my training. Then to La Dorada. There I start the serious stuff.'

Her last weekend there Ricardo Laverde arrived. He came by surprise, arranging it all himself, taking the train to La Dorada on his own and from there getting to Caparrapí by bus and then asking around for directions, describing the *gringos* whose existence, of course, everybody for miles around knew about. It didn't strike Elaine as at all strange that Ricardo Laverde and Mike Barbieri should get along so well: Barbieri gave Elaine the afternoon off to show her *bogotano* boyfriend around (that's what he called him, her *novio bogotano*) and said he'd see them in the evening, for dinner. And that night, in a matter of hours – hours spent, truth be told, in the middle of a field, around a campfire and in the presence of a jug of *guarapo* – Ricardo and Barbieri discovered how much they had in common, because Barbieri's father was an airmail pilot and Ricardo didn't like *aguardiente*, and they hugged and talked about planes and Ricardo opened his eyes wide as he talked about his courses and his instructors, and then Elaine interrupted to praise Ricardo and repeat the praise others had offered of his talent as a pilot, and then Ricardo and Mike talked about Elaine right in front of her, what a nice girl she was and how pretty, yes, pretty too, with those eyes, said Mike, yes, especially the eyes, said Ricardo and told secrets as if instead of having just met they'd roomed together in a frat house, and sang *For she's a jolly good fellow* and regretted in tandem that Elaine had to go to another site, *this site should be your site, fuck La Dorada, fuck The Golden One, fuck it all the way*, and they drank a toast to Elaine and to the Peace Corps, *for we're all jolly good fellows, which nobody can deny*. And the next day, in spite of the hangovers, Mike Barbieri accompanied them in person to catch the bus. The three of them arrived in the village plaza on horseback, like colonialists of times gone by (although theirs were squalid old nags, which would never have served colonialists of times gone by), and on Ricardo's face, as he politely carried her luggage, Elaine saw something she'd never seen before: admiration. Admiration for herself, for the ease with which she moved through the village, for the affection she'd earned from the people in three short weeks, for the natural and yet undeniably authoritative way she made herself understood by the locals. Elaine saw that admiration in his face and felt that she loved him, that she'd unexpectedly started to feel new and more intense things for this man who also seemed to love her, and at the same time felt that she'd arrived at a happy point: when this place could no longer surprise her too much. True, there would always be contingencies, in Colombia people always managed to be unpredictable (in their behaviour, in their manners: one never knew what they were actually thinking). But Elaine felt in charge of the situation. 'Ask me if I've got the hang of things here,' she said to Ricardo as they climbed aboard the bus. 'Have you *cogido el tiro a la vaina*, Elena Fritts?' he asked. And she answered, 'Yeah. I've got the hang of things here.'

She had no way of knowing just how mistaken she was.

5

What's There to Live For?

ELAINE WOULD REMEMBER THOSE last three weeks in Bogotá and in Ricardo Laverde's company the way one remembers the days of one's childhood, a cloud of images distorted by emotions, a promiscuous mixture of key dates without a well-established chronology. The return to the routine of classes at the CEUCA – there were very few left now, just a matter of refining certain bits of knowledge or perhaps justifying certain bits of bureaucracy – was broken by the disorder of her encounters with Ricardo, who might perfectly well be waiting for her behind a eucalyptus when she was on her way home or might have slipped a note into her book telling her to meet him at a dingy café at the corner of 17th and 8th. Elaine always showed up for these dates, and in the relative solitude of downtown cafés the two of them cast more or less lascivious glances at each other and then went into a cinema to sit in the back row and touch each other under a long black coat that had belonged to Ricardo's grandfather, the aviator hero of the war with Peru. Indoors, in the narrow house in Chapinero, in Don Julio and Doña Gloria's territory, they carried on the fiction that he was the son of the host family and she, the innocent apprentice of the moment; the son's nocturnal visits to the apprentice carried on as well, of course, with their silent nocturnal orgasms. So they began to live a double life, a life of clandestine lovers who didn't arouse anyone's suspicion, a life in which Ricardo Laverde was Dustin Hoffman's character in *The Graduate* and Miss Fritts was Mrs Robinson and her daughter at the same time, who was also called Elaine: that must mean something, wasn't it too much of a coincidence? During those few days in Bogotá, Elaine and Ricardo protested against the Vietnam War whenever a demonstration was called, and also attended parties organized by the American community in Bogotá, social events that seemed arranged deliberately so the volunteers could go back to talking their own language, ask out loud how the Mets or the Vikings were doing or take out a guitar and sing, all together and around a fireplace while passing a joint that was finished in two rounds, Frank Zappa's song:

What's there to live for?
Who needs the Peace Corps?

The three weeks ended on 1 November, when, at eight thirty in the morning, a new litter of apprentices swore loyalty to the statutes of the Peace Corps, after more promises and a vague declaration of intentions, and received their official appointment as volunteers. It was a rainy cold morning, and Ricardo was wearing a leather jacket that, upon contact with the rain, began to give off an intense smell. 'They were all there,' Elaine wrote to her grandparents. 'Among those graduating were Dale

Cartwright and the son of the Wallaces (the elder one, you remember). Among the audience were the Ambassador's wife and a tall man in a tie who, I seem to have understood, is an important Democrat from Boston.' Elaine also mentioned the deputy director of Peace Corps Colombia (his Kissinger glasses, his knitted tie), the directors of the CEUCA and even a bored municipal functionary, but at no point in the letter did Ricardo Laverde appear. Which, seen with years' worth of distance, is nothing short of ironic, for on that very night, under the pretext of congratulating her and at the same time saying farewell in the name of the whole Laverde family, Ricardo invited her to dinner at the Gato Negro restaurant, and by the light of some precarious candles that threatened to topple into the plates of food, taking advantage of a silence when the string trio finished singing 'Pueblito Viejo', knelt in the middle of the aisle where the bow-tied waiters kept walking up and down and in more sentences than strictly necessary asked her to marry him. In a flash, Elaine thought of her grandparents, regretted that they were so far away and that at their age and in their states of health even considering the trip would be impossible, felt the kind of sadness we tolerate because it appears at happy moments and, once the sadness passed, bent down to kiss Ricardo hard. As she did so she inhaled the wet leather smell of his jacket and tasted meunière sauce. 'Does that mean yes?' said Ricardo after the kiss, still kneeling and still in the waiters' way. Elaine burst into tears in reply, but smiling and crying at the same time. 'Of course,' she said. 'What a stupid question.'

So Elaine had to delay her departure for La Dorada by fifteen days, and in this cruelly short time organized, with the help of her future mother-in-law (after convincing her that no, she wasn't pregnant), a small and almost clandestine wedding in San Francisco Church. Elaine had liked this church since the beginning of her life in Bogotá. She liked its thick, damp stone walls, and she also liked going in off the street and coming out onto the avenue, that violent clash of light with darkness and noise with silence. The day before her wedding, Elaine went for a walk through the centre (a reconnaissance mission, Ricardo would say); as she crossed the threshold of the church, she thought of the silence and noise and the darkness and light, and the illuminated altar caught her eye. The place seemed familiar to her that day, not as if she'd been there before, but in a more profound or private way, as if she'd read a description of it in a novel. She stared at the timid flames of the candles, at the weak yellow lamps fastened like torches to the columns. The light of the stained-glass windows lit up two beggars who were sleeping with legs crossed and hands together on top of their bellies like marble tombs of popes. To her right, a life-sized Christ on all fours, as if he were crawling; the day pouring in through the other door struck him full in the face, and the thorns of his crown and the drops of emerald green that the Christ was crying or perspiring glistened in the light. Elaine went on, walked along the left aisle towards the set-in altar at the far end, and then she saw the cage. In it, enclosed like an animal on show, there was a second Christ, with longer hair, yellower skin, darker blood. 'It's the best in Bogotá,' Ricardo had told her once. 'I swear, Monserrate's got nothing on this.' Elaine bent down, read the little plaque: *Señor de la agonía*. She took two more steps towards the pulpit, found the tin box and another inscription: *Deposit your offering here and the image will be illuminated*. She put her hand in her pocket, found a coin and lifted it in two fingers, as if it were a host, to let there be light: it was one peso, the coat of arms blackened as if the coin had been through fire. She dropped it into the slot. The Christ figure came to life beneath the brief blast of the spotlights. Elaine felt, or rather knew, that she was going to be happy all her life.

Then came the reception, which Elaine went through in a fog, as if it were all happening to someone else. The Laverde family held it in their house: Doña Gloria explained to Elaine that it had been impossible, at such short notice, to rent the hall of a social club or some other decent place, but Ricardo, who listened to the laborious explanation in silence, nodding, waited until his mother had gone to tell Elaine the truth. 'They're fucked for money,' he said. 'The Laverdes have pawned their whole lives.' The revelation shocked Elaine less than she might have expected: a thousand different signals over the last few months had prepared her for it. But she was struck by Ricardo referring to his family in the third person, as if their bankruptcy didn't affect him. 'And us?' asked Elaine. 'What about us?' 'What are we going to do?' said Elaine. 'My work doesn't pay very much.' Ricardo looked her in the eye, put a hand on her forehead as if she might have a temperature. 'It's enough for a little while,' he said, 'and then we'll see. If I were you I wouldn't worry.' Elaine thought for a second, and found she wasn't worried. And she wondered why not. And then she asked him, 'Why wouldn't you be worried if you were me?' 'Because a pilot like me is never going to be short of work, Elena Fritts. It's a fact and that's just how it is.'

Later, when all the guests had gone, Ricardo led her up to the room where they'd slept together for the first time, sat her down on the bed (swept aside the few wedding presents) and then Elaine thought he was going to talk to her about money, that he was going to tell her they couldn't go anywhere on a honeymoon. He didn't though. He tied a blindfold over her eyes, a thick cloth that smelled of mothballs that might have been an old scarf, and said, 'From here on you don't see anything.' And so, blindly, Elaine let herself be led downstairs, and blindly heard the family's goodbyes (she thought Doña Gloria was crying), and blindly went out into the cold night air and got into a car someone else was driving, and thought it was a taxi, and on the way to who knows where asked what all this was and Ricardo told her to be quiet, not to spoil her surprise. Elaine blindly felt the taxi coming to a stop and a window opening and Ricardo identifying himself and being greeted with respect and a big gate opening with a metallic sound. As she got out of the taxi, seconds later, she felt a rough surface under her feet and a gust of cold wind messed up her hair. 'There are some stairs,' said Ricardo. 'Careful, take it slow, we don't want you falling.' Ricardo pressed her head as one does to keep someone from banging their head on a low roof, like the police do so their prisoners won't bang their heads on the doorframes of the patrol cars. Elaine let herself be led, her hand touched something new that soon turned into a seat and she felt something rigid against her knee, and as she sat down an image came into her head, the first clear idea of where she was and what was about to happen. And it was confirmed when Ricardo started to talk to the control tower and the light aircraft began to taxi down the runway, but Ricardo only gave her permission to take off the blindfold later, after take-off, and when she did so Elaine found herself facing the horizon, a world she'd never seen before bathed in a light she'd never seen before, and that same light was bathing Ricardo's face, whose hands moved over the panel and who looked at instruments (needles that were spinning, coloured lights) she didn't understand. They were going to the Palanquero base, in Puerto Salgar, a few kilometres from La Dorada: this was his wedding gift to her, these minutes spent on board a borrowed plane, a Cessna Skylark that the groom's grandfather had obtained in order to impress his bride. Elaine thought it was the best gift imaginable and that no other Peace Corps volunteer had ever arrived at their workplace in a light aircraft. A gust of wind shook them. Then they touched down. *This is my new life*, thought Elaine. *I've just landed in my new life.*

And it was. The honeymoon blended into the arrival at the permanent site, the first sanctioned shagging blended into the new volunteer's first missions: the first steps towards extending the sewer system, the first meetings with Acción Comunal. Elaine and Ricardo allowed themselves the luxury, courtesy of her CEUCA class, to spend a couple of nights in a tourist inn in La Dorada, surrounded by families from Bogotá or Antioquia cattle ranchers, and during those days even had time to find a single-storey house at a price that seemed reasonable. The house – a clear improvement, now that they were a married couple, compared to the little room in Caparrapí – was salmon pink and had an overgrown, 9-square-metre patio that nobody had taken any care of for a long time and that Elaine immediately set about salvaging. She discovered that now, in her new life, mornings had taken on a new character, and she started waking up at first light just to feel the freshness of the air before the brutal heat began to devour the day. 'I wash early in the morning with cold water,' she wrote to her grandparents, 'after all my griping about the cold water in Bogotá. We use a hollow gourd called a *totuma* to shower with. I'm sending a photo.' In the first days she acquired something that would prove to be essential: a horse to take her to neighbouring villages. He was called Tapahueco, but Elaine found the name so hard to pronounce that she ended up calling him Truman, and he had three speeds: a slow trot, a fast trot and a gallop. 'For 50 pesos a month,' Elaine wrote, 'a *campesino* looks after him for me and feeds him and brings him to me every morning at eight o'clock. I have blisters on my rear and every muscle in my body aches, but I'm learning to ride better all the time. Truman knows more than I do and is helping to teach me. We understand each other, and that's what matters. With a horse a person learns to manage time better. I don't have to depend on anyone and it's cheaper.

I'm not one of the Magnificent Seven, but I haven't lost my enthusiasm.'

She also spent time making contacts: with the help of her predecessor, a volunteer from Ohio who was on his way home and who Elaine looked down on from the first moment (he had an apostle's beard, but never took any initiative), she compiled a list of thirty notable locals: there was the priest, the heads of the most influential families, the mayor, the landowners who resided in Bogotá and Medellín, absent powers of a sort who had land but were never on it, and lived off it but never paid the taxes they should have: Elaine complained about this at night, in her matrimonial bed, and then complained that in Colombia all the citizens were political but no politician wanted to do anything for the citizens. Ricardo, who was now acting as if he knew it all, was openly amused and called her ingenuous and naïve and a gullible *gringa*, and after making fun of her and her pretensions to be a social missionary, a Good Samaritan for the Third World, he'd put on an unbearably paternalistic expression and sing, in a terrible accent, *What's there to live for? Who needs the Peace Corps?* And the more annoyed Elaine got – she no longer found the song's sarcasm amusing – the more enthusiastically he'd sing:

I'm completely stoned,
I'm hippy and I'm trippy,
I'm a gypsy on my own.

'Go fuck yourself,' she'd tell him, and he understood perfectly.

A couple of days before Christmas, after a long and frustrating meeting with a local doctor, Elaine arrived home dying for a shower to wash off the dust and sweat, and found they had visitors. The sun was setting and the faint lights of the neighbours' windows were beginning to come on. She tied Truman to the nearest post and, going through the little garden, in the kitchen door, and while she looked for a Coke in the propane refrigerator the voices reached her ear. Since they came from the living room, and since they were male voices, she supposed that they were some acquaintances who'd shown up to ask the *gringa* for something. This had already happened on several occasions: Colombians, Elaine complained, thought the Peace Corps' work was to do anything they couldn't be bothered to do or found difficult. 'It's the colonial mentality,' she used to say to Ricardo when they talked about the subject. 'So many years of being used to other people doing things for them can't be erased just like that.' Suddenly the idea of having to greet one of these people, the idea of having to go through a series of banalities and ask about their family and children and get out the rum or the beer (because one never knew when that person might be useful in the future, and because in Colombia things didn't get done through hard work but through real or feigned friendship), made her feel infinitely tired. But then she heard an accent in one of the voices, a vague tone that sounded familiar, and when she leaned round the corner, still unseen, she recognized first Mike Barbieri and then, almost automatically, Carlos, the harelipped man who'd helped them so much in Caparrapí. Then the men must have heard her or sensed her presence, because all three turned their heads at the same time.

'Oh, finally,' said Ricardo. 'Come in, come in, don't just stand there. These people are here to see you.'

A long time later, remembering that day, Elaine still marvelled at the certainty with which she knew, without any proof or reason to suspect, that Ricardo had lied to her. No, they hadn't come to see her: Elaine knew it the moment the words were out of his mouth. It was a shiver, an uncomfortable feeling as she shook Carlos's hand while Carlos didn't meet her gaze, a certain anxiousness or mistrust at greeting Mike Barbieri in Spanish, asking him how he was, how things were going, why he hadn't been at the last departmental meeting. Ricardo was sitting in a wicker rocking chair they'd got for a good price at a handicrafts market; the two guests, on wooden stools. In the centre, on the glass top of the table, were some papers that Ricardo snatched up, but on which Elaine managed to see a disorganized drawing, a sort of big ectoplasm in the shape of the American continent, or the shape of the American continent drawn by a child. 'Hi. What's up?' asked Elaine.

'Mike's coming to spend Christmas with us,' said Ricardo.

'If you don't mind,' said Mike.

'No, of course not,' said Elaine. 'And are you coming on your own?'

'Yeah, just me,' said Mike. 'With the two of you, who else could I need?'

Then Carlos stood up, offered Elaine his seat and mumbled something that might or might not have been goodbye, and, raising a fat-fingered hand, began to walk towards the door. A big sweat stain ran down his back. Elaine looked him up and down and noticed that he'd missed a belt loop of his well-pressed trousers and the noise his sandals made and the grey colour of the skin on his heels. Mike Barbieri stayed a while longer, long enough to drink two rum and Cokes and to tell them that a volunteer from Sacramento had come to spend Thanksgiving with him, and showed him how to call the United States with a ham radio. It was magic, pure magic. You had to find a radio buff here and another one in the United States, friendly people willing to lend their radio set and telephone to make the connection, and that way you could talk to your family back home without paying a cent, but it was completely legal, not fraudulent at all, or maybe a little, but who cares: he had talked to his younger sister, to a friend he owed some money and even with an ex-girlfriend from university days, who once threw him out of her life and who now, with time and distance, had forgiven him his worst sins. And all completely free, wasn't it amazing?

Mike Barbieri spent Christmas Eve with them, and Christmas Day as well, and the rest of the week as well, and New Year's Eve and New Year's Day too, and on 2 January he said goodbye as if he were saying goodbye to his family, with tears in his eyes and whole sentences devoted to thanking them for their hospitality, company, affection and the rum and Cokes. They were long days for Elaine, who couldn't manage to get excited by the holidays in the absence of candy canes and stockings hung by the fireplace and still couldn't quite understand at what moment this disoriented *gringo* had settled in with them. But Ricardo seemed to have a marvellous time: 'He's the brother I never had,' he'd say, hugging him. In the evenings, after a couple of drinks, Mike Barbieri took out the weed and rolled a joint, Ricardo would turn on the fan and the three of them would start talking politics, about Nixon and Rojas Pinilla and Misael Pastrana and Edward Kennedy, whose car went off the bridge and into the water, and about Mary Jo Kopechne, the poor girl who was with him and who drowned. Finally Elaine, exhausted, would go to bed. For her, as for the *campesinos* in her zone, the last week of the year was not a holiday, and she still had to leave the house as early as she could to get to her appointments. When she came home in the evening, dirty and frustrated by the lack of progress and with her calves aching from the hours spent on top of Truman, Ricardo and Mike were waiting for her with a meal almost ready. And after dinner, the same routine: windows wide open, rum, marijuana, Nixon, Rojas Pinilla, the Sea of Tranquillity and how it would change the world, the death of Ho Chi Minh and how it would change the war.

The first Monday of 1970 – a dry, tough, hot day, a day of so much light that the heavens seemed white instead of blue – Elaine rode off on Truman in the direction of Guarinocito, where they were building a school and she was going to talk about a literacy programme the volunteers in the department had begun to coordinate, and when she came around a corner she thought she saw Carlos and Mike Barbieri in the distance. That evening, when she got home, Ricardo had news for her: they'd got him a job, he was going to be away for a couple of days. He was going to bring a couple of televisions from San Andrés, nothing easier, but he would have to sleep over at the destination. That's how he put it, 'at the destination'. Elaine was pleased that he was starting to get work: maybe, after all, it wasn't going to be so hard to make a living as a pilot. 'Everything's going well,' Elaine wrote at the beginning of February. 'Of course, it's a thousand times easier to fly a light aircraft once you know how to read the instruments than to make village politicians cooperate with each other.' She added: 'And harder still for a woman.' And then:

> One thing I have learned: since the people are used to being told what to do, I have begun to act like a *patrón*. I'm very sorry to have to report that it gets results. I got the women of Victoria (a nearby village) to demand the doctor organize a nutrition and dental-health campaign. Yes, it's odd to see the two together, but feeding themselves on sugar-water would destroy anyone's teeth. So, at least I've accomplished something. It's not much, but it's a start.
>
> Ricardo is happy, that's for sure. Like a kid in a candy store. He's starting to get jobs, not a lot, but enough. He doesn't have the flying hours to become a

commercial pilot yet, but that's better, because he charges less and they prefer him for that (in Colombia everything's better if it's done under the counter). Of course, I see less of him. He leaves very early, flying out of Bogotá and these jobs eat up his day. Sometimes he has to sleep over at his old house, at his parents' house, on his way out or on his way back, or both. And me here by myself. Sometimes it's infuriating but I have no right to complain.

Between workdays Ricardo had weeks of leisure time, so in the evenings, when Elaine got home from her frustrating attempts to change the world, Ricardo had had time to get bored and bored again and to start doing things around the house with his toolbox, and the house began to look like a construction site. In March Ricardo built Elaine a shower stall in the patio, which was now a little garden: a wooden cubicle attached to the outside wall of the house that allowed Elaine to take a hose and have a shower under the night sky. In May he built a tool cupboard, and put an impregnable lock the size of a deck of cards on it to discourage any thieves. In June he didn't build anything, because he was away more than usual: after talking it over with Elaine, he decided to go back to the Flying Club to get his commercial pilot's licence, which would allow him to transport cargo and, most importantly, passengers. 'So we're going to take a serious step,' he said. Obtaining the licence meant getting almost a hundred more flying hours, as well as ten hours of flying instruction with dual controls, so he spent the weekdays in Bogotá (slept at his old house, got his parents' news, gave them news of his newlywed life, they all drank a toast and were happy) and went back to La Dorada on Friday afternoons, by train or by bus and once in a chartered taxi. 'That must have cost a fortune,' said Elaine. 'What does it matter,' he said. 'I wanted to see you. I wanted to see my wife.' One of those days he arrived after midnight, not by bus or train or even by taxi, but in a white jeep that invaded the tranquillity of the street with the roar of its engine and the glare of its headlights. 'I thought you weren't coming,' Elaine said. 'It's late, I was worried.' She gestured towards the jeep. 'Whose is that?'

'You like it?' said Ricardo.

'It's a jeep.'

'Yes,' he said. 'But do you like it?'

'It's big,' Elaine said. 'It's white. It's noisy.'

'But it's yours,' said Ricardo. 'Merry Christmas.'

'It's June.'

'No, it's December now. You don't notice because the weather's the same. You really should have known, you with your Colombian ways.'

'But where did it come from?' said Elaine, pronouncing every syllable. 'And how can we, when . . .'

'Too many questions. This is a horse, Elena Fritts, it just goes faster and if it rains you don't get wet. Come on, let's go for a spin.'

It was a 1968 Nissan Patrol, as Elaine found out, and the official colour was not white, but ivory. But this information interested her less than the two back doors and the passenger compartment, which was so spacious that a mattress could fit on the floor. Except that wouldn't be necessary since the jeep had two fold-down cushioned beige benches on which a child could comfortably lie down. The front seat was a sort of big sofa, and Elaine made herself comfortable there, and saw the long, thin gear lever coming up from the floor and its black knob with three speeds marked on it, and she saw the white dashboard and thought it wasn't white, but ivory, and saw the black steering wheel that Ricardo now started to move, and she grabbed hold of the handrail she found above the glove compartment. The Nissan began to move along the streets of La Dorada and soon out onto the highway. Ricardo turned in the direction of Medellín. 'Things are going well for me,' he said then. The Nissan left behind the lights of the town and plunged into the black night. In the beams of the headlights leafy trees sprang up and disappeared, a dog with shining eyes was startled, a puddle of dirty water twinkled. The night was humid and Ricardo opened the vents and a gust of warm air blew into the cabin. 'Things are going well,' he repeated. Elaine looked at his profile, saw the intense expression on his face in the darkness: Ricardo was trying to look at her at the same time as keep control of the vehicle on a road full of surprises (there could be other distracted animals, potholes that were more like craters, the odd drunk on a bicycle). 'Things are going well,' Ricardo said for the third time. And just when Elaine was thinking: *he's trying to tell me something*, just when she was starting to get frightened by this revelation that was coming down on top of her as if out of the black night, just when she was about to change the subject out of vertigo or fear, Ricardo spoke in a tone that left no room for doubt: 'I want to have a baby.'

'You're crazy,' said Elaine.

'Why?'

Elaine's hands started to wave around. 'Because having a child costs money. Because I'm a Peace Corps volunteer and make barely enough money to survive on. Because first I have to finish my *voluntariado*.' *Voluntariado*: the word gave her tongue a terribly tough time, like a racetrack full of curves, and for a moment she thought she'd got it wrong. 'I like this,' she said then, 'I like what I'm doing.'

'You can keep doing it,' said Ricardo. 'Afterwards.'

'And where are we going to live? We can't have a baby in this house.'

'Well, we'll move.'

'But, with what money?' said Elaine, and in her voice there was something resembling irritation. She was talking to Ricardo the way one talks to a stubborn child. 'I don't know what world you live in, *cariño*, but this isn't something you improvise.' She grabbed her long hair with both hands. Then she looked in her bag, took out an elastic band and put her hair up in a ponytail to get it off her sweaty neck. 'Having a baby is not something you improvise. You don't. You just don't.'

Ricardo didn't answer. A dense silence settled inside the jeep: the Nissan was the only thing audible, the rumbling of its engine, the friction of its wheels against the rough tarmac. Beside the road an immense field opened up then. Elaine thought she saw a couple of cows lying underneath a ceiba tree, the white of their horns breaking the uniform black of the pasture. In the background, above a low mist, the jagged hills stood out against the sky. The Nissan moved over the uneven road, the world was grey and blue outside the illuminated space, and then the highway went into a sort of brown and green tunnel, a corridor of trees whose branches met in the air like a gigantic dome. Elaine would always remember that image, the tropical vegetation completely surrounding them and hiding the sky, because that was the moment Ricardo told her – his eyes fixed on the road, without even glancing at Elaine, even avoiding her gaze – about the business he was doing with Mike Barbieri, about the future these business deals had and the plans this business had allowed him to make. 'I'm not improvising, Elena Fritts,' he said. 'I've thought about all this for a long time. It's all planned out down to the last detail. Now, your not finding out about the plans until just now is another detail, and that's, well, because you didn't need to. Now you do. It's to do with you now too. I'm going to explain the whole thing. And then you can tell me if we can have a baby or not. Deal?'

'OK,' said Elaine. 'Deal.'

'Good. So let me tell you what's going on with marijuana.'

And he told her. He told her about the closure, the year before, of the Mexican border (Nixon trying to free the United States from the invasion of weed); he told her about the distributors whose business had been hindered, hundreds of intermediaries whose clients couldn't wait and started looking in new directions; he told her about Jamaica, one of the alternatives closest to hand the consumers had, but most of all about the Sierra Nevada, the department of La Guajira, the Magdalena Valley. He told her about the people who had come, in a matter of months, from San Francisco, from Miami, from Boston, looking for suitable partners for a business with guaranteed profitability, and they were lucky: they found Mike Barbieri. Elaine thought briefly of the regional coordinator of volunteers for Caldas, an Episcopalian from South Bend, Indiana, who had already vetoed the sex education programmes in rural zones: what would he think if he knew? But Ricardo kept talking. Mike Barbieri, he told her, was much more than a partner: he was a real pioneer. He had taught things to the *campesinos*. Along with some other volunteers with agricultural skills, he'd taught them techniques, where to plant so the mountains protect the plants, what fertilizer to use, how to tell the male plants from the females. And now, well, now he had contacts with 10 or 15 hectares scattered between here and Medellín, and they could produce 400 kilos per harvest. He'd changed those *campesinos*' lives, there was not the slightest doubt about that, they were earning more than ever and with less work, and all that thanks to weed, thanks to what's going on with weed. 'They put it in plastic bags, put the bags on a plane, we provide the simplest thing, a twin-engine Cessna. I get in the plane, take it full of one thing and bring it back with something else. Mike pays about 25 dollars for a kilo, let's say. Ten thousand in total, and that's just for the top-quality stuff. No matter how bad it goes, from every trip we come back with sixty, seventy grand, sometimes more. How many trips can be done? You do the maths. What I'm trying to tell you is that they need me. I was in the right place at the right time, and it was a stroke of luck. But it's not about luck any more. They need me, I've become indispensable, and this is only just getting started. I'm the one who knows where to land, where you can take off. I'm the one who knows how to load one of these planes, how much it'll take, how to distribute the cargo, how to conceal fuel tanks in the fuselage to be able to make longer journeys. And you can't imagine, Elena Fritts, you just can't imagine what it's like to take off at night, the rush of adrenalin you get taking off at night in between the mountain ranges, with the river down below like a stream of molten silver, the Magdalena River on a moonlit night is the most striking thing you can ever see. And you don't know what it's like to see it from above and follow it, and come out over the open sea, the infinite space of the sea, when dawn hasn't broken yet, and watch the sun come up over the sea, the horizon flares up as if it's on fire, the light so bright it's blinding. I've only done it a couple of times so far, but I know the itinerary now, I know the winds and the distances, I know the plane's tics like I know this jeep's. And the others are noticing. That I can take off and land that machine anywhere I want, take off from 2 metres of shoreline and land it in the stony desert of California. I can get it into spaces radar doesn't reach: doesn't matter how small they are, my plane fits there. A Cessna or whatever you give me, a Beechcraft, whatever. If there's a hole between two radar beams, I'll find it and get my plane in there. I'm good, Elena Fritts, I'm really good. And I'm going to get better every time, with every flight. It almost scares me to think about it.'

One day at the end of September, during a week of unseasonal downpours when the streams flooded and several hamlets were undergoing sanitation emergencies, Elaine attended a departmental meeting of volunteers at the Peace Corps headquarters in Manizales, and was in the middle of a rather agitated debate on the constitution of cooperatives for local artisans when she felt something in her stomach. She didn't manage to get even as far as the door: the rest of the volunteers saw her crouch down with one hand on the back of a chair and the other holding her hair and vomit a gelatinous yellow mass across the red-tile floor. Her colleagues tried to take her to a doctor, but she resisted successfully ('There's nothing wrong with me, it's just a woman thing, leave me alone'), and a few hours later she was sneaking into room 225 of the Escorial Hotel and calling Ricardo to come and pick her up because she didn't feel able to get on a bus. While she waited for him she went out for a walk near the cathedral and ended up sitting down on a bench in the Plaza Bolívar and watching the passers-by, the children in their school uniforms, old men in their ponchos and vendors with their carts. A young boy with a wooden crate under his arm approached to offer her a shoe-shine, and she agreed wordlessly, to keep her accent from giving her away. She swept the square with her gaze and wondered how many of the people could tell by looking at her that she was American, how many could tell she'd been in Colombia for not much more than a year, how many could tell she'd married a Colombian, how many could tell she was pregnant. Then, with her patent-leather shoes so shiny she could see the Manizales sky reflected in the toes, she went back to the hotel, wrote a letter on the hotel's letterhead and lay back to think of names. None occurred to her: before she knew it, she'd fallen asleep. Never had she felt so tired as on that afternoon.

When she woke up, Ricardo was at her side, naked and asleep. She hadn't heard him come in. It was three in the morning: what kind of doorman or night watchman do these hotels have? What right did they have to let a stranger into her room without warning her? How had Ricardo proved that she was his wife, that he had a right to be in her bed? Elaine stood up with her gaze fixed on a point on the wall, so she wouldn't faint. She leaned out the window, saw a corner of the deserted square, placed a hand on her belly and burst into silent tears. She thought the first thing she'd do when she got back to La Dorada would be to look for someone to take in Truman, because horseback riding would be forbidden for the next few months, maybe for a whole year. Yes, that would be the first thing, and the second would be to start looking seriously for a house, a family house. She wondered if she should advise the volunteer coordinator, or even call Bogotá. She decided it wasn't necessary, that she'd work as long as her body allowed her to, and then circumstances would dictate her strategy. She looked at Ricardo, who was sleeping open-mouthed. She approached the bed and lifted up the sheet with two fingers. She saw his sleeping penis, the curly hair. Her other hand moved to her sex and then to her belly, as if to protect it. *What's there to live for?* she thought all of a sudden, and hummed in her head: *Who needs the Peace Corps?* And then she went back to sleep.

Elaine worked until she couldn't any more. Her belly grew more than expected in the first months, but, apart from the violent tiredness that forced her to take long morning naps, her pregnancy didn't modify her routines. Other things changed, however. Elaine started to be aware of the heat and humidity as she never had before; in fact, she started to be aware of her body, which was no longer silent and discreet and from one day to the next suddenly insisted on desperately drawing attention to itself, like a problematic teenager or a drunk. Elaine hated the pressure her own weight put on her calves, hated the tension that appeared in her thighs every time she had to climb four measly steps, hated that her small nipples, which she'd always liked, grew bigger and darker all of a sudden. Embarrassed, guilt-ridden, she began to skip meetings saying she wasn't feeling well, and she'd go to the expensive hotel to spend the afternoon in the pool just for the pleasure of tricking gravity for a few hours, of feeling, afloat in the cool water, that her body was back to being the light thing it had always been before.

Ricardo devoted himself to her: he made only one trip during the entire pregnancy, but it must have been a big shipment, because he came back with a tennis bag – dark blue imitation leather, gold zipper, a white panther leaping up – full of bundles of dollar notes so clean and shiny they looked fake, like the toy money of a board game. Not just the bag was full, but also the racket cover, which in this particular bag was sewn to the outside as a separate compartment. Ricardo locked it up in the tool cupboard he'd built himself and a couple of times a month he'd go up to Bogotá to change some of the dollars into pesos. He showered Elaine with attention. He drove her everywhere and picked her up in the Nissan, he went with her to her doctor's appointments, he watched her step onto the scales and saw the hesitant needle and wrote down the latest result in a notebook, as if the doctor's annotation might be imprecise or less reliable. He also went with her to work: if there was a school to be built, he would willingly pick up a trowel and put cement on the bricks, or carry wheelbarrow loads of gravel from one place to another, or fix with his own hands the broken mesh of a sieve; if she had to talk to Acción Comunal people, he would sit at the back of the room and listen to his wife's ever-improving Spanish and sometimes offer the translation of a word Elaine didn't remember. On one occasion Elaine had to visit a community leader in Doradal, a man with a luxuriant moustache and shirt open to his belly button who, in spite of his *paisa* snake oil hawker's patter, couldn't get a polio-vaccination campaign approved. It was a bureaucratic matter, things were going slowly and the children couldn't wait. They said goodbye with a feeling of failure. Elaine climbed laboriously into the jeep, leaning on the door handle, grabbing hold of the back of the seat, and was just getting comfortable when Ricardo said, 'Wait for me a moment, I'll be right back.' 'Where are you going?' 'I'll be right back. Wait one second.' And she saw him walk back in and say something to the man in the open shirt, and then they both disappeared behind a door. Four days later, when Elaine got the news that the campaign had been approved in record time, an image came into Elaine's head: that of Ricardo reaching into his pocket, taking out an incentive for public functionaries and promising more. She could have confirmed her suspicions, confronted Ricardo and demanded a confession, but she decided not to. The objective, after all, had been achieved. Children, think of the children. Children were what mattered.

When she was thirty weeks and the size of her belly was becoming an obstacle in her work, Elaine obtained a special permit from the volunteer coordinator and then authorization from Peace Corps headquarters in Bogotá, for which she had to send a medical report by post, hurriedly and badly written by a young doctor doing his year of rural service in La Dorada and who wanted, with no knowledge of obstetrics or any medical justification at all, to give her a genital examination. Elaine, who by that point in the appointment was half undressed, objected and even got angry, and the first thing she thought was that she'd better not say anything to Ricardo, whose reactions could be unpredictable. But later, coming home in the Nissan, looking at her husband's profile and his hands with their long fingers and dark hairs, she felt a fit of desire. Ricardo's right hand was resting on the gear lever; Elaine grabbed his wrist and opened her legs and his hand understood, Ricardo's hand understood. They arrived home without a word and hurried in like thieves, and closed the curtains and bolted the back door, and Ricardo threw his clothes on the floor without caring that they'd soon be covered in ants. Elaine, meanwhile, lay down on her side on top of the sheets, facing the white curtains, the illuminated square of the curtains. The daylight was so strong that there were shadows in spite of the curtains being closed; Elaine looked at her belly as big as a half-moon, her smooth, strained skin and the violet line from top to bottom as if drawn on with a felt-tip pen, and she saw the shadows that her swollen breasts made on the sheet. She thought how her breasts had never cast shadows on anything ever before and then her breasts disappeared under Ricardo's hand. Elaine felt her darkened nipples close at the contact of those fingers and then felt Ricardo's mouth on her shoulder and then felt him enter her from behind. And so, connected like puzzle pieces, they made love for the last time before she gave birth.

Maya Laverde was born in the Palermo Clinic in Bogotá in July 1971, more or less at the same time President Nixon used the words *War on Drugs* for the first time in a public speech. Elaine and Ricardo had moved into the Laverdes' house three weeks earlier, in spite of Elaine's protests: 'If the clinic in La Dorada is good enough for the poorest mothers,' she said, 'I don't see why it's not going to be good enough for me.'

'Ay, Elena Fritts,' Ricardo said, 'why don't you do us a favour and stop trying to change the world all the time.'

Then events proved him right: the baby girl was born with an intestinal problem and needed immediate surgery, and everyone agreed that a rural clinic would not have had either the surgeons or the neonatal instruments necessary to guarantee the child's survival. Maya was kept under observation for several days, stuck in an incubator that had once, long ago, had transparent walls, which were now scratched and opaque like glasses that get too much use; when it was time to feed her, Elaine would sit in a chair beside the machine and a nurse would take the little girl out and put her in Elaine's arms. The nurse was an older woman with wide hips who seemed to take her time on purpose when she was carrying Maya. She smiled down at her so sweetly that Elaine felt jealous for the first time, and was amazed that something like that – the threatening presence of another mother, the savage reaction of the blood – was possible.

A little while after the baby was discharged, Ricardo had to make another trip. But it was still too soon to take her to La Dorada, and the idea of Elaine and their daughter staying alone filled him with terror, so Ricardo suggested they stay in Bogotá, in his parents' house, under the care of Doña Gloria and the dark-skinned woman with the long black braid who floated like a phantom through the house cleaning and putting everything in order as she went. 'If they ask, tell them I'm transporting flowers,' Ricardo told her. 'Carnations, roses, even orchids. Yes, orchids, that sounds good, orchids are exported, everyone knows that. You *gringos* love orchids to death.' Elaine smiled. They were lying in the same narrow bed where they'd talked after making love for the first time. It was very late, one or two in the morning; Maya had woken them up crying for food, crying with her thin little nasal voice, and could only calm down once she'd clamped her tiny mouth around her mother's erect nipple. After nursing she'd fallen asleep between the two of them, forcing them to make a space for her, to balance precariously on the edge of the little bed; and that's how they stayed, half hanging over the edge of the bed, face to face but in the dark, so each could barely see the other's silhouette in the shadows. They were wide awake now. The baby was sleeping: Elaine smelled her scent of sweet powders, soap and new wool. She raised a hand and stroked Ricardo's face like a blind woman and then she started to whisper. 'I want to go with you,' said Elaine.

'One day,' said Ricardo.

'I want to see what you do. To know it's not dangerous. Would you tell me if it was dangerous?'

'Of course I would.'

'Can I ask you something?'

'Ask me something.'

'What happens if they catch you?'

'They're not going to catch me.'

'But what happens if they do?'

Ricardo's voice changed, there was a note of falsetto in it, something projected. 'People want a product,' he said. 'There are people who grow that product. Mike gives it to me, I take it in a plane, someone receives it and that's all. We give people what people want.' He kept quiet for a second and then added, 'Also, it's going to be legalized sooner or later.'

'But it's hard for me to imagine,' said Elaine. 'When you're not here I think about you, try to imagine what you're doing, where, and I can't. And that's what I don't like.'

Maya sighed so quietly and briefly that it took them an instant to realize where it had come from. 'She's dreaming,' said Elaine. She saw Ricardo bring his big face – his hard chin, his thick lips – up close to the baby's tiny face; she saw him give her an inaudible kiss, and then another. 'My little girl,' she heard him say. 'Our little girl.' And then, with no segue whatsoever, she saw him start to talk about the trips, about a cattle ranch that stretched out from the banks of the Magdalena and on the pastures of which an airport could be built, about a Cessna 310 Skyknight that over the last little while had become Ricardo's favourite ride. That's how he put it: 'My favourite ride. They don't make that model any more, Elena Fritts, that baby's going to be a relic before we know it.' He also told her about the solitude he felt while he was in the air, and how different a plane loaded with cargo felt to an empty one: 'The air gets cold, it's noisier, you feel more alone. Even if someone's there. Yeah, even if there's someone with you.' He told her of the enormity of the Caribbean and of the fear of getting lost, the fear of the mere idea of getting lost over such a huge thing as the sea, even someone like him, who never ever got lost. He told her of the detour he had to take to avoid Cuban airspace – 'so they don't shoot me down thinking I'm a *gringo*,' he said – and how familiar, how curiously familiar, everything seemed to him from there on, as if he were coming home instead of about to land in Nassau. 'In Nassau?' said Elaine. 'In the Bahamas?' 'Yes,' said Ricardo, 'the only Nassau there is,' and went on to say that there, in the airport, before the air-traffic controllers who saw without seeing (their vision and memories conveniently modified by a few thousand dollars), an olive-coloured Chevrolet pick-up truck and a big strong *gringo*, who looked just like Joe Frazier, were waiting to take him to a hotel where the only luxury was the lack of questions. The arrival always fell on a Friday. After spending two nights there – the function of those two nights was not to arouse suspicion, to turn Ricardo into just another millionaire who comes to spend a weekend with friends or lovers – after two nights of living shut up in a charmless hotel, drinking rum and eating fish and rice, Ricardo returned to the airport, admired the controllers' blindness again, requested permission to take off for Miami like any other millionaire returning home with his mistress, and in minutes he was in the air, but not in the direction of Miami, but rather skirting around the coast and going in over the beaches of Beaufort and flying over a pattern of disperse rivers like the veins on an anatomy diagram. Then it was a matter of exchanging the cargo for dollars and taking off again and heading south, towards the Caribbean coast of Colombia, towards Barranquilla and the grey waters of Bocas de Ceniza and the brown serpent that moves through a green background, towards a town in the interior, that town placed there, between two mountain ranges, placed in the wide valley like a die that a player has dropped, that town with its unbearable climate where the hot air burns your nostrils, where the bugs are capable of biting through a mosquito net, and where Ricardo arrives with his heart in his hands, because in that town the two people he loves most in the world are waiting for him.

'But those two people are not in that town,' said Elaine. 'They're here, in Bogotá.'

'Not for much longer.'

'Frankly, they're freezing to death. They're in a house that isn't theirs.'

'Not for much longer.'

Four days later he came to pick them up. He parked the Nissan in front of the iron gate and the little brick wall, jumped out quickly as if he were blocking traffic and opened the passenger door for Elaine. She, who was carrying Maya wrapped in white shawls and with her face covered so she wouldn't get chilled from the wind, walked right past him. 'No, not in the front seat,' she said. 'We girls are sitting in the back.' And so, sitting on one of the fold-down seats, with the baby in her arms and her feet resting on the other seat, looking at Ricardo from behind (the hairs on the back of his neck, below the line of his well-cut hair, were like triangular table legs), she travelled from Bogotá to La Dorada. They only stopped once, halfway there, at a roadside restaurant where three empty tables looked at them from a terrace of polished cement. Elaine went into the bathroom and found an open oval hole in the floor and two footprints to indicate where she should place her feet; she crouched down and peed, holding up her skirt in both hands and smelling her own urine; and there she realized, with a bit of a start, that it was the first time since the birth that she hadn't had any other women around. She was alone in a world of men, she and Maya were on their own, and she'd never thought that before, she'd been in Colombia for more than two years and she'd never had such a thought before.

When they were coming down into the Magdalena Valley and the heat burst in on them, Ricardo opened both windows and conversation was no longer possible, so they covered the last stretch to La Dorada in silence. The plains appeared on both sides, the hills like sleeping hippopotami, the grazing cows, the vultures tracing circles in the air and smelling something that Elaine neither smelled nor saw. She felt a drop of sweat, then another, slip down her side and disappear into her still-thick waist; Maya had started to sweat too, so she took off the blankets and stroked her chubby little thighs with one finger, the folds of her pale skin, and stared for a moment at those grey eyes that weren't looking at her, or rather looked at everything with the same alarmed disregard. When she looked up again she saw a landscape she didn't recognize. Had they passed the entrance to the town without her noticing? Did Ricardo have something to do before going home? She called to him from the back, 'Where are we? What's going on?' But he didn't answer, or he hadn't been able to hear her questions over the noise. They had turned off the main road and were now driving through some meadows, following a track made by the passing of cars, going under trees that didn't let the light through, driving along the edge of a property marked by fences: wooden stakes – some leaning so far over they were almost touching the ground – barbed wire that, when it was taut, served as a perch for colourful birds. 'Where are we going?' said Elaine. 'The baby's hot, I need to give her a bath.' Then the Nissan stopped and, in the absence of a breeze, the inside of the jeep immediately felt a jolt of the tropics. 'Ricardo?' she said. He got out without looking at her, walked around to the other side of the jeep, opened the door. 'Come on out,' he said.

'What for? Where are we, Ricardo? I have to get home, I'm thirsty, and so is the baby.'

'Come out for a second.'

'And I have to pee.'

'We won't be long,' he said. 'Come on out, please.'

She obeyed. Ricardo reached out a hand, but then realized Elaine had her hands full. Then he put a hand on her back (Elaine felt the sweat that was already soaking through her shirt) and led her to the edge of the track, where the fence turned into a wooden frame, a square made of thin tree trunks that served as a gate. With great difficulty Ricardo lifted the structure to make it swing open. 'Come in,' he said to Elaine.

'In where?' she asked. 'Into this pasture?'

'It's not a pasture, it's a house. It's our house. It's just that we haven't built it yet.'

'I don't understand.'

'There are 6 hectares, with access to the river. I've already paid half and I'll pay the other half in six months. We'll start building as soon as you know.'

'As soon as I know what?'

'How you want your house to be?'

Elaine tried to look as far into the distance as she could and realized only the grey shadow of the mountain range blocked the view. The land, their land, was gently sloped, and there, behind the trees, a hill began to roll gently down towards the wide valley, towards the bank of the Magdalena. 'It can't be,' she said. She felt the heat on her forehead and cheeks and knew she was blushing. She looked up at the cloudless sky. She closed her eyes, took a deep breath; she felt, or thought she felt, a breeze on her face. She leaned over to Ricardo and kissed him. Briefly, because Maya had started to cry.

The new house had white walls like the midday sky and a terrace of smooth, light tiles, so clean you could see a line of ants along the edge of the wall. The construction took longer than expected, in part because Ricardo wanted to do some of it himself, in part because the land lacked services, and not even the generous bribes that Ricardo distributed left, right and centre helped the electricity cables and water pipes arrive any faster (sewage pipes were impossible, but there, so close to the river, it was easy to dig a good septic tank). Ricardo built a stable for two horses, in case Elaine wanted to go back to horseback riding in the future; he built a swimming pool and had them put in a slide for Maya, even though the little girl wasn't even walking yet, and had them plant *carreto* and ceiba trees where there was no shade, and watched undaunted as the workers painted the bottoms of the palm tree trunks white, in spite of Elaine's protests. He also built a shed 12 metres from the house, or what he called a shed despite the cement walls being as solid as the house itself, and there, in that windowless cell, in three padlocked cupboards, he kept the impenetrable bags filled with 50- and 100-dollar bills held tightly together by elastic bands. In 1973, shortly after the creation of the Drug Enforcement Agency, Ricardo had a board etched and singed with the name of the property: Villa Elena. When Elaine said that it was very nice but she had nowhere to put such a big board, Ricardo had a brick gate built with two columns covered in stucco and whitewashed and a crossbeam with clay roof tiles, and had the sign hung there by two iron chains that looked like they'd been taken off a shipwreck. Then he had them put in a green-painted wooden door the size of a man and with a well-oiled bolt. It was a useless addition, since a person could just squeeze through the barbed wire to get onto the property, but it allowed Ricardo to go on his trips with the feeling – artificial and even ridiculous – that his family was protected. 'Protected from what?' said Elaine. 'What's going to happen to us here, where everybody loves us?' Ricardo looked at her in that paternalistic way he had that Elaine loathed and said, 'It's not always going to be like that.' But Elaine realized that he meant something else, that he was also telling her something else.

A long time later, remembering them for her daughter or for herself, Elaine had to accept that the next three years, the three monotonous and routine years that followed the construction of Villa Elena, were the happiest of her life in Colombia. Taking over the land that Ricardo had bought, getting used to the idea that it was theirs, wasn't easy: Elaine used to go out walking among the palms and sit down in a hut and drink cold juice while thinking about the course her life had taken, about the unfathomable distance between her origins and this destiny. Then she would start to walk – even in full sunlight, it didn't bother her – towards the river, and saw the neighbouring ranches far away in the distance, the *campesinos* in their sandals cut from old tyres driving the cattle with shouts, each with their own voice as unmistakable as fingerprints. The couple who worked for her now had previously made their living by driving other people's cattle. Now they cleaned the pool, kept the whole property in good shape (fixed the hinges on the doors, got rid of a spider's nest from the baby's room), made fish or chicken stew on the weekends. Walking through the fields, stomping hard because they'd told her it frightened away the snakes, Elaine was pleased about having worked to improve the lot of those *campesinos*, although she'd done so for less time than planned, and then, like a shadow, like the shadow of a low-flying vulture, it crossed her mind that she had now turned into the same kind of person who, as a Peace Corps volunteer, she'd fought against indefatigably.

The Peace Corps. Elaine got back in touch with the

Bogotá office when she thought she could leave Maya in good hands and go back to work; by telephone, deputy director Valenzuela listened to her explanations, congratulated her on her new family and told her to call back in a few days, after he'd had a chance to talk to head office back in the United States, not wanting to violate protocol. When Elaine did so, Valenzuela's secretary told Elaine that the deputy director had gone away unexpectedly and would phone her when he got back, but days passed and the call didn't come. Elaine didn't let that discourage her, and one day she went out herself and found the Acción Comunal people, who welcomed her as if barely a day had passed, and she started working again in a matter of hours on two new projects: a fishing cooperative and the construction of latrines. During the hours she spent with the community leaders – or with the fishermen, or drinking beer on the terraces of La Dorada, because that's how business got done – she left Maya with her cook's little boy, or brought her with her to work so she could play with other babies, but she didn't tell Ricardo, who had very fixed opinions about the indiscriminate mixing of social classes. She began to use English again, so her daughter would not be deprived of her own language, and Maya would drop Spanish perfectly naturally when talking to her, going into and coming out of each of her languages as if she were going into or coming out of a game. She had turned into a lively and clever and bold little girl: she had long, narrow eyebrows and a cheekiness about her that could disarm anyone, but she also had her own world, and would go off among the *carreto* trees and reappear with a lizard in a glass, or completely naked having left her clothes, out of solidarity, on top of an egg. It was around that time when Ricardo, coming back from one of his trips to the Bahamas, brought her a gift of a three-banded armadillo in a cage full of fresh shit. He never explained how he'd got it, but he spent several days telling Maya the same things, obviously, that he'd been told: armadillos live in holes they dig with their own claws, armadillos roll up into a ball when they're scared, armadillos can stay under water for more than five minutes. Maya looked at the animal with the same fascination – her mouth half open, eyebrows arched – with which she listened to her father. After seeing her get up early to feed the creature, seeing her spend hours snuggled up to him with a shy hand on the rough shell, Elaine asked, 'So, what's your armadillo's name?'

'He doesn't have a name,' said Maya.

'What do you mean? He's yours. You have to name him.'

Maya looked up, looked at Elaine, blinked twice. 'Mike,' she said. 'He's called Mike the armadillo.'

And that's how Elaine found out that Barbieri had come to visit a couple of weeks earlier, while she was out managing projects with no future with the departmental boss. Ricardo hadn't said anything to her: why? She asked him as soon as she could, and he fended her off with three simple words: 'Because I forgot.' Elaine didn't let it go at that. 'But what did he come for?'

'To say hello, Elena Fritts,' said Ricardo. 'And he might

come again, so don't be surprised. As if he wasn't a friend of ours.'

'But the thing is he's not a friend of ours.'

'He's a friend of mine,' said Ricardo. 'He is my friend.'

Just as Ricardo had announced, Mike Barbieri visited them again. But the circumstances of the visit were not ideal. During the month of April in 1976, the rainy season had turned into a civil disaster: in the shantytowns of all the big cities houses were collapsing and burying the squatters who'd built them, on the mountain roads the landslides blocked traffic and isolated towns, and in one case there was the cruel paradox of a village, which had no system of rainwater collection, being left with no drinking water while a flood of biblical proportions rained down on them. The Miel River flooded and Elaine and Ricardo were helping to open ditches to clear the water from the flooded houses. From the television screen, the weather forecaster told them of trade winds and chaos in the Pacific currents, of hurricanes with stupid names that were beginning to form in the Caribbean, and the relationship that all that had with the downpours that were devastating Villa Elena, disrupting the household routines and also their domestic lives. The humidity was so intense that their clothes would never dry once they were washed and the drainpipes got clogged with fallen leaves and drowned insects and the terrace flooded three or four times, so that Elaine and Ricardo had to get up in the middle of the night to defend themselves, naked but for the rags and brooms, from the water that was already threatening to invade the dining-room.

At the end of the month Ricardo had to go on one of his trips, and Elaine had to struggle alone against the threat of water. Afterwards she'd go back to bed to try to get a bit more sleep, but she never could, and would turn on the television to watch, as if hypnotized, a screen where another rain rained, an electrical rain in black and white whose static sound had a curious sedative effect on her.

The day Ricardo should have come home went by without Ricardo arriving. It wasn't the first time it had happened – delays of two and even three days were acceptable, since Ricardo's business was not without its unforeseen contingencies – and she mustn't worry about them. After eating a plate of rice and fish and a few slices of fried plantain, Elaine put Maya to bed, read her a few pages of *The Little Prince* (the part about drawing the sheep, which made Maya laugh and laugh) and, when the little girl turned over and fell asleep, Elaine kept reading out of inertia. She liked Saint-Exupéry's illustrations and she liked, because it reminded her of Ricardo, the passage where the Little Prince asks the pilot what that thing is and the pilot says, 'It's not a thing. It flies. It's a plane. My plane.' And she was reading the Little Prince's alarmed reaction, the moment when he asks the pilot if he fell out of the sky too, when she heard an engine and a man's voice, a greeting, a shout. But when she came out she didn't find Ricardo, but Mike Barbieri, who had arrived by motorcycle and was drenched from head to toe, his hair stuck to his forehead, his shirt stuck to his chest, his legs and back and the insides of his forearms covered in big gobs of fresh mud.

'Do you know what time it is?' Elaine said to him.

Mike Barbieri was standing on the terrace dripping wet and rubbing his hands together. The olive green knapsack he'd brought was lying beside him on the floor, like a dead dog, and Mike was staring at Elaine with a blank expression on his face, like the way the *campesinos* looked at her, Elaine thought, they looked without seeing. After a couple of long seconds, he seemed to wake up, to snap out of the torpor his journey had brought on. 'I've come from Medellín,' he said, 'I never expected to get caught in a downpour like this. My hands feel like they're falling off from the cold. I don't know how it can be so cold in such a hot place. The world must be coming to an end.'

'From Medellín,' said Elaine, but not as a question. 'And you're here to see Ricardo.'

Mike Barbieri was going to say something (she was perfectly well aware that he was going to say something) but he didn't. His gaze left her face and glided past her like a paper plane; Elaine, turning around to see what he was looking at, found Maya, a little ghost in a lace nightie. In one hand she had a stuffed animal – a rabbit with very long ears and a ballerina's tutu that had once been white – and with the other she was pushing her chestnut hair off her face. 'Hello, beautiful,' said Mike, and Elaine was surprised by the sweetness in his tone. 'Hello, sweetie,' she said to her. 'What happened? Did we wake you up? Can't you sleep?'

'I'm thirsty,' said Maya. 'Why is Uncle Mike here?'

'Mike came to see Daddy. Go to your room, I'll bring you a glass of water.'

'Is Daddy back?'

'No, he's not back yet. But Mike came to see all of us.'

'Me too?'

'Yes, you too. But now it's time to sleep, say goodnight, you'll see him another day.'

'Goodbye, Uncle Mike.'

'Goodnight, lovely,' said Mike.

'Sleep tight,' said Elaine.

'She's so big,' said Mike. 'How old is she now?'

'Five. She's about to turn five.'

'Holy smoke. How time flies.'

The cliché annoyed Elaine. Annoyed her more than it should have, it almost made her angry, it was like an affront, and suddenly her annoyance turned into surprise: at her disproportionate reaction, at the strangeness of the scene with Mike Barbieri, at the fact that her daughter had called him Uncle. She asked Mike to wait for her there, because the floor was too slippery and if he came in soaking wet he risked hurting himself; she brought him a towel from the servants' bathroom and went to get a glass of water from the kitchen. *Uncle Mike*, she was thinking, *what's he doing here?* And she thought it in Spanish too, *what the hell is he doing here?* And suddenly there was that song again, *What's there to live for? Who needs the Peace Corps?* When she walked into Maya's room, when she breathed in her scent that was different from all others, she felt an inexplicable desire to spend the night with her, and thought that later, when Mike had left, she'd carry Maya to her bed so she could keep her company until Ricardo got back. Maya had fallen asleep again. Elaine bent down over the head of her bed, looked at her, brought her face up close, breathed in her breath. 'Here's your water,' she said, 'do you want a sip?' But the little girl didn't say anything. Elaine left the glass on her bedside table, beside the string merry-go-round where a horse with a broken head was trying, slowly but tirelessly, to catch up with a clown. And then she went back to the front of the house.

Mike was using the towel vigorously, rubbing his ankles and shins. 'I'm getting it all muddy,' he said when he saw Elaine come back. 'The towel, I mean.'

'That's what it's for,' said Elaine. And then, 'So you came to see Ricardo.'

'Yeah,' he said. He looked at her with the same empty expression. 'Yeah,' he repeated. He looked at her again: Elaine saw the drops running down his neck, his beard dripping like a leaky tap, the mud. 'I came to see Ricardo. And it seems like he's not here, right?'

'He should have been back today. Sometimes these things happen.'

'Sometimes he gets delayed.'

'Yeah, sometimes. He doesn't fly by a precise itinerary. Did he know you were coming?'

Mike didn't answer straight away. He was concentrating on his own body, on the muddy towel. Outside, in the dark night, in that night that blended with the rocky hills and became infinite, another downpour was unleashed. 'Well, I think so,' said Mike. 'Maybe I'm the one who's confused.' But he didn't look at her as he spoke: he dried off with the towel and had that absent expression, like a cat cleaning itself with strokes of its tongue. And then Elaine thought that Mike might keep drying himself till the end of time if she didn't do something. 'Well, come in and sit down and have a drink,' she said then. 'Rum?'

'OK, but no ice,' said Mike. 'See if it'll warm me up. I can't believe how cold it is.'

'Do you want one of Ricardo's shirts?'

'That's not a bad idea, Elena Fritts. That's what he calls you, isn't it? Elena Fritts. A shirt, yeah, not a bad idea.'

And so, wearing a shirt that wasn't his (short-sleeved with blue checks on a white background, a breast pocket with a missing button), Mike Barbieri drank not one, but four glasses of rum. Elaine watched him. She felt comfortable with him: yes, that's what it was, comfort. It was the language, perhaps, coming back to her language, or perhaps the codes they shared and the disappearance, while they were together, of the necessity of explaining themselves that was always there with Colombians. Being with him had something of indisputable familiarity, like coming home. Elaine had a drink too and felt accompanied and she felt that Mike Barbieri was also accompanying her daughter. They talked about their country and politics back home just as they'd done years before, before Maya existed and before Villa Elena existed, and they told stories of their families, their personal histories and also recent news, and doing so was comfortable and agreeable, like putting on a nice wool coat on a winter's evening. Although it wasn't easy to know where the pleasure came from in talking about the

2-dollar bill that had just been reissued back home, or about the bicentennial celebrations of independence, or about Sara Jane Moore, the muddle-headed woman who had tried to assassinate the president. It had stopped raining and a cool breeze came in from the night heavy with the scent of hibiscus. Elaine felt light-hearted, even cosy, so she didn't hesitate for a second when Mike asked if there was a guitar around and in a matter of seconds he was tuning it up and started singing Bob Dylan and Simon and Garfunkel songs.

It must have been two or three in the morning when something happened that didn't shock Elaine (she'd think later) as much as it should have shocked her. Mike was singing the part of 'America' where the couple gets on a Greyhound bus when they heard a sound outside, in the distance, in the quiet night, and the dogs began to bark. Elaine opened her eyes and Mike stopped playing; both of them sat still, listening to the silence. 'Don't worry, nothing ever happens around here,' said Elaine, but Mike was already on his feet and had gone to find the olive green knapsack he'd brought with him and taken out a big, silver-plated pistol, or a silver pistol that looked big to Elaine, and had gone outside, raised his arm and fired two shots at the sky, one, two, two explosions. Elaine's first reaction was to protect Maya or to neutralize her unease or her fear, but when she reached her daughter's room in four strides she found her asleep, deep in an imperturbable sleep and far from all sounds and noises and worries, incredible. When she got back to the living room, however, something had broken in the atmosphere. Mike was justifying himself with a twisted sentence: 'If it was nothing before, now it's even less.' But Elaine had lost the urge to hear the song about the Greyhound bus and the New Jersey Turnpike: she felt tired; it had been a long day. She said goodnight and told Mike to sleep in the guest room, the bed was made, tomorrow they could have breakfast together. 'Who knows, maybe even with Ricardo.'

'Yeah,' said Mike Barbieri. 'With any luck.'

But when she woke up, Mike Barbieri had gone. A note, that was all he'd left, a note on a paper napkin, and in the note three words on three lines: 'Thanks, Love, Mike.' Later, remembering that strange and hazy night, Elaine would feel two things: first, a profound hatred towards Mike Barbieri, the most profound hatred she'd ever felt; and second, a sort of involuntary admiration for the ease with which that man had gone through the night, for the massive deception he'd carried out for so many and such intimate hours without giving himself away for a moment, for the incombustible serenity with which he'd pronounced those final words. *With any luck*, Elaine would think, or rather the words would repeat themselves in her head tirelessly, *with any luck*, that's what Mike Barbieri had said to her without a muscle in his face twitching, a feat worthy of a champion poker player or a Russian roulette enthusiast, because Mike Barbieri knew perfectly well that Ricardo wasn't going to return to Villa Elena that night and he'd known it from the start, from the time he arrived by motorcycle at Elaine's house. In fact, that's precisely why he'd come:

to tell Elaine. He'd come to tell her that Ricardo wasn't going to come back.

He knew very well.

He knew very well, he who'd been to see Ricardo days earlier to tell him about the new business opportunity they could not afford to miss, to convince him that the shipments of marijuana were bringing in pocket money compared to what they could be earning now, to explain what this *coca* paste that was coming in from Bolivia and Peru was and how in some magic places it was transformed into the luminous white powder for which all of Hollywood, no, all of California, no, all of the United States, from Los Angeles to New York, from Chicago to Miami, were willing to pay whatever they had to. He knew very well, having direct contact with those places, where a few Peace Corps veterans, who had just spent three years in the Cauca Valley and in Putumayo, had turned into overnight experts in ether and acetone and hydrochloric acid, and where they assembled bricks of the product that could illuminate a dark room with their phosphorescence. He knew very well, he who'd done some numbers on a piece of paper with Ricardo and calculated that any Cessna, with the passenger seats removed, could carry some twelve canvas rucksacks full of bricks, 300 kilos in total, and that, at 100 dollars a gram, a single trip could produce 90 million dollars of which the pilot, who ran so many risks and was so indispensable to the operation, could keep two. He knew very well, having listened to Ricardo's enthusiasm, his plans to make this trip and just this trip and then retire, retire forever, retire from piloting cargo planes and also passenger planes and all piloting except flying for pleasure, retire from everything except his family, a millionaire forever before the age of thirty.

He knew very well.

He knew very well, he who accompanied Ricardo in the Nissan to a ranch in Doradal with its property lines too far away to see, this side of Medellín, and there introduced him to the Colombian side of the business, two men with wavy black hair and moustaches who spoke softly and gave the impression of feeling very much at ease with their consciences and after greeting Ricardo they attended to and entertained him as he'd never been entertained or attended to in his life. He knew very well, he who'd been at Ricardo's side while the bosses showed him around the property, the *paso fino* horses and the luxurious stables, the bullring and barns, the swimming pool like a cut emerald, the fields that stretched further than the eye could see. He knew very well, having helped load the Cessna 310-R with his own hands, having taken the rucksacks out of a black Land Rover with his own hands and put them into the plane, he who couldn't contain himself and had given Ricardo a big hug, a hug of true comrades, feeling as he did so that he'd never loved any Colombian this much. He knew very well, having watched the Cessna take off and followed it with his gaze, its white shape against the grey background of the clouds that were now threatening rain, and having watched it get smaller and smaller until it disappeared in the distance, and then got back into the Land Rover and let them drive him out to the main road where he caught the first bus heading in the direction of La Dorada.

He knew very well.

He knew very well, having received the phone call twelve hours before arriving at Villa Elena that gave him the news, and in an urgent and then threatening tone demanded explanations. And he couldn't give any, of course, because nobody could explain how DEA agents were waiting for Ricardo in the very spot he landed, or how the two dealers – one from Miami Beach, the other from the university zone of Massachusetts – waiting for Ricardo's shipment in a covered Ford pick-up truck hadn't noticed their presence. It was said that Ricardo was the first to notice that something was wrong. It was said that he tried to get back to the cockpit, but he must have realized his effort would be futile, for he'd never be able to get the Cessna in motion in time to escape. So he ran down the runway towards the woods that surrounded it, chased by two agents and three German shepherds who caught up with him 30 metres from the edge of the woods. He had already lost at the moment of running off, it was obvious that he'd lost, and that's why no one could explain what happened next. It's possible to think it was out of fear, a reaction to the moment's vulnerability, to the agents' shouts and to their own weapons pointing at him, or perhaps it was out of despair or rage or powerlessness. Of course, Ricardo couldn't have thought that firing a random shot could help him in any way, but that's what he did, using a .22-calibre Taurus he'd started carrying in January: it was a random shot and only one shot, over his shoulder without bothering to aim and with no desire to hurt anyone, with such bad luck that the bullet pierced the right hand of one of the agents, and that same hand in a plaster cast would be enough later, during the trial for drug trafficking, to increase the sentence, even though it was a first offence. Ricardo dropped the Taurus on the way into the woods and shouted something, they say he shouted something, but those who heard him didn't understand what he said. When the dogs and the second agent found him, Ricardo was lying in a puddle with a broken ankle, his hands black with dirt, his clothes torn and covered in pine gum and his face disfigured by sadness.

6

Up, Up, Up

ADULTHOOD BRINGS WITH IT the pernicious illusion of control, and perhaps even depends on it. I mean that mirage of dominion over our own life that allows us to feel like adults, for we associate maturity with autonomy, the sovereign right to determine what is going to happen to us next. Disillusion comes sooner or later, but it always comes, it doesn't miss an appointment, it never has. When it arrives we receive it without too much surprise, for no one who lives long enough can be surprised to find their life has been moulded by distant events, by other people's wills, with little or no participation from their own decisions. Those long processes that end up running into our life – sometimes to give it the shove it needed, sometimes to blow to smithereens our most splendid plans – tend to be hidden like subterranean currents, like tiny shifts of tectonic plates, and when the earthquake finally comes we invoke the words we've learned to calm ourselves, *accident*, *fluke*, and sometimes *fate*. Right now there is a chain of circumstances, of guilty mistakes or lucky decisions, whose consequences await me around the corner; and even though I know it, although I have the uncomfortable certainty that those things are happening and will affect me, there is no way I can anticipate them. Struggling against their effects is all I can do: repair the damage, take best advantage of the benefits. We know it, we know it very well; nevertheless it's always somewhat dreadful when someone reveals to us the chain that has turned us into what we are, it's always disconcerting to discover, when it's another person who brings us the revelation, the slight or complete lack of control we have over our own experience.

That's what happened to me over the course of that second afternoon at Las Acacias, the property formerly known as Villa Elena, whose name no longer suited it one fine day and had to be urgently replaced. That was what happened to me during that Saturday night when Maya and I were talking about the documents in the wicker chest, about every letter and every photo, about every telegram and every bill. The conversation taught me all that the documents hadn't confessed, or rather organized the contents of the documents, gave an order and a meaning and filled in a few of its gaps, although not all of them, with the stories that Maya had inherited from her mother in the years they lived together. And also, of course, with the stories her mother had made up.

'Made up?' I said.

'Oh, yeah,' said Maya. 'Starting with Dad. She invented him entirely, or rather, he was an invention of hers. A novel, understand? A flesh-and-blood novel, her novel. She did it because of me, of course, or for me.'

'You mean you didn't know the truth?' I said. 'Elaine didn't tell you?'

'She must have thought it would be better that way. And maybe she was right, Antonio. I don't have children.

I can't imagine what it's like to have children. I don't know what a person might be capable of doing for them. My imagination doesn't stretch that far. Have you got kids, Antonio?'

Maya asked me that. It was Sunday morning, that day Christians call Easter and on which they celebrate or commemorate the Resurrection of Jesus of Nazareth, who had been crucified two days before (more or less at the same time as I began my first conversation with Ricardo Laverde's daughter) and who from this moment on began to appear to the living: to his mother, to the Apostles and to certain women well chosen for their merit. 'Have you got kids, Antonio?' We'd had an early breakfast: lots of coffee, lots of freshly squeezed orange juice, lots of chunks of papaya and pineapple and sapodilla plums, and a cooked breakfast with a very hot *arepa*, which I put in my mouth too hot and left a blister on my tongue that came back to life every time my tongue touched my teeth. It wasn't hot yet, but the world was a place that smelled of vegetation, humid and colourful, and there, at the table on the terrace, surrounded by hanging vines, talking a few metres from a trunk with some bromeliads growing out of it, I felt good, I thought I was feeling good on this Easter Sunday. 'Have you got kids, Antonio?' I thought of Aura and Leticia, or rather I thought of Aura taking Leticia to the closest church and showing her the candle that represented the light of Christ. She'll take advantage of my absence to do it: in spite of several attempts, I was never able to recover the faith I had as a little boy, much less the dedication with which my family followed the rituals of these days, from the ashes on the forehead on the first day of Lent to the Ascension (which I pictured in my head according to an encyclopedia illustration, a painting full of angels that I've never found since). And I had therefore never wanted my daughter to grow up in this tradition, which now seemed so alien to me. *Where are you, Aura?* I thought. *Where is my family?* I looked up, let myself be dazzled by the clarity of the sky, felt a stabbing in my eyes. Maya was looking at me, waiting, hadn't forgotten her question.

'No,' I said, 'I don't. It must be very strange, having kids. I can't imagine it either.'

I don't know why I did that. Maybe because it was too late to start talking about the family that was waiting for me in Bogotá; those are things you mention in the first moments of a friendship, when you introduce yourself and hand over two or three pieces of information to give the illusion of intimacy. One introduces oneself: the word must come from that, not pronouncing one's own name and hearing the other's name and shaking hands, not from kissing a cheek or two or bowing, but from those first minutes in which certain insubstantial pieces of information are exchanged, certain unimportant generalities, to give the other the sensation they know us, that we're no longer strangers. We speak of our nationality; we speak of our profession, what we do to make a living, because the way we make our living is eloquent, it defines us, structures us; we talk about our family. Well anyway, that moment was already long past with Maya, and to start talking about the woman I lived with and our daughter two days after having arrived at Las Acacias would have raised unnecessary suspicions or required long explanations or stupid justifications, or simply seemed odd, and after all it wouldn't be without consequences: Maya would lose the trust she'd felt until now, or I would lose the ground I'd gained so far, and she would stop talking and Ricardo Laverde's past would go back to being the past, would go back to hiding in other people's memories. I couldn't allow that.

Or perhaps there was another reason.

Because keeping Aura and Leticia out of Las Acacias, remote from Maya Fritts and her tale and her documents, distant therefore from the truth about Ricardo Laverde, was to protect their purity, or rather avoid their contamination, the contamination that I'd suffered one afternoon in 1996 the causes of which I'd barely begun to understand now, the unsuspected intensity of which was just now beginning to emerge like an object falling from the sky. My contaminated life was mine alone: my family was still safe: safe from the plague of my country, from its afflicted recent history: safe from what had hunted me down along with so many of my generation (and others, too, yes, but most of all mine, the generation that was born with planes, with the flights full of bags of marijuana, the generation that was born with the War on Drugs and later experienced the consequences). This world that had come back to life in the words and documents of Maya Fritts could stay there, I thought, could stay there in Las Acacias, could stay in La Dorada, could stay in the Magdalena Valley, could stay a four-hour drive from Bogotá, far from the apartment where my wife and daughter were waiting for me, perhaps with some concern, yes, perhaps with worried expressions on their faces, but pure, uncontaminated, free of our particular Colombian story, and I wouldn't be a good father or a good husband if I brought this story to them, or allowed them to enter this story, enter Las Acacias and the life of Maya Fritts in any way, enter into contact with Ricardo Laverde. Aura had had the strange luck to be absent during the difficult years, to have grown up in Santo Domingo and Mexico and Santiago de Chile: was it not my obligation to preserve that luck, to be vigilant to keep anything from ruining that sort of exemption that the eventful life of her parents had granted her? I was going to protect her, I thought, her and my little girl, I was protecting them. This was the right thing to do, I thought, and I did so with real conviction, with almost religious zeal.

'It's true, isn't it?' Maya said. 'It's one of those things that can't be shared, so everyone tells me. Anyway. The thing is she did it for me. She invented my dad, invented him entirely.'

'For example?'

'Well,' said Maya, 'for example, his death.'

And so, with the white light of the Magdalena Valley shining in my face, I learned about the day that Elaine or Elena Fritts explained to her daughter what had happened to her father. During the previous year, father and daughter had talked a lot about death: one afternoon, Maya had come upon the slaughter of a Cebú cow, and almost immediately began to ask questions. Ricardo had resolved the matter in four words: 'Her years were up.' Everyone and everything runs out of years eventually, he explained: animals, people, everyone. Armadillos? asked Maya. Yes, Ricardo told her, armadillos too. Grandpa Julio? asked Maya. Yes, Grandpa Julio too, Ricardo told her. So, one afternoon towards the end of 1976, when the girl's questions about her father's absence were starting to get unbearable, Elaine Fritts sat Maya on her lap and told her, 'Daddy's years were up.'

'I don't know why she chose that moment, I don't know if she got tired of waiting for something, I don't know anything,' Maya told me. 'Maybe some news arrived from the United States. From the lawyers or from my dad.'

'You don't know?'

'There aren't any letters from that time, my mother burnt them all. What I'm telling you is what I imagine happened: she got some news. From my dad. From the lawyers. And decided to change her life, or that her life with my dad was over and she was going to start another different one.'

She explained that Ricardo had got lost in the sky. Sometimes that happened to pilots, she explained: it's rare, but it happened. The sky was very big and the sea was very big too and a plane was a very small thing and the planes that Daddy flew were the smallest ones of all, and the world was full of planes like those, little white planes that took off and flew over the land and then went out and flew over the sea, and went far, very far away, far from everything, completely alone, without anyone to tell them how to get back to land again. And sometimes something happened, and they got lost. They forgot where ahead was and where was back, or they got confused and started flying in circles without knowing which way was ahead and which was back, where the left was and where the right, until the plane ran out of gasoline and fell into the sea, fell out of the sky like a little girl diving into a pool. And it sank without a sound or a noise, sank unseen because out in those places there isn't anyone to see, and out there, at the bottom of the sea, pilots ran out of years. 'Why don't they swim?' asked Maya. And Elena Fritts said, 'Because the sea is very deep.' And Maya, 'But Daddy's out there?' And Elena Fritts, 'Yes, Daddy's there. At the bottom of the sea. His plane fell, Daddy fell asleep and his years ran out.'

Maya Fritts never questioned that version of events. That was the last Christmas they spent at Villa Elena, the last time Elaine had them cut down a yellowing shrub to decorate with the fragile coloured balls the little girl loved, with reindeer and sleighs and fake candy canes that bent the branches with their weight. In January 1977 several things happened: Elaine received a letter from her grandparents telling her that it had snowed in Miami for the first time in history; President Jimmy Carter pardoned the Vietnam draft dodgers; and Mike Barbieri – who Elaine had always secretly considered a draft dodger – showed up dead in La Miel River, shot in the back of the neck, his naked body thrown face down on the riverbank, the water playing with his long hair, his beard wet and reddened with blood. The *campesinos* who found him went in search of Elaine even before they went to the authorities: she was the other *gringa* in the region. Elaine had to be present at the first judicial proceedings, had to go to a municipal court with open windows and fans that messed up the records to say that yes, she knew him, and that no, she didn't know who might have killed him. The next day she packed up the Nissan with everything she could fit in it, her clothes and her daughter's, the suitcases full of money and an armadillo with the name of a murdered *gringo*, and went to Bogotá.

'Twelve years, Antonio,' Maya Fritts said to me, 'twelve years I lived with my mother, just the two of us, practically in hiding. She didn't just take my dad away from me, but my grandparents too. We didn't see them again. They just came to visit a couple of times, and it would always end in a fight, I didn't understand why. But other people came. It was a tiny little apartment, in La Perseverancia. Lots of people came to visit us, the house was always full of *gringos*, people from the Peace Corps, people from the Embassy. Did Mom talk to them about drugs, about what was happening with drugs? I don't know, I wouldn't have been aware of something like that. It's perfectly possible they talked about cocaine. Or about the volunteers who had taught the *campesinos* to process the *coca* paste just as they'd taught them techniques for growing better marijuana before. But the business wasn't yet what it became later. How would I have known? A child doesn't catch things like that.'

'And no one asked about Ricardo? None of those visitors spoke of him?'

'No, nobody. Incredible, isn't it? Mom constructed a world in which Ricardo Laverde didn't exist, that takes talent. As difficult as it is to maintain a little tiny lie, she built up something huge, an actual pyramid. I imagine her giving instructions to all her visitors: in this house we don't speak of the dead. What dead? Well, the dead. The dead who are dead.'

It was around that time that she killed the armadillo. Maya didn't remember the absence of her father upsetting her too much: she didn't remember any bad feelings, any aggression, any desire for revenge, but one day (she would have been about eight) she grabbed the armadillo and took him to the laundry patio. 'It was one of those old-fashioned patios apartments used to have, you know, uncomfortable and tiny, with a stone sink and clothes lines and a window. Do you remember those laundry sinks? On one side was where you scrubbed the clothes against the ridged surface, on the other was a sort of tank, for a child it was like a deep well of cold water. I brought a bench over from the kitchen, leaned over the water and pushed Mike down with both hands, without letting go of him, and I put both my hands on his back so he wouldn't move. I'd been told that armadillos could spend a long time under water. I wanted to see how long. The armadillo started struggling, but I held him down there, pressed against the bottom of the sink with my whole body weight, an armadillo is strong, but not that strong, I was already a good-sized girl. I wanted to see how long he could stay under water, that was all, it seemed to me that's all it was. I remember the roughness of his body very well, my hands hurt from the pressure and then they went on hurting, it was like holding a knotty tree trunk in place so the current wouldn't carry it off. What a struggle the creature put up, I remember perfectly. Until he stopped struggling. The maid found him later, you should have heard her scream. I was punished. Mom slapped me hard and cut my lip with her ring. Later she asked me why I'd done it and I said, To see how many minutes he could stay under. And Mom answered, Then why didn't you have a watch? I didn't know what to say. And that question hasn't completely gone away, Antonio, it still runs around my head every once in a while, always at the worst moments, when life isn't working out for me. This question appears to me and I've never been able to answer it.'

She thought for a moment and said, 'Anyway, what was an armadillo doing in an apartment in La Perseverancia? How absurd, the house smelled like shit.'

'And did you never have any suspicions?'

'About what?'

'That Ricardo was alive. About him being in jail.'

'Never, no. I've since discovered that I wasn't the only one, that my story wasn't unique. In those years they were legion those who arrived in the United States and stayed there, I don't know if you know what I mean. Those who arrived, not with shipments like my dad, though there were those as well, but as simple passengers of a commercial plane, an Avianca or American Airlines plane. And the families who were left behind in Colombia had to tell the children something, didn't they? So they killed the father, never better said. The guy, stuck in jail in the United States, died all of a sudden without anyone ever knowing he was there. It was the easiest thing to do, easier than struggling with the shame, the humiliation of having a mule in the family. Hundreds of cases like this one. Hundreds of fictitious orphans, I was just one. That's the great thing about Colombia, nobody's ever alone with their fate. Shit, is it ever hot. It's incredible. Aren't you hot, Antonio, being from a cool climate?'

'A little, yes. But I can take it.'

'Here you feel every pore open. I like the early mornings, first thing. But then it gets unbearable. No matter how used to it you get.'

'You must be pretty used to it by now.'

'Yes, it's true. Maybe I just like to complain.'

'How did you end up living here?' I asked. 'I mean, after all that time.'

'Oh, well,' said Maya. 'That's a long story.'

Maya had just turned eleven when a classmate told her about the Hacienda Nápoles for the first time. This was the vast property, more than 3,000 hectares, that Pablo Escobar had bought towards the end of the 1970s on which to build his personal paradise, a paradise that was an empire at the same time: a tropical lowland Xanadu, with animals instead of sculptures and armed thugs instead of a *No Trespassing* sign. The hacienda's land stretched over two departments; a river crossed it from one side to the other. Of course that wasn't the information Maya's classmate gave her, for in 1982 the name Pablo Escobar was not yet on the lips of eleven-year-old children, nor did eleven-year-old children know the characteristics of the gigantic territory or the collection of antique cars that would soon be growing in special carports or the existence of several runways designed for the business (for the taking off and landing of planes like the one Ricardo Laverde had piloted), much less had they seen *Citizen Kane*. No, eleven-year-old children didn't know about those things. But they did know about the zoo: in a matter of months the zoo became a legend on a national scale, and it was the zoo that Maya's classmate told her about one day in 1982. She told her about giraffes, elephants, rhinoceroses, huge birds of every colour; she told her about a kangaroo that kicked a football. For Maya it was a revelation so extraordinary, and it turned into a desire so important, that she had the good sense to wait until Christmas to ask to be taken to the Hacienda Nápoles as a Christmas present.

Her mother's reply was emphatic: 'Don't even dream about going to see that place.'

'But everyone in my class has been,' said Maya.

'Well you're not going,' said Elaine Fritts. 'Don't even think of mentioning it again.'

'And so I went on the sly,' Maya told me. 'What else could I do? A friend invited me and I said yes. My mom thought I was going to spend the weekend in Villa de Leyva.'

'You're kidding,' I said. 'You sneaked off to the Hacienda Nápoles too? How many of us must have done the same thing?'

'Oh, so you . . .'

'Yeah, I did too,' I said. 'I wasn't allowed to go, so I made up some lie too, and went to see what was forbidden. A taboo place, Hacienda Nápoles.'

'And when did you go there?'

I made some calculations in my head, summoning up certain memories, and the conclusion made a shiver of pleasure run up my spine. 'I was twelve. I'm a year older than you. We went there around the same time, Maya.'

'You went in December?'

'Yes.'

'December 1982?'

'Yes.'

'We were there at the same time,' she said. 'Incredible. Isn't it incredible?'

'Well, yeah, but I'm not sure . . .'

'We went on the same day, Antonio,' said Maya. 'I'm sure of it.'

'But it might have been any day.'

'Don't be silly. It was before Christmas, right?'

'Right. But . . .'

'And after school broke up, right?'

'Yes, that's right.'

'Well, it had to be a weekend, otherwise there wouldn't have been adults to take us. People work. And how many weekends are there before Christmas? Let's say three. And what day was it, a Saturday or a Sunday? It was a Saturday, because Bogotá people always went to the zoo on Saturdays, grown-ups don't like to make a trip like that and then have to go to the office the next day.'

'Well, there are still three days,' I said, 'three possible Saturdays. Nothing guarantees we chose the same one.'

'I know we did.'

'Why?'

'I just do. Don't bug me any more. Do you want me to keep telling you?' But Maya didn't wait for my answer. 'OK,' she said, 'so, I went to see the zoo and then I went home, and the first thing I did when I walked in was to ask my mother exactly where our house was in La Dorada. I think I recognized something along the way, the landscape, I recognized a mountain or a curve in the road, or the turn-off onto the main road to Villa Elena, because to get to the Hacienda Nápoles you pass right by that road. I must have recognized something, and when I saw my mother I wouldn't stop asking her questions. It was the first time I'd talked about it since we left, Mom was quite shocked. And as the years went by I kept asking questions, saying I wanted to go back, asking when we could go back. The house in La Dorada turned into a sort of Promised Land for me, you see? And I began little by little to do everything necessary to go back. And it all began with that visit to the zoo at the Hacienda Nápoles. And now you tell me that maybe we saw each other there, at the zoo. Without knowing you were you and I was me, without knowing we'd meet one day.'

Something happened in that instant in her gaze, her green eyes opened slightly wider, her narrow eyebrows arched as if they'd been drawn on again, and her mouth, her mouth with blood-red lips, gestured in a way I'd not seen before. I had no way of proving it, and commenting on it would have been imprudent or stupid, but at that moment I thought: *That's a little girl's expression. That's what you were like when you were little.*

And then I heard her say, 'And have you been back since then? Because I haven't, I've never been back. The place is falling to pieces, from what I've heard. But we could go anyway, see what's there, see what we remember. How's that sound?'

Soon we were driving down the highway towards Medellín at the hottest hour of the day, moving along the ribbon of asphalt just as Ricardo Laverde and Elaine Fritts had done twenty-nine years earlier, and not only that, but doing so in the same bone-coloured Nissan in which they'd driven. In a country where it's quite common to see cars from the 1960s in the streets – a Renault 4, a Fiat here and there, Chevrolet trucks that might even be fifteen years older – the survival of a jeep was neither miraculous nor extraordinary, there are hundreds like this on the roads. But anyone could see that this was not just any Nissan jeep, but rather the first big present Ricardo Laverde bought for his wife with the money from the flights, the marijuana money. Twenty-nine years before, the two of them had travelled around the Magdalena Valley as we were doing now; they had kissed while sitting on this seat; right here they'd talked about having children. And now their child and I were occupying those same places and perhaps feeling the same humid heat and the same relief at accelerating and getting air to blow in the windows, so we had to raise our voices to hear each other. It was either raise our voices or die of heat with the windows rolled up, and we preferred the former. 'This jeep still exists,' I said in a forced tone, sounding like an actor in a theatre that was too big.

'How about that,' said Maya. Then she raised a hand and pointed to the sky. 'Look, military planes.'

I heard the sound of the planes that were passing over our heads, but when I looked up I only saw a flock of turkey vultures tracing circles against the sky. 'I try not to think of Dad when I see them,' said Maya, 'but I can't help it.' Another squadron flew over in formation and this time I saw them: the grey shadows crossing the sky, the jet engines shaking the air. 'That was the inheritance he wanted,' said Maya. 'The hero's grandson.' The road was suddenly filled with uniformed lads armed with rifles that hung across their chests like sleeping animals. Before driving onto the bridge over the Magdalena we slowed down so much and passed so close to the soldiers that the wing mirror almost brushed the barrels of their rifles. They were boys, sweaty, scared kids whose mission, guarding the military base, seemed too big for them, just as their helmets and uniforms were, and those stiff leather boots in these cruel tropics. As we passed beside the fence that surrounded the base, a structure covered in green canvas and crowned with an elaborate labyrinth of barbed wire, I saw a green sign with white letters, *No Photography*, and another in black letters on a white background: *Human rights, the responsibility of all*. On the other side of the fence military trucks could be seen driving on a paved road; beyond them, exhibited like a relic in a museum, a Canadair Sabre balanced on a sort of pedestal. In my memory the image of this plane, which Ricardo Laverde liked so much, is forever linked to Maya's question: 'Where were you when they killed Lara Bonilla?'

People of my generation do these things: we ask each other what our lives were like at the moment of those events – almost all of which occurred in the 1980s – which defined or diverted them before we knew what was happening to us. I've always believed that in this way, verifying that we're not the only ones, we neutralize the consequences of having grown up in that decade, or we mitigate the feeling of vulnerability that has always accompanied us. And those conversations tend to begin with Lara Bonilla, the Minister of Justice. He had been the first public enemy of drug trafficking, and the most powerful of the legal ones; the method of the hit man on the back of a motorbike, where a teenager approaches the car in which the victim is travelling and empties a Mini Uzi into it without even slowing down, began with his murder. 'I was in my room, doing my chemistry homework,' I said. 'And you?'

'I was ill,' said Maya. 'Appendicitis, imagine, I'd just had surgery.'

'Do kids get that?'

'It's so cruel, but yes. And I remember the commotion at the clinic, the nurses rushing in and out. It was like being in a war movie. Because they'd killed Lara Bonilla and everyone knew who'd done it, but no one knew that could happen.'

'It was something new,' I said. 'I remember my dad in the dining room. His head in his hands, elbows on the table. He didn't eat anything. He didn't say anything either. It was something new.'

'Yes, that day we went to bed changed,' said Maya. 'A different country, wasn't it? At least that's how I remember it. Mom was scared. I looked at her and saw her fear. Of course, she knew all sorts of things that I didn't.' Maya was quiet for a moment. 'And when Galán was killed?'

'That was at night. It was a Friday in the middle of the year. I was . . . Well, I was with a friend.'

'Oh, very nice,' said Maya with a slanted smile. 'You having a fine old time while the country falls to pieces. Were you in Bogotá?'

'Yes.'

'Was she your girlfriend?'

'No. Well, she was going to be. Or that's what I thought.'

'Oops, a frustrated love,' Maya laughed.

'At least we spent the night together. Even though it was obligatory.'

'The After Curfew Hour Lovers,' said Maya. 'Not a bad title, don't you think?'

I liked seeing her like this, suddenly cheerful, I liked the little barely visible lines that appeared beside her eyes when she smiled. In front of us there was now a truck loaded with huge milk containers, big metal cylinders like unexploded bombs on top of which three shirtless teenagers were riding. Seeing us caused them inexplicable laughter. They waved to Maya, blew kisses at her, and she put the jeep into second gear and pulled into the other lane to overtake them. As she did so she blew a kiss back to them. It was a teasing, playful act, but there was something in the melodramatic way she closed her lips (and in the whole movie-star gesture) that filled the moment with an unexpected sensuality, or at least that's how it seemed to me. On my side of the road, two water buffalo were bathing in a sort of marsh that opened up between the shrubs. Their wet horns glistened under the sun, their manes stuck to their faces. 'And the day of the Avianca plane?' I said.

'Oh, the famous plane,' said Maya. 'That really fucked everything up, didn't it.'

Once the presidential candidate Galán was dead, his policies, and among them the fight against drug trafficking, were inherited by a very young provincial politician: César Gaviria. In his attempt to take Gaviria out of the picture, Pablo Escobar had a bomb planted on a passenger airline that flew – that would have flown – the Bogotá–Cali route. Gaviria, however, did not even board the plane. The bomb exploded just after take-off, and the remains of the disintegrated plane – including three passengers who were apparently not killed by the bomb but by the impact – fell over Soacha, the same place where Galán had fallen, shot on the wooden campaign platform. But I don't think this coincidence means anything.

'That's when we knew,' said Maya, 'that the war was against us too. Or that was the confirmation, at least. Beyond any doubt. There'd been other bombs in public places, of course, but they'd seemed like accidents, I don't know if the same thing happened to you. Well, I'm not entirely sure *accidents* is the right word either. Things that happen to people with bad luck. The plane was different. It was the same deep down, but for some reason it seemed different to me, as if they'd changed the rules of the game. I'd started university that year. Agronomy, I was going to study agronomy, I suppose I was already sure that I was going to reclaim the house in La Dorada. The fact is I'd started university. And it took me the whole year to notice.'

'Notice what?'

'The fear. Or rather, that this thing I got in my stomach, the occasional faint feelings, the irritation, weren't the typical symptoms of first-year jitters, but pure fear. And Mom was scared too, of course, maybe even more than I was. And then came the rest, the other attacks, the other bombs. The DAS one with its hundred dead. That one at the shopping mall with fifteen. Then the other shopping mall with however many there were. A special time, no? Not knowing when it might be your turn. Worrying when someone who was supposed to arrive wasn't there. Always knowing where the closest pay phone is to let someone know you're OK. If there were no pay phones, knowing that anybody would lend you their phone, all you had to do was knock on a door. Living like that, always with the possibility that people close to us might be killed, always having to reassure our loved ones so they don't think we are among the dead. Our lives were conducted inside houses, remember. We avoided public places. Friends' houses, friends of friends, houses of distant acquaintances, any house was better than a public place. Well, I don't know if you know what I mean. Maybe in our house it was different. We were two women on our own, after all. Maybe it wasn't like that for you.'

'It was exactly like that,' I said.

She turned to look at me. 'Really?'

'Really.'

'So you understand me then,' said Maya.

And I said a couple of words whose scope I didn't manage to fully determine: 'I understand you perfectly.'

The landscape repeated itself around us, green plains with grey mountains in the background, like a Gonzalo Ariza painting. My arm stretched along the back of the front seat, which in those models is bulky and undivided, so you feel like you're sitting on a sofa. With the shifting breezes and the rolling of the Nissan, sometimes Maya's hair brushed my hand, brushed the skin of my hand, and I liked the sensation and looked forward to it from then on. We left the straight line of cattle ranches with their drinking troughs with roofs and armies of cows lying around the trunks of the acacias. We passed over the Negrito River, a stream of dark waters and dirty banks, with clouds of foam sparkling here and there, the remains of the accumulated contamination from villages and towns upstream where they dumped their waste water into the same water in which they washed their clothes. When we got to the toll booth and the Nissan came to a stop, the sudden absence of air circulating raised the temperature inside the vehicle, and I felt – in my armpits, but also on my nose and under my eyes – that I was beginning to sweat. And when we got back in motion, as we approached another bridge over the Magdalena, Maya began to tell me about her mother, about what happened with her mother at the end of 1989. I was looking at the river beyond the bridge's yellow railings, looking at the little sandy islands that soon, when the rainy season arrived, would be covered by brown water, and meanwhile Maya was telling me about the evening when she came home from university and found Elaine Fritts in the bathroom, so drunk she'd almost passed out and clutching the toilet bowl as if it might be leaving at any moment. 'My baby,' she said to Maya, 'my baby's home. My little girl is big now. My little girl is a big girl.' Maya picked her up as best she could and put her to bed and stayed with her, watching her sleep and touching her forehead every once in a while; she made her a herbal tea at two in the morning; put a bottle of water on the bedside table and brought her two painkillers for her hangover; and at the end of the night heard her say that she couldn't take it any more, that she'd tried but she couldn't do it any longer, that Maya was a grown-up now and could make her own decisions just as she'd made hers. And six days later she boarded a plane and returned home to Jacksonville, Florida, to the same house she'd left twenty years earlier with a single idea in her head: to be a Peace Corps volunteer in Colombia. To have an enriching experience, leave her mark, do her bit, small as it might be. All those things.

'The country changed on her,' said Maya. 'She arrived in a place and twenty years later she no longer recognized it. There is a letter that's always fascinated me, it's from late 1969, one of the first. My mother says that Bogotá is a boring city. She doesn't know how long she can live in a place where nothing ever happens.'

'Where nothing ever happens.'

'Yeah,' said Maya. 'Where nothing ever happens.'

'Jacksonville,' I said. 'Where's that?'

'North of Miami, way north. I only know from seeing it on maps, because I've never been. I've never been to the States.'

'Why didn't you go with her?'

'I don't know. I was eighteen,' Maya told me. 'At that age life's just starting, you're only just discovering it. I didn't want to leave my friends, I'd just started seeing someone . . . It's funny because as soon as Mom left I realized Bogotá was not for me. One thing led to another, as they say in movies, and here I am, Antonio. Here I am. Twenty-eight years old, alone and single, all my body parts still in good working order and living alone with my bees. Here I am. Melting in the heat and taking a stranger to see a dead Mafioso's zoo.'

'A stranger,' I repeated.

Maya shrugged and said something that didn't mean anything.

'Well, no, but anyway.'

When we got to the Hacienda Nápoles the sky had begun to cloud over and the air was sweltering. It would soon rain. The name of the property was painted in now peeling letters on the arch of the unnecessarily huge white gate – an eighteen-wheeler could easily have driven through – and on the crossbeam, precariously balanced, was a light aircraft, white and blue like the gate: it was the Piper that Escobar used during the early years and to which, he used to say, he owed his wealth. Passing beneath that plane, reading the registration number stencilled on the underside of the wing, was like entering a timeless world. Time, however, was present. To be more precise: it had wreaked havoc. Since 1993, when Escobar was shot dead on a Medellín rooftop, the property had gone into a vertiginous decline, and that, above all, was what Maya and I saw as the Nissan advanced along the paved track between the fields of lemon trees. There were no cattle grazing in these meadows, which, among other things, explained why the grass was so long. The weeds were devouring the wooden posts. That's what I was staring at, the wooden posts, when I saw the first dinosaurs.

They were what I'd liked most on my first long-ago visit. Escobar had ordered their construction for his children, a tyrannosaurus and a brontosaurus built to scale, a friendly-looking mammoth (grey and bearded like a tired grandfather) and even a pterodactyl floating over the pond with an anachronistic snake in its talons. Now their bodies were crumbling into bits, and there was something very sad and perhaps somewhat indecent in the vision of those cement-and-iron structures out in the open. The pond itself had turned into a lifeless puddle, or at least that's what it looked like from the path. After leaving the Nissan on a patch of neglected land, in front of a wire fence that might once have been electrified, Maya and I began to walk through the same places we had gone through in a car years ago, as children, almost teenagers, who didn't yet understand very well what the owner of all that did for a living or why their parents wouldn't allow them such innocent fun. 'Back then you weren't allowed to walk, remember? Nobody got out of their car.'

'It was forbidden,' I said.

'Yes. I'm shocked.'

'By what?'

'Everything seems smaller.'

She was right. We told a soldier we wanted to see the animals and asked him where they were, and Maya openly handed him a 10,000-peso note as encouragement. And so, guided or accompanied or escorted by a beardless youngster in camouflage cap and uniform who moved lazily, his left hand resting on his rifle, we arrived at the cages in which the animals were sleeping. The humid air filled with a dirty smell, a mixture of excrement and rotting food. We saw a cheetah lying at the back of his cage. We saw a chimpanzee scratching his head and another running in circles with nothing to chase. We saw an empty cage, the door open and an aluminium basin leaning against the bars.

But we didn't see the kangaroo who kicked the football, or the famous parrot who could recite the line-up of the Colombian national team, or the emus, or the lions and elephants Escobar had bought from a travelling circus, or the miniature horses or the rhinoceroses, or the incredible pink dolphin Maya dreamt of for a week straight after that first visit. Where were the animals we'd seen as kids? I don't know why our own disappointment should have surprised us, for the deterioration of the Hacienda Nápoles was well known, and in the years gone by since Escobar's death various testimonies had circulated in the Colombian press, a sort of extremely slow-motion film on the rise and fall of the criminal empire. But maybe it wasn't our disappointment that surprised us, but the way we experienced it together, the unexpected and especially unjustified solidarity that suddenly united us: we had both come to this place at the same time, this place had been a symbol of the same things for both of us. That must have been why later, when Maya asked if we could go as far as Escobar's house, I felt as if she'd taken the words out of my mouth, and it was me who pulled out some wrinkled and grimy money to bribe the soldier with this time.

'Oh no. You can't go in there,' he said.

'And why not?' asked Maya.

'You just can't,' he said. 'But you can walk around it and you can look in the windows.'

That's what we did. We walked around the perimeter of the construction and together saw its ruined walls, its dirty or broken windows, the splintering wood of its beams and columns, the broken and chipped tiles of the outside bathrooms. We saw the billiard tables inexplicably still there six years later: in those salons that time had darkened and dirtied, the green felt shone like jewels. We saw the pool empty of water, but full of dry leaves and pieces of bark and sticks that the wind had blown in. We saw the garage where the collection of antique cars was rotting away, we saw the flaking paint and broken headlights and dented bodywork and missing cushions and seats converted into a disorder of popping springs, and we remembered that according to legend one of these machines, a Pontiac, had belonged to Al Capone and another, again according to legend, to Bonnie and Clyde. And later we saw a car that had never been luxurious but basic and cheap, however its value was undoubtedly great: the famous Renault 4 in which the young Pablo Escobar, long before cocaine became the source of his riches, competed in local races as a novice driver. The Renault 4 Cup, that amateur trophy was called: the first time Escobar's name appeared in the Colombian press, long before the planes and the bombs and the debates about extradition, was as a racing-car driver in this competition, a young provincial in a country that was still a small province in the world, a young trafficker who was still making the news for activities other than that incipient trafficking. And there was the car, asleep and broken and devoured by neglect and time, the bodywork cracked open, another dead animal whose skin was full of worms.

But maybe the strangest thing that afternoon was that everything we saw we saw in silence. We looked at each other frequently, but we never spoke anything more than an interjection or an expletive, perhaps because all that we were seeing was evoking different memories and different fears for each of us, and it seemed imprudent or perhaps rash to go rummaging around in each other's pasts. Because it was that, our common past, that was there without being there, like the unseen rust that was right in front of us eating away at the car doors and rims and fenders and dashboards and steering wheels. As for the property's past, we weren't overly interested: the things that had happened there, the deals that were made and the lives that were extinguished and the parties that were held and the violence that was planned, all that was a backdrop, scenery. Without a word we agreed we'd seen enough and began to walk towards the Nissan. And this I remember: Maya took my arm, or slipped her arm in mine like women used to do in times gone by, and in the anachronism of her gesture there was an intimacy I could not have predicted, that nothing had foretold.

Then it began to rain.

It was just drizzle at first, although with fat drops, but in a matter of seconds the sky turned as black as a donkey's belly and a downpour drenched our shirts before we had time to seek shelter anywhere. 'Shit, that's the end of our stroll,' said Maya. By the time we got to the Nissan, we were soaked to the skin; since we'd run (shoulders raised, one arm up to shield our eyes), the fronts of our trousers were wet through, while the back, almost dry, seemed made of a different fabric. The windows of the jeep fogged up immediately with the heat of our breathing, and Maya had to get a box of tissues out of the glove compartment to clean the windscreen so we wouldn't crash. She opened the vents, a black grille in the middle of the dashboard, and we began to move cautiously forward. But we had only gone about 100 metres when Maya stopped suddenly, rolled down the window as fast as she could so I, from the passenger seat, could see what she was looking at: thirty steps away from us, halfway between the Nissan and the pond, a hippopotamus was studying us gravely.

'What a beauty,' said Maya.

'Beauty?' I said. 'That's the ugliest animal in the world.'

But Maya paid me no attention. 'I don't think it's an adult,' she went on. 'She's too little, just a baby. I wonder if she's lost.'

'And how do you know it's female?'

But Maya was already out of the jeep, in spite of the downpour that was still falling and in spite of a wooden fence between us and the piece of land where the creature was. Its hide was dark iridescent grey, or that's how it looked to me in the diminished afternoon light. The raindrops hit and bounced off as if they were falling against a pane of glass. The hippopotamus, male or female, juvenile or full-grown, didn't bat an eyelid: it looked at us, or looked at Maya who was leaning over the wooden fence and looking at it in turn. I don't know how much time went by: one minute, two, which in such circumstances is a long time. Water dripped off Maya's hair and all her clothes were a different colour now. Then the hippopotamus began a heavy movement, a ship trying to turn around in the sea, and I was surprised to see such a long animal in profile. And then I didn't any more, or rather I saw its powerful arse and thought I saw streams of water sliding over its smooth, shiny skin. It wandered away through the tall grass, with its legs hidden by the weeds in such a way that it seemed not to make any progress, but just to get smaller. When it reached the pond and got into the water, Maya returned to the jeep.

'How long are those creatures going to last, that's what I wonder,' she said. 'There's no one to feed them, no one to take care of them. They must be so expensive.'

She wasn't talking to me, that was clear: she was thinking out loud. And I couldn't help but remember another comment identical in spirit and even in form that I had heard a long time ago, when the world, or at least my world, was a very different one, when I still felt in charge of my life.

'Ricardo said the same thing,' I told Maya. 'That's how I met him, when he commented how sorry he felt for the animals from the zoo.'

'I can imagine,' said Maya. 'He worried about animals.'

'He said they weren't to blame for anything.'

'And it's true,' said Maya. 'It's one of the few, very few, real memories I have. My dad looking after the horses. My dad stroking my mom's dog. My dad telling me off for not feeding my armadillo. The only real memories. The rest are invented, Antonio, false memories, made-up memories. The saddest thing that can happen to a person is to find out their memories are lies.'

Her voice was twanging, but that could have been due to the change in temperature. There were tears in her eyes, or maybe it was rainwater running down her cheeks, around her lips. 'Maya,' I asked then, 'why was he killed? I know this piece of the puzzle is missing, but what do you think?' The Nissan was on the move again and we were travelling the kilometres that separated us from the entrance gate, Maya's hand closed over the black knob of the gear lever, water ran down her face and neck. I insisted: 'Why, Maya?' Without looking at me, without taking her eyes off the drenched panorama, Maya said those five words I'd heard from so many mouths, 'He must have done something.' But this time they seemed unworthy of what Maya knew. 'Yes,' I said, 'but what? Maybe you don't want to know.' Maya looked at me with pity. I tried to add something but she cut me off. 'Look, I don't want to talk any more.' The black blades moved across the windscreen and swept the water and leaves away. 'I want us to stay quiet for a while, I'm tired of talking. Do you understand, Antonio? We've talked too much. I'm sick of talking. I want to be silent for a while.'

So in silence we arrived at the gate and passed beneath the white and blue Piper, and in silence we turned left and headed for La Dorada. In silence we drove along the part where the trees met over the top of the road, keeping the light from passing through and on rainy days lessening the difficulties drivers faced. In silence we came back out into the bad weather, in silence we saw the yellow railings of the bridge over the Magdalena, in silence we crossed it. The surface of the river bristled under the downpour, it wasn't smooth like the hippopotamus's hide but rough like that of a gigantic sleeping alligator, and on one of the little islands a white boat was getting wet with its motor pulled up. Maya was sad: her sadness filled the Nissan like the smell of our wet clothes, and I could have said something to her, but I didn't. I kept silent: she wanted to be in silence. And so, in the middle of that obliging silence, accompanied only by the thundering of the rain on the jeep's metal roof, we went through the toll booth and headed south through the cattle ranches. Two long hours in which the sky gradually darkened, not due to the dense rain clouds but because night fell halfway there. By the time the Nissan lit up the white façade of the house, it was completely dark. The last thing we saw were the eyes of the German shepherd gleaming in the beam of the headlights.

'Nobody's home,' I said.

'Of course not,' said Maya. 'It's Sunday.'

'Thanks for the outing.'

But Maya didn't say anything. She walked in and took off her wet clothes as she went, skirting around the furniture without turning on any lights, voluntarily blind. I followed her, or followed her shadow, and realized that she wanted me to follow her. The world was blue and black, made not of figures but of outlines; one of them was Maya's silhouette. In my memory it was her hand that reached for mine, not the other way around, and then Maya said these words: *I'm tired of sleeping alone.* I think she also said something simple and very understandable: *Tonight I don't want to be so alone.* I don't remember having walked to Maya's bed, but I see myself perfectly sitting on the edge of it, beside a bedside table with three drawers. Maya turned down the sheets and her spectral silhouette stood out against the wall, in front of the mirror on the wardrobe, and it seemed like she was looking in the mirror and as she did so her reflection was looking at me. While I was attending to this parallel reality, that fleeting scene that elapsed in my absence, I got into her bed, and I didn't resist when Maya got in beside me and her hands undid my clothes, her suntanned hands acted as naturally and deftly as my own hands. She kissed me and I felt her breath at once fresh and fatigued, an end-of-the-day breath, and I thought (a ridiculous thought and also indemonstrable) that this woman hadn't kissed anyone for a long time. And then she stopped kissing me. Maya touched me futilely, took me futilely in her mouth, her futile tongue ran over my body without a sound, and then her resigned mouth returned to my mouth and only then did I realize she was naked. In the semi-darkness her nipples were a violet tone, a dark violet like the red scuba divers see at the bottom of the sea. *Have you been underwater in the sea, Maya?* I asked her or think I asked her. *Way down deep in the sea, deep enough for colours to change?* She lay down beside me, face up, and at that moment I was overcome by the absurd idea that Maya was cold. *Are you cold?* I asked. But she didn't answer. *Do you want me to go?* She didn't answer this question either, but it was a pointless question, because Maya didn't want to be alone and she'd already settled that. I didn't want to be alone at that moment either: Maya's company had become indispensable to me, just as the disappearance of her sadness had become urgent. I thought how the two of us were alone in this room and in this house, but alone with a shared solitude, each of us alone with our own pain deep in our flesh but mitigating it at the same time by the strange arts of nakedness. And then Maya did something that only one person in the world had ever done before: her hand rested on my belly and found my scar and caressed it as if she were painting with one finger, as if she'd dipped her finger in tempera and were trying to make a strange and symmetrical design on my skin. I kissed her, in order to close my eyes more than to kiss her, and then my hand moved over her breasts and Maya took it in hers, took my hand in hers and put it between her legs and my hand touched her smooth straight hair, and then her soft inner thighs, and then her sex. My fingers under her fingers penetrated her and her body tensed and her legs opened like wings. *I'm tired of sleeping alone*, she'd told me, this woman who was now looking at me with wide-open eyes in the darkness of her room, wrinkling her brow like someone who's on the verge of understanding something.

Maya Fritts did not sleep alone that night, I wouldn't have let her. I don't know when her well-being began to matter so much to me, I don't know when I began to regret that there could be no possible life together for us, that our common past did not necessarily imply a common future. We'd had the same life and nevertheless had very different lives, or at least I did, a life with people who were waiting for me on the other side of the Cordillera, four hours from Las Acacias, 2,600 metres above sea level . . . In the darkness of the bedroom I thought of that, although thinking in the darkness is not advisable: things seem bigger or more serious in the darkness, illnesses more destructive, the presence of evil closer, indifference more intense, solitude more profound. That's why we like to have someone to sleep with, and that's why I wouldn't have left her alone that night for anything in the world. I could have got dressed and left in silence, carrying my shoes and leaving the doors ajar, like a thief. But I didn't: I saw her fall into a deep sleep, undoubtedly because she was so tired both from all the driving and from all the emotions. Remembering tires a person out, this is something they don't teach us, exercising one's memory is an exhausting activity, it drains our energy and wears down our muscles. So I watched Maya sleep on her side, facing me, and I watched her hand slide under her pillow once she was asleep and hug it or cling to it, and it happened again: I saw her as she'd been as a girl. I didn't have the slightest doubt that this gesture contained or embodied the little girl she'd once been, and I loved her in some imprecise and absurd way. And then I fell asleep too.

When I woke up, it was still dark. I didn't know how much time had passed. I hadn't been woken by the light, or the sounds of the tropical dawn, rather by the distant murmur of voices. I followed the sounds to the living room and was not surprised to find her as I did, sitting on the sofa with her head in her hands and a recording playing from her tiny stereo. I didn't have to hear more than a few seconds, only a couple of those phrases spoken by strangers in English had to reach me to recognize the recording, for deep down I'd never stopped hearing that dialogue that spoke of weather conditions and then of work and of how many hours pilots could fly before they were obliged to rest, deep down I recognized it as if I'd heard it yesterday. 'Well, let's see,' said the first officer just as he'd done some time ago, in Consu's house. 'We've got 136 miles to the VOR, and 32,000 feet to lose, and slow down to boot so we might as well get started.' And the captain said, 'Bogotá, American nine six five request descent.' And Operations said, 'Go ahead, American nine six five, this is Cali ops.' And the captain said, 'All right, Cali. We will be there in just about twenty-five minutes from now.' And I thought, just as I'd thought before: *No you won't. You won't be there in twenty-five minutes. You'll be dead, and that will change my life.*

Maya didn't look at me when I sat down beside her, but she lifted her face as if she'd been waiting for me, and on her cheeks I saw the trail of her tears and I stupidly wanted to protect her from what was going to happen at the end of the tape. They'd be parking at gate two and landing on runway zero one, the plane's headlights were on because there was a lot of visual traffic in the area, and I sat beside Maya on the sofa and put my arm around her back and hugged her and held her close to me, and the two of us sank into the sofa like a couple of old insomniacs, that's what we were, an old married couple who can't sleep and meet like ghosts in the early hours to share their insomnia. 'I'm going to talk to the people,' said the voice, and then, 'Ladies and gentlemen, this is your captain. We have begun our descent.' And then I felt her sob. 'There goes my mom,' she said. I thought she wouldn't say anything else. 'She's going to be killed,' she said then, 'she's going to leave me all alone. And I can't do anything, Antonio. Why did she have to be on that flight? Why didn't she get a direct flight? How much bad luck can one person have?' and I held her, what else could I do but hold her tight, I couldn't change what had happened or stop the flow of time on the tape, time that advanced towards what had already happened, towards the definitive. 'I'd like to wish everyone a very, very happy holiday and a healthy and prosperous 1996,' the captain said from the tape. 'Thank you for flying with us.'

And with those false words – the year 1996 would not exist for Elaine Fritts – Maya went back to remembering, back to the exhausting work of memory. Was it for my benefit, Maya Fritts, or maybe you'd discovered you could use me, that nobody else would allow you this return to the past, that nobody but me would invite those memories, listen to them with the discipline and dedication I listened to them? And so she told me of the December afternoon she came back into the house, after a long day of work in the apiary, ready to take a shower. She'd had an outbreak of acariasis in the beehives and had spent the week trying to minimize the damage and preparing concoctions of anemone and coltsfoot; she still had the intense odour of the mixture on her hands and was desperate for a wash. 'Then the phone rang,' she said. 'I almost didn't answer it. But I thought: what if it's important? I heard Mom's voice and actually thought, well, at least it's not that. It's nothing important. Mom always called at Christmas, that's one thing we hadn't lost in spite of the years. We talked five times a year: on her birthday, on mine, at Christmas, on New Year's Day and on Dad's birthday. The birthday of the deceased, you understand, that the living mark because he's not here to celebrate it. That time we were talking for quite a while, telling each other unimportant things, and at some point my mother said look, we have to talk.' And that's how Maya found out, during a long-distance telephone call, down the line from Jacksonville, Florida, the truth about her father. 'He hadn't died when I was five. He was alive. He'd been in prison, and now he was out. He was alive, Antonio. And not only that, but he was in Bogotá. And not only that but he'd tracked down my mother, who knows how. And he wanted us all to get together.' 'Pretty night, huh?' says the captain from the black box. And the first officer, 'Yeah, it is. Looking nice out here.' 'For us to get together, Antonio, get that,' said Maya. 'As if he'd gone out for a couple of hours to pick up some groceries.' And the captain, '*Feliz Navidad, señorita.*'

I don't know if there are any studies of people's reactions to revelations such as that one, how a person behaves in the face of such a brutal change in circumstances, in the face of the disappearance of the world as they'd known it. One might think that in many cases a gradual readjustment would follow, the search for a new place in the elaborate system of our lives, a re-evaluation of our relationships and of what we call the past. Perhaps that might be the most difficult and least acceptable aspect, the change to the past, which we used to believe was fixed. In Maya Fritts's case the first thing was incredulity, but that didn't last long: in a matter of seconds she had yielded to the evidence. This was followed by a sort of contained fury, partially caused by the vulnerability of this life in which a mere phone call can topple everything in such a brief space of time: all you have to do is pick up the receiver and a new fact comes through it into the house, something we've neither sought nor requested and that sweeps us along like an avalanche. And the contained fury was followed by open fury, the shouts down the telephone, and the insults. And the open fury was followed by hatred and hateful words: 'I don't want to see anybody,' Maya said to her mother. 'Whether he believes it or not, I'm warning you. If he shows up here, I'll shoot him.' Maya spoke with a broken voice, very different from what it must have been then, what I was now seeing on the sofa, the soft even serene sobbing. 'Uh, where are we?' asked the first officer on the black box, and in his voice there is some alarm, the anticipation of what's to come. 'This is where it starts,' Maya said to me. And she was right, it was starting there. 'Where we headed?' said the first officer. 'I don't know,' said the captain. 'What's this? What happened here?' And there, with the first disoriented lurches of the Boeing 757, with its movements of a lost bird at 13,000 feet in the Andean night, Elaine Fritts's death was beginning. There were those voices again that have now realized something, those voices that feign serenity and control when they've lost all control and serenity is a façade. 'Left turn. So you want a left turn back around?' 'Naw . . . Hell no, let's press on to . . .' 'Press on to where, though?' 'Tuluá.' 'That's a right.' 'Where we going? Come to the right. Let's go to Cali. We got fucked up here, didn't we?' 'Yeah.' 'How did we get fucked up here? Come to the right, right now. Come to the right, right now.'

'They fucked up here,' Maya said or rather whispered. 'And Mom was on board.'

'But she didn't know what was going on,' I said. 'She didn't know the pilots were lost. At least she wouldn't have been scared.'

Maya considered the idea. 'It's true,' she said. 'At least she wasn't scared.'

'What would she have been thinking of?' I said. 'Have you ever wondered, Maya? What would Elaine have been thinking of at that moment?'

Sounds of anguish began to be heard. An electronic voice delivered desperate warnings to the pilots: 'Terrain, terrain.' 'I've asked myself a thousand times,' said Maya. 'I had told her quite clearly that I didn't want to see him, that my dad had died when I was five and that was that, nothing was going to change that. Not to try to change things for me at this stage. But then I was a wreck for several days. I got sick. I had a fever, a high fever, and feverish and all I still went out to work in the hives out of fear of being home when my dad arrived. What would she have been thinking? Maybe that it was worth a try. That my dad had loved me very much, had loved us both, and that it was worth trying. She called back another time and tried to justify what my dad had done, said that in those days everything was different, the world of drug trafficking, all that. That they were a bunch of innocents, that's what she told me. Not that they were *innocent*, no, that they were *innocents*, I'm not sure if you realize what a distance there is between the two concepts. Anyway, it's the same. As if innocence might exist in this country of ours . . . Anyway, that was when my mother decided to get on a plane and fix things up in person. She told me she was going to get on the first flight she could. That if her own daughter was going to shoot her, well she'd just take it. That's what she said to me, her own daughter. That she was just going to endure it, but she wasn't going to be left wondering what might have happened, full of doubts. Oh, now we're at this part. It's so painful, incredible, after all this time.' 'Shit,' said the pilot on the recording. 'Up, baby,' said the pilot. 'Up.'

'The plane is crashing,' said Maya.

'Up,' said the captain in the black box.

'It's OK,' said the first officer.

'They're going to be killed,' said Maya, 'and there's nothing to be done.'

'Up,' said the captain. 'Easy does it, easy.'

'And I didn't get to say goodbye,' said Maya.

'More, more,' said the captain.

'OK,' said the first officer.

'How was I supposed to know?' said Maya. 'How could I have known, Antonio?'

And the captain, 'Up, up, up.'

The cool early morning filled up with Maya's weeping, soft and fine, and also with the singing of the first birds, and also with the sound that was the mother of all sounds, the sound of lives disappearing as they pitch over the edge into the abyss, the sound made by Flight 965 and all it contained as they fall into the Andes and that in some absurd way was also the sound of Laverde's life, tied irremediably to that of Elena Fritts. And my life? Did my own life not begin to throw itself to the ground at this very instant, was that sound not the sound of my own downfall, which began there without my knowledge? 'So you fell out of the sky, too?' the Little Prince asks the pilot who tells the story, and I thought yes, I'd fallen out of the sky too, but there was no possible testimony of my fall, there was no black box that anybody could consult, nor was there any black box of Ricardo Laverde's fall, human lives don't have these technological luxuries to fall back on. 'Maya, how is it that we're hearing this?' I said. She looked at me in silence (her eyes red and flooded, her mouth looking devastated). I thought she hadn't understood me. 'I don't mean . . . What I want to know is how this recording came . . .' Maya took a deep breath. 'He always liked maps,' she said.

'What?'

'Maps,' said Maya. 'He always liked them.'

Ricardo Laverde had always liked maps. In school he always did well (always in the top three of his class), but he did nothing as well as he drew maps, those exercises in which the student had to draw, with a soft leaded pencil or a nib or a drawing pen, on tracing paper and sometimes on wax paper, the geographies of Colombia. He liked the sudden straight line of the Amazon trapezoid, he liked the tempered Pacific coast like a bow without an arrow, he could draw from memory the peninsula of La Guajira and blindfolded he could stick a pin in a sketch, as others might pin the tail on the donkey, without a second thought, to show the exact location of the Nudo de Almaguer. In all of Ricardo's scholastic history, the only calls from the discipline prefect came when they had to draw maps, for Ricardo would finish his in half the allotted time and for the rest of the class he'd draw his friends' maps in exchange for a 50-centavo coin, if it was a map of the political administrative division of Colombia, or a peso, if it was hydrography or a distribution of thermic levels.

'Why are you telling me this?' I said. 'What's it got to do with?'

When he came back to Colombia, after nineteen years in prison, and had to find work, the most logical thing was to look where there were planes. He knocked on various doors: flying clubs, aviation academies and found them all closed. Then, following a sort of epiphany, went to the Agustín Codazzi Geographical Institute. They gave him a couple of tests, and two weeks later he was flying a twin-engine Commander 690A whose crew was composed of a pilot and co-pilot, two geographers, two specialized technicians and sophisticated aero-photography equipment. And that's what he was doing for the last months of his life: taking off in the early morning from El Dorado Airport, flying over Colombian airspace while the camera in the back took 23 by 23 negatives that would eventually, after a long laboratory and classification process, end up in the atlases from which thousands of children would learn the tributaries of the River Cauca and where the Occidental Cordillera begins. 'Children like our children,' said Maya, 'if either of us ever has any kids.'

'They'll study Ricardo's photos.'

'It's nice to think,' said Maya. And then, 'My father had made good friends with his photographer.'

His name was Iragorri. Francisco Iragorri, but everyone called him Pacho. 'A skinny guy, about our age, more or less, one of those with the features of the baby Jesus, pink cheeks, upturned nose, not a single hair to shave.' Maya tracked him down and called him and invited him to come to Las Acacias at the beginning of 1998, and he was the one who told her what happened on Ricardo Laverde's last night. 'They always flew together, after the flight they'd have a beer and say goodbye. And a couple of weeks later they'd meet up at the Institute, at the Institute laboratory, and work together on the photos. Or rather Iragorri would work and let my father watch and learn. To do photo finishing. To analyse a photo in three dimensions. How to use a stereoscopic viewfinder. My father enjoyed all that with childlike enthusiasm, Iragorri told me.' The day before he was killed Ricardo Laverde had showed up at the lab looking for Iragorri. It was late. Iragorri thought the visit wasn't to do with work, and a couple of sentences, a couple of glances later, understood that the pilot was going to ask him for a loan: nothing easier than anticipating financial favours. But he wouldn't have guessed the reason in a thousand years: Laverde was going to buy a recording, a black box recording. He explained to Iragorri what flight it was from. He explained who had died on that flight.

'The money was for some bureaucrat who was going to get him a copy of the cassette,' said Maya. 'It seems something like that is not so difficult if you have the right contacts.'

The problem was the amount of the loan: Laverde needed a lot of money, more, obviously, than anyone would have on hand, but also more than a person could withdraw from a cash machine. So the two friends, the pilot and the photographer, made a decision: they stayed there, wasting time in the facilities of the Agustín Codazzi Geographical Institute, in the darkroom and the restoration offices, amusing themselves with old contact sheets or fixing the topography on a job they were behind on or rectifying wrong coordinates, and at about eleven thirty they went to the nearest cash machine to withdraw the maximum amount allowed and did so twice: once before and once after midnight. So they tricked the machine's computer, that poor apparatus that only understands digits; that's how Ricardo Laverde acquired the amount of money he needed. 'Iragorri told me all that. It was the last piece of information I could find,' Maya told me, 'until I learned that my father was not alone when he was shot.'

'Until you learned that I existed.'

'Yes. Until I found that out.'

'Well Ricardo never spoke to me about that job,' I said. 'Never mentioned maps or aerial photos or a twin-engine Commander.'

'Never?'

'Never. And not because I didn't ask.'

'I see,' said Maya.

But it was obvious: she was seeing something that escaped me. In the living-room window the trees were beginning to appear, the silhouettes of their branches were beginning to detach themselves from the dark background of that long night, and also inside, around us, things recovered the lives they had during the day. 'What do you see?' I asked Maya. She seemed tired. We were both tired, I thought; I thought that under my eyes there would also be grey circles like the ones under Maya's eyes. 'Iragorri sat there the day he came,' she said. She pointed at the empty armchair across from us, the nearest to the stereo system from which no sound was now coming. 'He just stayed for lunch. He didn't ask me to tell him anything in return. Or to show him my family's papers. Much less sleep with me.' I looked down, guessed that she was doing the same. And Maya added, 'The truth is that you, my dear friend, are a user.'

'Sorry,' I said.

'You should be ashamed of yourself.' Maya smiled: in the dawn's blue light I saw her smile. 'The thing is I remember perfectly, he was sitting there and we'd just been brought some *lulo* juice, because Iragorri was teetotal, and he'd added a spoonful of sugar and he was stirring it like this, slowly, when we got to the thing about the cash machine. Then he told me that of course, of course he'd lent my dad that money, but he didn't really have money to spare. So he said look, Ricardo, don't take this the wrong way, but I have to ask you how you're going to pay me back. When you're going to pay me back, and how? And that's when my dad, according to Iragorri, told him, Oh, don't worry about that. I've just done a job that I'll be getting good money for. I'm going to pay you all this back with interest.'

Maya stood up, took a couple of steps towards the rustic table her little stereo sat on and pressed rewind. The silence filled with that mechanical murmur, as monotonous as running water. 'That sentence is like a hole, everything goes down it,' said Maya. '*I've just done a job*, my dad said to Iragorri, *that I'll be getting good money for.* Not very many words, but they're fuckers.'

'Because we don't know.'

'Exactly,' said Maya. 'Because we don't know. Iragorri didn't ask me at first, he was discreet or shy, but eventually he couldn't help it. What kind of job would it have been, Señorita Fritts? I can see him there, looking away. See that piece of furniture, Antonio?' Maya pointed to a wicker structure with four shelves. 'See the pre-Columbian pieces up top?' There was a little man sitting cross-legged with an enormous phallus; at his side, two pots with heads and prominent bellies. 'Iragorri stared at them up there, far from my eyes, he couldn't look at me as he said what he said, he didn't dare. And what he said was: Your dad wouldn't have been mixed up in something fishy? Fishy like what? I asked. And he, looking up there the whole time, looking at the pre-Columbian figurines, blushed like a child and said, well, I don't know, it doesn't matter, what does it matter now. And you know what, Antonio? That's what I think too: what does it matter any more?' The murmur of the tape player stopped then. 'Shall we listen to it again?' said Maya. Her finger pressed a button, the dead pilots began to chat again in the distant night, in the middle of the night sky, at an altitude of 32,000 feet, and Maya Fritts came back to my side and put a hand on my leg and rested her head on my shoulder and I could smell her hair in which I could still detect the previous day's rain. It wasn't a clean smell, but I liked it, I felt comfortable with it. 'I have to go,' I said then.

'Are you sure?'

'I'm sure.'

I stood up, looked out the big window. Outside, behind the hills, the white stain of the sun was coming up.

There is just one direct route between La Dorada and Bogotá, just one way to make this journey without unnecessary detours or delays. It's the one used by all the transport, produce, merchandise and passengers too, for those companies rely on covering the distance in the shortest possible space of time, and that's also why a mishap on the only route can be very damaging. You turn south and take the straight road that runs by the river that takes you to Honda, the port where travellers used to arrive when no planes flew over the Andes. From London, from New York, from Havana, Colón or Barranquilla, they would arrive by sea at the mouth of the Magdalena, and change ship there or sometimes carry on in the same one. There followed long days of sailing upriver on tired steamships, which in the dry season, when the water level fell so low that the riverbed emerged, would get stranded on the banks between crocodiles and fishing boats. From Honda each traveller would get to Bogotá however they could, by mule or by train or in a private car, depending on the era and the resources, and that last leg could also take a while, from several hours to several days, for it's not easy to go, in barely 100 kilometres, from sea level to an altitude of 2,600 metres where that grey-skyed city rests. So far in my life no one has been able to explain convincingly, beyond banal historical causes, why a country should choose as its capital its most remote and hidden city. It's not our fault that we *bogotanos* are stuffy and cold and distant, because that's what our city is like, and you can't blame us for greeting strangers warily, for we're not used to them. I, of course, can't blame Maya Fritts for having left Bogotá when she got the chance, and more than once I've wondered how many people of my generation had done the same, escaped, not to a tropical lowland town like Maya had, but to Lima or Buenos Aires, to New York or Mexico, to Miami or Madrid. Colombia produces fugitives, that's true, but one day I'd like to find out how many of them were born as Maya and I were at the beginning of the 1970s, how many like Maya or like me had a calm or protected or at least unperturbed childhood, how many traversed their teenage years and fearfully became adults while the city around them sank into fear and the sound of gunshots and bombs without anyone having declared any war, or at least not a conventional war, if such a thing exists. That's what I'd like to know, how many left my city feeling in one way or another that they were saving themselves, and how many felt that by saving themselves they were betraying something, turning into proverbial rats fleeing the proverbial ship by the act of fleeing the city in flames. *I will tell you that / one day I saw a crazed, arrogant, swarming city / burn through the night,* says a poem by Aurelio Arturo. *Unblinking, I watched it collapse, / and fold like a rose petal / under a hoof.* Arturo published that in 1929: he had no way of knowing what would later happen to the city of his dream, the way Bogotá would adapt itself to his lines, entering into them and fulfilling their requisites, as iron adapts to its mould, yes, as molten iron always fills the mould it's poured into.

It burned like a loin, amid forests of flame
and cupolas fell and the walls fell
over the beloved voices and over the broad mirrors
. . . ten thousand howls of pure resplendence!

The beloved voices. I was thinking of them that strange Monday, when after the weekend at Maya Fritts's house, I found myself coming into Bogotá from the west, passing under the planes taking off from El Dorado Airport, passing over the river, and then driving up 26th Street. It was just after ten in the morning and the trip had gone without mishaps or collapses or traffic jams or accidents that would have held me up on a road so narrow in places that vehicles had to take it in turns to pass. I was thinking through everything I'd heard over the weekend and about the woman who had told it to me, and also about what I'd seen at the Hacienda Nápoles, whose cupolas and walls were falling down too, and also, of course, I was thinking about Arturo's poem and about my family, my family and Arturo's poem, my city and the poem and my family, the beloved voices of the poem, Aura's voice and Leticia's voice, which had filled my recent years, which in more than one sense had rescued me.

And the flames like my own hair,
red panthers set loose into the young city,
and the walls of my dream burning, toppling,
like a city collapsing in screams.

I drove into the parking garage of my building as if returning after a lengthy absence. Through the window a doorman I'd never seen before waved me in; I had to perform more manoeuvres than usual to get into my space. When I got out I felt cold, and I thought that the car's interior had conserved the warm air of the Magdalena Valley and that this contrast had undoubtedly led to the violent shutting of my pores. It smelled of cement (cement has a cold smell) and of fresh paint: they were doing some work I hadn't remembered they were starting over the weekend. But the workers had left, and there, in the parking garage of my building, in another car's space, was a gasoline barrel cut in half, and in it the remains of the fresh cement. As a child I had liked the feeling of wet cement on my hands, so I looked around – to make sure no one would see me and think I was crazy – and I approached the barrel and stuck two fingers carefully into the now almost hardened mixture. And I went up in the lift like that, looking at my dirty fingers and smelling them and enjoying that cold smell, and so I went up the ten floors to my apartment, and was about to ring the bell with the dirty fingers. I didn't, and not only so I wouldn't get the bell or the wall dirty, but because something (a quality of the silence on this high floor, the darkness of the panes of smoked glass in the door) told me that there was no one home to open the door for me.

Now, there is something that has happened to me all my life when I return from sea level to the altitude of Bogotá. It's not just me, of course, but happens to many and even the majority, but since I was little it always seemed that my symptoms were more intense than other people's. I'm talking about a certain difficulty in breathing for the first two days after my return, a slight tachycardia unleashed by efforts as minimal as climbing the stairs or getting down a suitcase, and that lasts while my lungs get used to this rarefied air again. That's what happened to me as I opened with my own keys the door to my apartment. My eyes mechanically registered the clean dining table (no envelopes to open, no letters or bills), the telephone table where the red light of the answering machine was blinking and the little screen indicated that there were four new messages, the swinging door into the kitchen (it had been left stuck half open, I should oil the hinges). All this I saw while feeling the lack of oxygen that my heart was demanding. What I didn't see, however, were any toys at all. Not in the carpeted corners or abandoned on the chairs or lost in the hall. There were none, not the plastic fruit in its basket, not the chipped little teacups, not the chalk for the board or any coloured paper. Everything was perfectly orderly, and that was when I took two steps towards the telephone and played the messages. The first was the dean's office, asking why I hadn't taught my 7 a.m. class, and asking me to report as soon as possible. The second was Aura.

'I'm calling so you won't worry,' said that voice, the beloved voice. 'We're fine, Antonio. Leticia and I are fine. It's Sunday now, eight o'clock at night, and you haven't come back. And I don't know where we can go from here. You and me, I mean, I don't know where you and I can go, what's left after what's happened to us. I've tried,

I've tried hard, you know I have. And I'm tired of trying, even I get tired. I can't do it any more. Forgive me, Antonio, but I can't do it any longer, and it's not fair on our little girl.' She said this: *It's not fair on our little girl.* And then she said other things, but the time the answering machine gave her had run out and her message was cut off. The next message was also from her: 'I got cut off,' she said with a broken voice, as if she'd been crying in between the two messages. 'Well, I don't have anything else to say anyway. I hope you're fine too, that you got home OK, and that you forgive me. I just can't do it any more. I'm sorry.' Then came the last message: it was the university again, but not the dean's office this time, but the secretary. They were asking if I'd supervise a thesis, an absurd project on revenge as a legal prototype in the *Iliad*.

I had listened to the messages standing by the phone with my eyes open but without looking at anything, and now I played them again so I could hear Aura's beloved voice while I walked around the apartment. I walked slowly, because I couldn't get enough air: no matter how deeply I inhaled, I couldn't get the feeling of breathing comfortably, with my constricted lungs, my rebellious bronchial tubes, my self-sabotaging alveoli refusing to receive the oxygen. In the kitchen there was not even one single dirty plate, not a glass or a piece of cutlery out of place. Aura's voice was saying she was tired, and I walked down the hall towards Leticia's room, and Aura's voice was saying it wasn't fair on our little girl and I sat down on Leticia's bed and thought that what would be fair would be that Leticia were here with me, so I could take care of her as I'd taken care of her until now.

I want to take care of you, I thought, *I want to take care of both of you, together we'll be protected, together nothing will happen to us.*

I opened the wardrobe: Aura had taken all of Leticia's clothes, a child of Leticia's age goes through several outfits a day, you have to be washing clothes all the time. My head hurt all of a sudden. I attributed it to the lack of oxygen. I thought I'd lie down for a few minutes before going to find a painkiller, because Aura was always complaining about my tendency to take medication at the first symptoms, and not give the body the chance to defend itself on its own. 'Forgive me,' said Aura's voice out there in the living room, from the other side of the wall. Aura was not in the living room, of course, and I had no way of knowing where she was. But she was fine, and Leticia was fine, and that's what mattered. Maybe, with a little luck, she'd phone back. I lay down on this bed that was too small for me, on which my long grown-up body did not fit, and my eyes focused on the mobile that hung from the ceiling, the first image that Leticia saw when she woke up in the morning, the last thing she probably saw when she went to bed at night. From the ceiling hung an aquamarine egg, four arms stuck out from the egg and from each arm hung a figure: an owl with big spiral eyes, a ladybird, a dragonfly with muslin wings, a smiling bee with long antennae. There, concentrating on the forms and colours that were moving in an imperceptible way, I thought of what I'd say if Aura called back. Would I ask her where she was, if I could go and pick her up or if I had the right to hope she'd come back? Would I keep quiet so she could realize she'd made a mistake abandoning our life? Or would I try to convince her, tell her that together we could defend ourselves better from the evil of the world, or that the world was too risky a place to be wandering on our own, without anyone waiting for us at home, who worries about us when we don't show up and who can go out to look for us?

AUTHOR'S NOTE

I began *The Sound of Things Falling* in June 2008, during six weeks I spent at the Santa Maddalena Foundation (Donnini, Italy), and would like to thank Beatrice Monti della Corte for her hospitality. I finished the novel in December 2010, in the house of Suzanne Laurenty (Xhoris, Belgium), and to her also go my grateful thanks. Between the two dates many people enriched and improved this novel. They know who they are.

TRANSLATOR'S NOTE

I would also like to thank Beatrice Monti della Corte for her gracious hospitality, as well as Lillian Nećakov for her co-translation of Aurelio Arturo's poem *Dream City*.

A NOTE ON THE TYPE

The text of this book is set in Bembo. This type was first used in 1495 by the Venetian printer Aldus Manutius for Cardinal Bembo's *De Aetna*, and was cut for Manutius by Francesco Griffo. It was one of the types used by Claude Garamond (1480–1561) as a model for his Romain de L'Université, and so it was the forerunner of what became standard European type for the following two centuries. Its modern form follows the original types and was designed for Monotype in 1929.

ALSO AVAILABLE BY JUAN GABRIEL VÁSQUEZ

THE SECRET HISTORY OF COSTAGUANA

'With wonderful panache, Vásquez has reinvented Conrad and his literary geography . . . A vivid, forceful, masterly book'
Alberto Manguel, GUARDIAN

London, 1903. Joseph Conrad is struggling with his new novel set in the South American Republic he calls 'Costaguana'. José Altamirano, Colombian by birth, has just arrived in London, and comes to the writer's aid by telling him his life story. When *Nostromo* is published the following year, however, José is outraged: his story is nowhere to be found. But the reader is about to discover the true story.

The Secret History of Costaguana is a comic, tragic, despairing, but above all exhilarating novel, told by a bumptious narrator with a score to settle. It is Latin America's lively riposte to Europe's limiting vision of the continent and confirms Juan Gabriel Vásquez's reputation as one of the leading novelists of his generation.

'Splendid'
DAILY TELEGRAPH

'Highly layered and intelligent . . . The most erudite and inventive Colombian novelist writing today'
INDEPENDENT

THE INFORMERS

'A fine and frightening study of how the past preys upon the present'
John Banville

When Gabriel Santoro publishes his first book, a biography of a Jewish family friend who fled Germany for Colombia shortly before World War Two, it never occurs to him that his father will write a devastating review in a national newspaper. Why does he attack him so viciously? Do the pages of his book unwittingly hide some dangerous secret? As Gabriel sets out to discover what lies behind his father's anger, he finds himself undertaking an examination of the guilt and complicity at the heart of Colombian society, as one treacherous act perpetrated in those dark days returns with a vengeance half a century later.

'Subtle, assured, artfully told and painted in delicate le Carré-style shades of ambiguity, *The Informers* shows how mightily the novel in Colombia is thriving after the Márquez era . . . Anne McLean's translation captures every shifting tone in the novel's silvery palette'
Boyd Tonkin, INDEPENDENT

'An intricate tale of deceit, loyalty and tarnished relationships, told in beautifully restrained prose'
TIMES LITERARY SUPPLEMENT